FOOL'S TAVERN

NED RESNIKOFF

D1545582

ibooks
new york
www.ibooks.net

DISTRIBUTED BY SIMON & SCHUSTER, INC.

An Original Publication of ibooks, inc.

Copyright © 2004 by Ned Resnikoff

An ibooks, inc. Book

Distributed by Simon & Schuster, Inc.
1230 Avenue of the Americas, New York, NY 10020

ibooks, inc.
24 West 25th Street
New York, NY 10010

The ibooks World Wide Web Site Address is:
http://www.ibooks.net

ISBN 0-7434-9295-1
First ibooks, inc. printing July 2004
10 9 8 7 6 5 4 3 2 1

Edited by Judy Gitenstein

Printed in the U.S.A.

PROLOGUE
Not Exactly a Standing Ovation

"So, eh, how's everybody tonight?" Aust Galanodel sat on a rickety wooden stool on a rickety wooden stage, with his silver harp resting in his lap. He was lanky, especially for an elf, wearing a pointed green hat with a red feather comically protruding from it, and light, flexible clothing. Several drawstring bags full of tricks lined his belt, and a rapier hung from the worn leather. The jaunty red feather and his sharp, dancing eyes looked extremely out of place in the bar, even though it was called the "Merry Walrus." True, its customers were sometimes walrus-sized, but you could never consider any of them "merry."

As Aust waited for a response to his question, he surveyed the room. The air was filled with pipe weed smoke, which made him gag, and the bar was poorly lit, with wax candles at each table. The customers, for the most part, were sweaty, unbathed, obese, hairy, male, and human, although a few Half-Orcs and Ogres lurked around. They were just big, dirty, and hairy enough to fit in.

1

"Good, good," Aust said finally, though he had received no reply. "Glad to see you all cheerful. Let's begin with a little ditty I picked up in Ludrock. It's called 'Dralock, Mieshaben Stromrye.' Roughly translated from Dwarven, it means 'The king has a strange odor about him, similar to that of livestock droppings in a room with no windows.' Now of course, since dwarves don't have livestock or windows, it's beyond me how—"

"Get on with the song, dimwit!" someone shouted from the audience, before promptly going back to sleep under the table.

"Alright, alright, I'm getting to it," Aust announced. "Hold on to your reins. Now..." He picked up the harp, and plucked it twice. "Theeeeeeeeeere once was a king who had an odor that..."

So caught up in his own performance was the man who billed himself as a "Master Bard," that he failed to notice the effect the song was having on the patrons. Well, not so much the song as the singer. The sound of Aust's voice was so indescribably horrible that it practically made their ears bleed—not quite the intended effect. But as far as the paying customers were concerned, Aust was the worst singer ever. Period.

Aust strummed his last chord on the harp, then looked at the audience with an enormous grin. "Did you like it?"

The audience stared on in stunned silence, mouths gaping, eyes brought to tears by the horrifying sound of his voice. "Get him!" one member shouted.

Two enormous meaty hands swiped at the bard,

and he leapt to the side, stuffing his harp back in his rucksack.

"Not exactly a standing ovation," he muttered, and slung the rucksack over his shoulder, ducking under three enormous fists moving in his direction. "I guess that means you won't be wanting an encore performance."

The three attackers lost their balance, and Aust swept his foot around in a circular kick beneath them, knocking them in all directions. He rolled away from their collective weight before it crushed him.

"Anybody else want some?" he asked.

That's when the rest of the patrons dove for him all at once.

Aust leapt up and grabbed a beam on the ceiling, swung from it and landed right on a drunk's face, knocking him over in the process. He whipped around and brought his palm up, snapping a charging man's nose, then kicked him in the shins to knock him over. Another grabbed Aust on the shoulder from behind, and the bard twisted around. He poked his attacker in the eyes, punched him in the stomach, then yanked his nose. The man fell forward, crying, and curled up in a fetal position.

Aust ducked and slid between another man's legs, leaping up behind to kick him in the back of the neck. He turned and saw the bartender standing there, distinguishable from the others in the bar only by his shiny bald head and greasy apron.

"Where's my money?" Aust demanded. Another fist came at him, and he knocked out his attacker's teeth with his elbow.

"You should give *me* money, you bastard!" the bartender snarled, and shattered a whiskey bottle against the bar, brandishing it like a dagger. He lunged at Aust, and the bard stepped to the right. In one fluid motion, he pulled the rapier from under his belt and brought the hilt down on the bartender's head. He grabbed the bartender by the neck, and jabbed the point of the weapon into his second chin.

"Sorry to put you in this kind of position, but fair is fair," Aust whispered in the bartender's ear. "You promised me twenty coppers for my performance. And now that I'm making my exit, I'd like them."

The bartender reached into his pocket and hurled five pieces of silver at Aust's face. "Keep them!" he sobbed. "But please don't kill me!"

Aust snorted. "I'm an artist, not a warrior."

And before anybody in the tavern could beg to differ, Aust pocketed the money and did a backflip out the window, disappearing into the night.

CHAPTER
ONE
Instructors Are Not Flotation Devices

"Mr. Welkland," Professor Mendell said skeptically, adjusting his glasses, "we already have several mages on our staff here at the Academy for Arcane Study. Why would you be of any particular interest to us?"

Cade Welkland sat in a large office facing a panel of professors. Most of them were large, bald, and neckless. Cade, on the other hand, was skinny, had some neatly combed hair, and an Adam's apple that bobbed up and down as he swallowed nervously.

The walls were lined with portraits of grand master mages at the Academy. Many of them were young by elven standards, but were hundreds of years old nonetheless. Cade, being human, was at a disadvantage. He had not a drop of elven blood to provide an affinity for magic, and he expected to live to, at the very most, a little under one century.

"I'll tell you why I'd be of particular interest," Cade

said with as much confidence as he could muster. "I have studied the most modern of the arts. Your teachers, with great respect to them, know only the magics that have flourished in the previous few centuries. I can bring students into a new age."

"And what would this new form of magic be?"

"Why...control of the elements." Cade hoped his near-panic wasn't visible. "I've prepared a presentation, if you'd like."

"Please."

"Alright, then." Cade got to his feet. "Nature itself is an element," he began, summoning a few vines that sprouted from the floor. So far, so good. "So is lightning." A lightning bolt appeared from nowhere and struck the vines, setting them on fire.

"Aren't you going to put that out?" a professor asked nervously.

"All in good time. You'll notice I am also manipulating the fire to burn in the direction I want it to. How about we smother it with some rock?"

Dirt and stones formed in the air above the fire, then fell on the flames, putting out the fire.

"What a mess!" another professor sneered.

"Yes, but we will use water to cleanse it all." Instantly, water began to pour throughout the room, cleaning away the dirt and charred vines.

"Everything's wet!"

"Yes, but I can easily draw the water particles back up from the rug, by—oh no!"

The water wasn't stopping. It continued to poor in, filling the whole room. Cade was up to his knees, and reminded himself uncomfortably that he couldn't swim. While desperately trying to perform the proper meditation ritual to excise the water, he pulled open the door, which turned out to be a bad move. More water roared through it. Now Cade was struggling blindly beneath the current, his best suit ruined. Sending a stream of bubbles to the surface, and panicking more than he ever had in his entire life (he had a fear of water, heights, spiders...well, just about everything), Cade grabbed at what looked like a large flotation device bobbing up and down near the ceiling.

He happened to have grabbed Professor Mendell's leg and proceeded to drag himself to the surface.

"Get off!" the professor screamed, and slammed one meaty fist onto the magician's head, stunning him.

The few seconds of unconsciousness gave Cade time to focus. Conjuring some wind currents and using the water molecules themselves, he managed to apply most of the pressure from the water to one wall. The wall begin to crack and splinter, until finally, with a great roar, it shattered to pieces, and an enormous jet of water sprayed out the side of the building, bringing five screaming professors and one terrified mage down with it.

All six of them were thrown against the now soaking and muddy campus lawn. Cade blacked out again, and when he woke up, five very angry professors were standing over him.

"So, uh," he said cheerfully, pulling his ragged, muddy body to its feet, "when should I start?"

"Young man," Professor Mendell said, wiping mud

from his glasses, "you're lucky we don't have you arrested. Now get off of my campus, and never come back."

"But—"

"Do you wish to be chased off by the guards?"

"No, but—"

"Then get off. Now."

Mournfully, Cade turned and trudged off.

TWO
Sir Bernard, the Better Than Everybody Else

"Let go of thine noble damsel, fiendish dragon!" Sir Bernard began to perform a bizarre dance in front of the red dragon, armor creaking despite a fresh oiling just that morning by one of Bernard's servants. Sword waving in the air, tower shield clumsily barking, Bernard finished and fell on his steel-coated knees.

Pendrick watched with a combination of boredom and amusement. Flaunting the flat spines on his back, a sign he didn't find this knight errant much of a threat, he turned to see the "damsel" in question.

She seemed to be equally unfazed by the fact that she was supposed to be held captive by an enormous fire-breathing dragon.

"What will you do if I don't let her go?" the dragon asked. He began to pick at his teeth with the rib bone of a cow.

"I'll, uh, be forced to vanquish you!"

"Go ahead."

"Could I just say something—" "Damsel" began.

"Be silent, woman!" Bernard replied confidently. "Your rescue is at hand!"

"But—"

"But first let me dispose of this hideous beast!"

"Well that's not very nice," Pendrick commented with mock indignation. These hero types, he thought. Yeesh. What a bunch of morons.

The knight errant let out a war cry, then charged. Pendrick, with one of his enormous claws, flicked the knight back, slamming him against the cave wall. Bernard collapsed in a heap of steel.

"How 'bout this," Pendrick suggested brightly. "I put my paws behind my back, and turn my head so I can't breath fire on you. How's that?"

Bernard, dismayed that the foe was trying to let him win, muttered something about "never trusting a dragon's honor," then charged. He thrust his mighty sword into Pendrick's chest, and—

The scale made an interesting chiming sound as the long sword bounced off and flew toward the end of the cave.

"Oh dear," Pendrick chuckled. "That tickled."

Bernard snarled, and made another thrust, this time slashing the blade across in a wide sweep. This made a full octave, and "Damsel" laughed and applauded.

Livid, Bernard went around to the other end, and struggled to get on the dragon's back. Alas, his armor was too heavy.

"Need a hand?" Pendrick allowed Bernard to scramble onto his paw, then gently placed the knight on his back. Angrier than ever, the knight began slashing the scales on Pendrick's spine. "Vile beast!" Bernard puffed as he hacked away at the hide. "You have soiled my honor!"

"If you don't shut up and go away, I'll soil your armor too." Pendrick yawned. Then, turning to the "Damsel," he muttered, "Think I should get vanquished now?"

"Damsel" shrugged. "Sure, why not. I'll tell him once we get outside the cave."

The dragon nodded. Then he let out an agonized roar (and a very realistic one, at that), and collapsed. Bernard stumbled, and fell off the beast, bouncing once in the dirt, and landing at "Damsel's" knees. Then, struggling to a kneeling position, he bowed his head before "Damsel."

"M'lady," he said, "I am but a humble servant of the gods. If you will grant me thy noble blessing—"

"Get up, you idiot," "Damsel" snapped.

Stunned, Bernard obeyed. "First of all," she continued, "I'm not a noble woman. I'm a biologist. Second of all, that dragon's not dead, in case you haven't noticed."

Bernard heard a deep snicker come from within the belly of the beast. He shivered.

"And third of all, I was in no danger at all. I was interviewing him!"

Bernard blinked. He looked at Pendrick. Then the biologist. The wheels in his mind started to work, searching desperately for some valiant way to make sure this misadventure never got out. Dragons lived in solitude, and this one didn't seem like the type to press charges. But the biologist posed a threat.

"Alas!" Bernard cried. "You have been put under a vile spell by that beast! I am sorry, m'lady, but this must be done."

With that, he drew his sword and approached the biologist. After all this trouble, he felt he needed to shed some blood in the name of his king, even if that blood was that of an innocent woman. He heaved his sword at her, expecting to run her through. The biologist slipped to Bernard's right, and the last thing he remembered was the sole of her shoe blocking his ability to see through his visor.

When he woke up, he was miles from the cave. Grumbling, he staggered to his feet, and then realized that his tower shield was missing. Oh well, he'd just say it was cut in half while he was battling a hydra…or maybe an army of orcs that decided not to invade the kingdom. Yeah, the orcs story sounded good.

Shoulders slumped, he trudged back to town, which was just over the hill.

"I have returned!" Sir Bernard announced as he strode into the court of King Devham.

"Ah," the king said, "very good. Now, tell me of your exploits for today." The hall was large and imposing, filled with the stench of ale mixed with ancient tomes and generations of rulers. The king himself sat on a throne made of solid gold (with some cushions for comfort), and despite his girth, made larger by years of gluttony and sloth, he still looked too small for the throne. While most kings had long, luxurious manes, Devham was still struggling to grow his facial hair, hoping it would make him look wise. Thus, his "beard" was little more than unkempt stubble, which had the undesired effect of making people wonder if he bathed often enough.

"Well," Bernard said, then dove into the speech he had crafted as he headed home. It was a long tale, involving an army of orcs, cowardly elves, and, of course, an evil dragon.

"And what happened to your helmet? How'd the boot print get there?"

Bernard cursed. He had forgotten about that blasted kick the biologist had given him. "Oh, uh, you see, an elf tried to ambush me by jumping out of a tree. He landed right on me. Fortunately for me, he was light, so I tore him off and cleft him in half."

"Of course," the king said with his unfailing suspension of disbelief. Sir Bernard was the "king's pet," and no lie, no matter how ridiculous, would change that.

"Well, no matter. Good knight, come closer. There is something I must show you."

Sir Bernard removed his helmet as he stepped forward. He was a handsome man, with blond hair and blue eyes, but his gaze had an irritating vacancy that made it look as if he'd been kicked in the head too many times.

As he approached, Devham thrust a piece of parchment into his hands. Bernard read it (slowly, since education had never been one of his priorities when he was a child), and his eyes widened. He looked up at the king and grinned. Devham tossed him a quill pen.

"Well," he said, "are you going to sign up?"

CHAPTER
THREE
The Imperfect Crime

"This is excellent." Milo chuckled to himself and rubbed his hands together. "I'll be right under their noses!"

He had spent weeks planning the robbery. It was to be his greatest—the greatest of all time. The grand ball at the castle of King Devham had been planned for months. And now Milo was going to crash the party by stealing the king's crown right off his fat, poorly shaven head. After spending nearly all his silvers on information from easily-bribed guards, and assembling the equipment to perform the job, Milo was ready. He'd have his money back a hundred times over once he purloined the precious headgear!

So there Milo stood, peering over the edge of the tallest tower, surveying the moat below. This would have made any normal-size person him easily seen. But Milo was a halfling and he was all but invisible to the those below.

Like most halflings, Milo disdained the "taller folk"

as clumsy brutes who could easily be taken advantage of. So he had become a thief. He stole from the rich, because, after all, they didn't really need all that cash, did they? And, with all the gouging those oversized monkey-brained monarchs did, they deserved to have a little cash lifted.

Milo peered down through the skylight. The king, he could see, was beginning his slow swagger down the grand hall.

Showtime.

Carefully Milo cut away one of the panes on the skylight and attached his anchor to the roof beside it. Then, strapping the harness to his waist, he flicked a switch on the anchor. The wheel inside the anchor began to turn, slackening the rope attached to Milo's waist. The idea was that the anchor would lower him down.

There was a speed dial and a reverse button on Milo's harness. He jumped through the window pane, praying the old wizard he had bought it from would make good on his promise of complete reliability.

At that moment, somebody looked up and shouted to the others. Milo smiled. The better the show, the bigger his name would be. Devham had broken into a run. Milo cranked up the speed, and came to a halt at the rope's end.

The king was already at the other end of the court. "State your name," he shouted.

"I'm the great Milo Pennywise," the thief replied. "The greatest thief in all the land."

"It looks like your luck's run out, thief. Guards!"

"Not exactly, King Devham. I'll be taking that

crown now." From his belt, Milo produced a long wooden rod with a button on it, another trinket from the wizard. When he pressed the button, a long, thin rope shot from the rod with a wad of adhesive on the end. The adhesive hit the crown, tore it right off of Devham's head, then quickly retracted. The king's eyes widened, and the guards dashed forward. Milo waved, and slammed down the reverse lever, cranking up the speed dial as far as it would go.

"Ta-ta," he howled as he shot toward the roof. "Now all will remember my name. The great Milo Pennywise, the one who stole the crown right off the king's—"

One of the guards had run up to the roof and had grabbed a lever on the device.

"—head!" The anchor stopped and Milo began to fall back to the hall. "Oop," he muttered. A guard must have gotten to the reverse switch at the anchor. Cursing, Milo pulled out the rod again, and fired it at the skylight.

The guards lunged for Milo all at the same time. When Milo popped up to the ceiling, they were subjected to a gloriously painful and brutally efficient head-butting, which put them all out like candles in a hurricane. Meanwhile, Milo was on the ceiling, unbuckling his harness and chuckling softly. Removing the other rod he always kept, he shot it out the skylight.

Jeremiah, the guard who had crawled up on the roof, had been watching the whole thing, and couldn't help but grin. He had stopped that thief. He would be a hero. Maybe he'd even be made a captain.

His nearly-toothless grin turned to a gape of horrified surprise when something sticky attached to a long rope hit him in the ankle. Gasping, he fell over, smashing his jaw against the ground.

"No!" Milo shouted, as he saw his glimmering trophy slip from his belt. He'd have only one chance to reach it as it fell. Otherwise, he'd leave empty-handed and on the run, or he simply wouldn't leave. He shot another rod at the crown, and missed, hitting the floor instead. The rod began to yank the howling thief toward a three-story drop.

Jeremiah's eyes snapped open. The first thing he realized was that his jaw hurt. The second was that he was being dragged toward the skylight. His hands fumbled along the cobblestone path, looking for a sturdy grip. He found none, and began to drop.

Milo realized he was slowing down, and sighed in relief. Then he turned and saw the guard he had knocked out struggling to get back inside, and moaned in despair. Two hammy legs kicked desperately at the wall, searching for a foothold as the rope grew tighter and tighter. Milo wasted no time in using the stall to shake loose the rod in his right hand. Now, thanks to his weight (he was a feather compared to Jeremiah), he snapped back, and landed directly on the guard's heel. The jolt made Jeremiah gasp in surprise, and he slipped.

Realizing that being crushed by a 270-pound man is not the most pleasant way to go, Milo leapt, shaking the rod loose as he did so. He soared all of two inches, then began twisting around to fire the rod. If he could make it shoot to the ceiling...

The rod fell just short. The halfling cursed, but a multi-syllabic word he had learned in a pub was cut off by a sharp pain in his back, followed by a dull thudding sound. The fog cleared quickly, and Milo leapt to his feet before quickly executing a high kick and running along the table he had just landed on. Lucky for him, he had landed in a particularly large green gelatin cake. Had he landed on the cheese tray, he would have been impaled by dozens of tiny toothpicks.

Jeremiah was not so lucky. He landed near the edge of one table, snapping it, and making the other end pop up like a seesaw. Unfortunately for him, one of the side dishes was boiled rice.

Everything else went flying off the table. Aristocrats shielded themselves from flying forks and knives. As for the food, suffice it to say it provided some cushioning for the impact of those metal platters. One aristocrat had been wearing a stylish hat with a large, circular platform at the top, on which a platter of roasted chicken landed. He shrieked, and the chicken slipped off the platter and landed on the floor. The next day it was found perfectly unscathed by servants. They didn't let on where it had been when they served it to the king for supper.

The rice met another fate. When the table flipped, the rice left the pan, and the pan hit Jeremiah on the head. He jumped up, causing the table to overturn. The rice had been kept warm by water boiling over a small twig fire , and the overturned table sent flaming twigs everywhere. The panic intensified.

This incident with the rice, boiling water, flipping

table, flaming twigs, flying entrees, deadly flying silverware, and lucky poultry all occurred within the space of one second. And by the time that second was up, Milo was gone, the crown, unfortunately, left on the floor. In the panic, even the great Milo Pennywise could not reach his loot.

FOUR
Recruiting Women is for the Elves

The woman who appeared in Frederick's recruiting center seemed quite serious about joining the royal guard. She was attractive, he had to admit, but clearly didn't know her place in the natural order of things. Everyone knew women were weak; why would this one be any different? He decided to humor her.

"Name," he said, not raising his eyes from the parchment on his desk. They were sitting in a musty cabin that served as the town recruitment center, sparsely decorated with two chairs and a wooden desk.

"Ana Anastacion," the woman replied.

"Date of birth."

Ana responded with the date.

This continued for a little while, cutting back and forth in brief sentences. Finally, Frederick stood, a bulky, broad-shouldered man whose hair was just beginning to thin. "Come with me," he said as he led her to a large room filled with obstacles, ropes, and weapons. Frederick expected the woman to be frightened at the sight of it (as he assumed most women did), but Ana seemed unfazed.

"The testing arena," Frederick explained, "is where we decide whether you're good enough to play in the big leagues. Three officers, one of which will be me, will come at you. You have to keep us at bay for as long as I see fit, in which case you'll be recruited. If we catch you, it will be marked on your record, and you won't be able to join, or even try to get recruited again for two years. Understand?"

"Yes."

"Then welcome to your challengers."

Two men appeared. They were slightly skinnier than Frederick, and both wore chain mail vests. Frederick introduced them as Mel and Benson. Ana looked at them with what Frederick thought was slight disappointment, but he knew they could crush her easily.

"When I give the word, it begins," Frederick said, backing up. "Ready...go!"

Mel and Benson began to charge . Ana didn't move. Frederick shook his head. She must be really slow. He knew from experience that they were rhinos.

Mel and Benson's fists flew forward as they got within range. Ana ducked right under them, and delivered two simultaneous uppercuts to their abdomens, grabbed their ankles, and flipped the two charging rhinos neatly over her head.

Frederick gasped. He had never seen anybody, much less a woman, move that fast. Well, he decided, she would have to be taught a real lesson now. He hated to lay his hands on a fragile inferior being, but she had earned it.

Benson and Mel staggered to their feet, but Ana was already running toward the rope at the far wall. A log was placed as an obstacle, and she leapt over it effortlessly, leaving the two men to stumble over it. Grabbing the rope, Ana kicked against the wall, and swung toward the two, grabbing a quarterstaff from the weapons rack on the way. She gave Mel a strong thwap on the head one way, and as she swung back, another for Benson. Now Frederick was taking chase, grabbing the rope and hopping onto it, climbing up. He, too, snatched up a quarterstaff. Ana glanced down and climbed higher.

Is she insane? Frederick thought. She's going to get killed if I drop her from that height.

Still, he sighed and climbed farther. As they reached the very top of the rope (two stories up, at the ceiling of the testing arena), Ana looked down, took in a deep breath, and jumped. Frederick shouted in surprise. As she fell, Ana hit the wall again, bounded off it, and grabbed the rope directly below Frederick. It swung from the impact, and Frederick swung with it. Losing his grip from the surprise, he landed on the matted floor, and though there was no serious injury, he got a bruise on the forehead he would never forget. Ana bounded down beside him, and pressed her quarterstaff to his throat.

"Ready to give—" she began, when Benson and Mel both leapt on her at the same time. She heard them shout an incoherent war cry as they lunged through the air, running toward them, whirling her quarterstaff, and knocking them out of the air. Then she turned back to Frederick.

"—up? Well?"

Frederick shuddered. "Get out," he muttered.

"I beat you. All three of you. I deserve to be recruited."

"I said that you had to keep at us for an allotted amount of time. It's not over yet."

"So you'd like to have another go? Fine with me. I haven't shown off all my moves yet."

Frederick stood up, and realized his tongue was bleeding. He spat at the floor, and wiped his mouth. Then, hefting his quarterstaff, he got into the fighting position. "You're good at evasion," he said, "but a woman can't stand and fight like a man."

"As we can see, fighting like a man isn't really a compliment."

Frederick roared, and struck with his quarterstaff, hoping to trip Ana. Her quarterstaff went down to block his before providing a quick jab at the side of his face. He jabbed and whirled and slashed, but he couldn't break through Ana's defenses. And every time he tried, she would respond by giving him a sharp slash with her quarterstaff. But she couldn't fight forever, and it looked like she was tiring. So Frederick pressed on. Finally, he broke through. The two quarterstaffs clashed together forming an "X" shape between the competitors. Ana drew hers away to make another blow, and Frederick attempted to block. But he knew she was too fast. And she wanted to end this.

Then Benson and Mel were up again, and each grabbed Ana by one arm, dragging her back. Her quarterstaff fell to the ground. Frederick, on reflex, smashed her in the stomach with his. It shattered. Ana went limp in the arms of Frederick's two companions. Their grips loosened. They realized too late that Ana was still conscious, and simply waiting for their grips to loosen. Ana's eyes lit up with pure rage—a look that Frederick would never forget—and she grabbed their shoulders, hurling them both at Frederick.

Looking down at the unconscious pile and ignoring the pain in her ribs, Ana considered what to do with them. She couldn't wait for them to wake up and claim recruitment, because the fact is, she had been out for a second or two from that blow Frederick had delivered. So, she decided to press on. In the capital city, maybe there would be a recruit center that would react reasonably. Unless her documentation got there first. Two years...

Grimacing, Ana told herself she could take the pain. It wasn't so long a walk, anyway.

CHAPTER
FIVE
Fool's Tavern

Cade nursed his wooden mug of seltzer, blocking out all but the swishing bubbles and the soft pitter-patter of rain outside. Fool's Tavern, as it was appropriately called, was far too loud and obnoxious for him, with lots of bawdy songs, shouting, and card playing.

A large hairy half-ogre was asleep next to Cade, his large, bulky arms spread out over the table, and a thin line of drool rolling toward the bartender who was absentmindedly mopping it up. "Don't mind ol' Grob there," he told Cade. "He's always passing out all over the tavern. Drools a stream, if y'know what I'm sayin'."

Cade knew exactly what he was saying.

"So," the bartender said, "what brings an educated man like yerself to a motley tavern like this?

Cade didn't look up. "I need a room," he muttered. "And a job."

The fact was, the tavern was the cheapest place in town, and Cade had very little money left. When he had gotten home from the Academy, he had seen an eviction notice nailed to his door. So, he had set out for the capital, hoping that he would be able to find a home and a source of income there.

The bartender nodded knowingly, which is something a bartender has to be good at, even if he's thinking about something else, such as sheepherding. Then he walked away.

The door banged open, and a crack of thunder made the entire room grow silent. Cade turned.

Swaggering into the room was Aust Galanodel, soaking wet, though his feather, oddly, was as red and perky as ever. He came over to Cade, dragged the half-ogre off his stool, letting him hit the ground with a thud. Then he climbed onto the stool himself, placing his harp on the ground as he did so.

"Drink," he announced, slapping the table. The bartender came over, and poured him some Black Whiskey, the finest he had.

The bartender saw Aust reaching for his a pouch of gold coins, and stopped him. "It's on the house, Mr. Galanodel," he said nervously. "You're famous around these parts." He chuckled nervously. "Just please, don't sing!"

"Ah, good man," Aust said to Cade. "Knows what it's like to be a great bard, I imagine. Doesn't want me to strain the vocal cords. Good man."

Cade, seeing the expression on the bartender's face, decided wisely not to argue.

"So what's your name?" Aust asked, clapping Cade roughly on the back.

"Cade Welkland."

"Good name. I am Aust Galanodel, great bard, poet, singer, and all around entertainer." He stuck out a hand, and before Cade could extend his own, Aust reached over and shook it. Then he turned toward the bartender.

"Sir, a drink for my new friend Cade here!" He slapped Cade on the back again, who gripped the edge of the bar, to protect his ribs from slamming against it.

"So," Aust said, "what's with the long face?"

"Uh—"

"Eviction notice? Looking for work in the capital? Yes, I thought so. I know what'd cheer you up, friend! Have some whiskey. I'm going to go look around for a nice little game goin' on. If you know how to cheat, you can make a fortune at those things. Be back in a jiffy."

Aust grabbed his mug and wandered around the bar, trying not to choke on pipe weed smoke. He saw a few games of cards, and decided to join one.

"So, fellows," he said cheerily, setting down his mug at the one empty spot of the table. "What are the stakes today? I'd be happy to add my pile to the share."

"Y'really wanna join in?" a large dwarf demanded.

"Sure, uh…"

"Brottor. Brottor Baldcrk."

"Aust Galanodel. Sure, why not? What are the stakes?"

"No money."

"Oh?"

"This is a gamble of a different kind."

The dwarf stroked his red beard thoughtfully, trying to clear his head of cobwebs and pipe weed. He was dressed in rusty chain mail, and a blackened horned helmet was on the table beside him. "There," he said, pointing at a piece of parchment nailed to the wall. "The losers have to sign that."

Aust looked over at the parchment.

HEROES NEEDED

A CONTEST WILL BE HELD AT THE KING'S COURT TOMORROW. ALL WHO WISH MAY JOIN. THE SIX WINNERS WILL BE GIVEN A QUEST TO SET OUT UPON. REPORT TO THE TAVERN AT WHICH THIS NOTICE IS PLACED AT NOON TOMORROW TO BE LED TO THE ROYAL COURT. BRING ALL AVAILABLE ARMOR AND WEAPONS. A YARD SALE WILL ALSO BE HELD BY THE BLACKSMITH AT THE FRONT GATES. CASH ONLY!

Following that was a price list for various weapons and armor.

Beneath that were no signatures.

Aust smiled to himself. He had always written about adventurers, but to be one: that was a death wish! And the contest itself would be back-breakingly painful. Only a lunatic would sign.

Fortunately, Aust knew how to cheat. Unfortunately, he was already going over his limit of alcohol and fatigue, a deadly mix when gambling.

"Alright then," he said.

"Good," Brottor replied. "Roll up your sleeves."

Aust hadn't been prepared for this. He always kept

a few extra cards up his sleeves. "Say again?" he asked innocently.

"Roll up your sleeves. Never trust an elf, I say. So, roll 'em up."

Aust sighed. "I'm offended that you would suggest that I'm a cheater. Ha! I'll not play with ruffians like yourself!"

And he marched off.

"So he's scared, is 'e," the dwarf's companion (a human) jeered. "Just as I suspected. The elf is a lyin' cheat, and doesn't wanna get caught!"

Aust froze, and whirled around.

"How dare you!" he shouted indignantly, folding his arms to hide his cards. "I'll prove I'm not afraid to lose! I'll sign the stinking parchment right now!"

Angrily, he scribbled his name on the paper with a fountain pen he always kept in one pouch. Then he whirled around and stormed away.

Aust took exactly two steps before he realized what he had done. His entire body stiffened. His eyes widened. His mouth fell open. His mouth closed, then opened again silently. Then he whirled around, and stared at the parchment for a while.

Brottor grinned. "Glad I ain't him," he muttered to his friend.

"Don't be too sure," the human said as he slapped his hand down on the table.

Brottor took one look at it, and began to dance much in the manner Aust did, except for pointing at his friend's hand rather than the parchment.

"You don't expect-expect-expect—"

"Expect you to sign it?" The human laughed. "Of course I do. And remember the rest of our agreement."

Brottor sighed miserably. "You get to call me 'Shorty' for a full year."

"That's right."

Aust, regaining his composure, smiled at the dwarf. "Need a pen?"

Brottor snatched it out of his grip, and signed his name. Aust snatched back his pen, smiled brightly, tipped his hat, and strode back to his table.

"Uh…what just happened over there, if you don't mind my asking?" Cade asked.

"Did you see that parchment over there when you walked in?"

"I can see it right now. I have the eyes of a hawk…with my glasses on, that is."

Aust looked at him blankly.

"They're magically augmented," Cade explained. "I've been studying ways to allow them to zoom in and out, and produce perfectly sharp images."

"Oh. Well, about that parchment…"

"Yeah?"

"I just signed it."

Now it was Cade's turn to look at his new friend blankly. "You…signed that parchment."

"Well, yeah."

"You, my friend, are screwed." Cade laughed and slammed his mug on the bar. The bartender ran over and filled it up some more.

"What are you doing?" Aust hissed, grabbing the bartender's apron. "That's a human! He can't handle that much beer! He's dead drunk!"

"Yeah," the bartender replied, grinning, "but I'm makin' a bundle offa him."

Aust sighed, and looked back at Cade. "Why don't you sign it?" he asked.

"Me?" The human snorted. "I'm not exactly the adventuresome type."

"Well, what've you got to lose? You don't have a job, or a house, or money."

Cade nursed his mug for a little while. "Alright," he said finally. "I'll do it." He rose to his feet, and stumbled over to the parchment. He wrote his name on it, then turned around, and like Aust, took two steps before the effect of the signing sank in. His reaction was slightly different though. He simply paused calmly, ran a slightly shaky hand through his hair, then whirled around and slammed himself against the wall, vigorously rubbing both hands against the parchment in a mad effort to wipe off his name, until two waiters, fearing he was damaging the parchment, dragged him to the floor and poured more alcohol down his throat until he went to sleep.

Aust watched all of this while shaking his head in half-amused pity, then helped one of the waiters carry the snoring mage up to his room.

A half hour later, Milo entered the tavern. He drank nothing, and wandered around miserably, picking a few pockets. He made four silvers, but his heart wasn't in it, considering the cash he could have been rolling in at that moment from a genuine king's crown on the black market.

Ana entered, played a few card games, and left the other players feeling dismayed that they had lost to a woman, of all genders. Then she met up with Brottor's companion.

"Sit down," he said, smiling at Ana as he shuffled his deck expertly. "I welcome new blood." When he grinned, his entire face twisted into a plastic mask. His teeth seemed to glow like white beacons. His eyes were a sickly yellow, much like his skin.

If Aust were there at the moment, he would have been puzzled by the sudden change that Brottor's friend seemed to have undergone. Before he had been a loud, boorish tavern rat. Now he was a polite card sharp. Strangest of all were the physical changes. As Brottor's friend had been thick-skinned, bald, and sadly lacking of a neck, now he was lanky, had a grotesquely long neck, and a light layer of unhealthy, straw-like hair. Still, the eyes were the same. Those yellow, sharp eyes.

Unfortunately, Aust was not present to notice this distinct change, as he was lying on a lumpy mattress in an upstairs room, staring at the ceiling and trying to recall all those songs he had heard about brave elven adventurers, who got lots of cash, got the girl, and became famous. Unfortunately, only the stories about morons getting themselves killed while trying to fight dragons came to mind.

Ana pulled over a chair and sat at the table. "Stakes?" she asked.

"Not money, if that's what you're thinking. I have something more interesting in mind."

"I'm listening."

"See that parchment over there?"

Ana glanced at it.

"Let me guess," she said, "loser has to sign that?" She laughed cynically. "Sorry, but I'm not that stupid. I'd rather play for profit."

"You're right." The man sighed as Ana turned to join another game. "I don't know why I bothered asking you anyway. Adventuring is a man's job, really."

He struck the right nerve with those words, and he clearly knew what he was doing, judging from his broad grin.

Ana stiffened, then whirled around and slammed a fist on the table. It was full of silvers. "For the signature," she said, "and five silvers."

The man flipped five silvers out onto the table. "Deal," he said primly.

Five minutes later, Ana signed the parchment, rented a room with what little money she had left, then walked upstairs and began slamming her forehead against the doorframe until it began to splinter.

Milo walked up to Brottor's companion, sat down, gulped down a beer he had bought with his stolen silvers. He had no intention of playing cards, and much to his surprise, Brottor's friend didn't ask.

"What'd you get that poor woman into?" Milo chuckled. Brottor's friend shrugged, smiling himself. Milo noticed that although he wasn't a halfling, the human was pretty short, not like a lot of the other big clumsy lugs that felt so special for being able to see over the bar without the aid of stools. He had thick hair that hadn't been cut in a while, and a halfling's sharp eyes—except, of course, for their putrid yellow colr, nothing like the pleasant softer colors that halflings usually have.

Milo looked over at the parchment, then looked back at the human. "Sounds pretty exciting, doesn't it?" he commented.

"Why don't you sign, then?"

Milo snorted. "Me? Y'really want to know what I do for a living, friend? I'm a thief. Thieves have no place in adventuring."

"Lots of thieves get into adventurin'. There's a big fat profit to be made from it, I can tell ya that, and most heroes don't live long, considerin' they try to run straight for the baddies. But thieves, folks like yerself, are different. You're smart. You can go around the orcs just as easily as goin' right at them. You can go in, get the gold, and get out without ever bein' noticed. That's how an adventurer makes real money!"

Milo thought about that, then gulped down some more beer.

"Alright then," he said, "I have nothing to lose!"Milo scribbled his name on the parchment, then raised his mug high as he whirled around. "To adventurin'!" he shouted, jumping up onto a table. Several people who had nothing to do with adventuring but needed an excuse to toast something, repeated this cry.

"Say, friend," Milo said to the human, "you never told me yer name."

"My name's Loki."

"Loki..."

"Nothing else. Just Loki."

Milo stared blankly at him for a while, then started to get a bit dizzy and fell off the table, fast asleep.

CHAPTER
SIX
The Contest Begins

Morning. Sunlight streamed through the windows of Fool's Tavern. The bartender was mopping vomit and beer off the floor, humming and waiting for somebody from the rooms upstairs to come down and ask what had happened to all his clothes and money the previous night.

There was a knock on the door, a heavy one, one that almost knocked the rickety old door off its hinges. The bartender answered it. A royal guard appeared, clothed in formal plate mail, studded with rubies and painted gold, with the seal of House Devham painted on the chest plate. His face was obscured, and his voice muffled by an enormous helmet.

"Do you have the list?"

"The list? Uh...oh...the list!" The bartender ambled over to the parchment which Ana, Aust, Brottor, Cade, and Milo had all signed, tore it from its nail, and handed it to the guard. The guard's eyes went to the bottom name on the list.

"Where is this Miia Bohnvwize? Strange name. One of your regulars?"

"Lemme see that," he said, and grabbed the paper. "Oh! Milo Pennywise. Yeh, he was a little far gone when he signed his name. I remember that well. He passed out under that table o'er there. He's a small one, so you can't see him from here, but he's there."

Sure enough, a halfling was snoring contentedly under the table. The guard loomed over him.

"Get up," he said gruffly. The halfling rubbed his eyes and looked up. Then he began to scream his lungs out.

A bad day, in Milo's definition, is one in which you wake up with a horrible hangover. A worse day is one in which you know you've done something bad, but can't remember what it was, but know you'll suffer for it. A really terrible day is one where you wake up a wanted man. Today, Milo had the feeling he was about to find a new low in bad days, one which only the most sadistic could ever imagine possible.

Since all of these requirements were met, it was perfectly reasonable for Milo to scream his lungs out. "Maybe we can cut a deal!" Milo sputtered, jumping back from the guard.

"I could get in serious trouble if I don't deliver you to the king! How's that for a deal?"

Milo felt sick. He was getting sent right to the king, where he'd probably get his head removed.

"Of course there's a chance you could live," the guard said, "a small one, but there is that chance—if you win this thing."

Win this thing? Milo felt briefly confused, then realized he must be talking about some kind of court case. "But the king himself is judge!" he shrieked.

The guard shrugged. "I can't help that," he said. "Now come quietly, and maybe I won't break your nose."

Miserably, Milo followed the guard, who sat him down in a wooden chair.

"I'll go get the others," the guard said as he headed upstairs. Milo was once again briefly confused by the lack of anything to restrain him. He considered making a break for it, then saw the burly half-ogre bartender blocking the doorway. Small and maneuverable as he was, Milo would have no advantage in the situation.

Two minutes later, the guard was leading the woman from the bar down the stairs. He sat her down in one of the chairs, and went back up again.

"Hey," Milo whispered, "what did you get caught for?"

The woman looked a little confused. "I didn't do anything," she said.

She looks honestly bewildered, Milo thought. *That was some good acting on her part.* "That was good," he said, "but really, what did you do?"

"Nothing!"

"Right. Okay, I get it. Never mind. Good luck trying that shtick in court, though."

"Court? What are you talking about?" The woman looked genuinely annoyed at Milo.

Next came down a nervous-looking young man with glasses.

"Great," Milo muttered as the guard went back upstairs. "More of them. What, did I walk in on, a thief's convention or something?"

The man with glasses looked confused too.

"We're being arrested?" he cried.

"What tipped you off, genius?" Milo muttered.

"Bu-bu-but, I thought we were going to the contest. The one I signed up for on that sheet!"

"What the hell are you talking about?" Milo demanded. And before Cade could respond, Milo remembered: the parchment! This did not improve Milo's mood, though, because it dawned on him he would be coming face-to-face with King Devham anyway. The last person he wanted to see.

The castle was five stories tall, except for the center, where the skylight dipped to a mere three stories in height. In daylight, it was a dull gray, appearing more like a big, dumb older brother than the fearsome fortress it was at night.

"Halt!" a voice called from the tower to the left of the gate. A small fish flew from the tower, and hit Aust in the face.

"Sorry!" the guard called. "I was feedin' the alligators in the moat and my hand slipped! Now then, who goes there?"

The escort stared angrily up at the guard. "These people are here for the competition," he growled. "Lower the bridge!"

Recognizing the gold-plated armor, the guards mumbled some "yes, sirs" and "aye ayes" before the bridge dropped and the gate creaked open.

The throne room had been cleaned up since the previous night's misadventures, Milo noted. Even the skylight had been repaired. The broken tables had been cleared out to make way for the adventurers standing on either side of a brand-new red carpet. They stood rigidly, their eyes fixed straight ahead. The patrons of Fool's Tavern assumed similar positions.

"Adventurers!" a man holding a large scroll shouted from the doorway, making Cade jump. "I bring you...His Royal Highness King Devham!"

From behind a curtain, trumpets began to play a loud, majestic theme. Devham strolled through a large door, and over to his throne, his royal chin raise arrogantly.

"Heroes!" Devham proclaimed. "Adventurers! Wanderers, mercenaries, drifters, and thugs. Today, you will all compete for the greatest honor of all. Hundreds of you today are competing for the chance to go forth and complete a marvelous quest to spread the glory of this kingdom."

Oh wonderful, Ana, Milo, and Cade thought at once. Aust thought it too, but with more enthusiasm, and, as usual, Brottor's mind was on killing large, green, ugly people.

While this speech went on, Cade scanned the crowd. Most of them were thugs or mercenaries. There were a few knights and some miserable fools who looked like they had signed their parchments on drunken dares. His eyes went to the man to Devham's left, and his mouth dropped.

That bastard, he thought. So it's true. No wonder he looks so happy.

Sir Bernard saw Cade gaping at him, and smiled arrogantly.

"The contest," Devham continued, "will continue far into the night, and test the mettle, as well as the metal, you all must possess. It will range from jousting to horseback racing, to one-on-one free-for-all combat. And the six victors, the glorious champions, will be heroes—not just normal heroes, but heroes sponsored by this kingdom! And who among you will succeed? Will it be the noble knight? The ruthless barbarian? The cunning mercenary? The quick-footed scout? We shall see! And now, to the field!"

Nearly everybody, with the exception of Ana, Cade, and Milo began to cheer. The king smiled, then strolled down the carpet and through the door. Everybody else followed him.

"Cade!" Bernard cried in mock surprise, running toward the wizard. "How's everything been going for you? Trying to join the great adventurers of our age?" He laughed uproariously. "You must be desperate!" Then his face turned serious. "I'll crush you like the pathetic worm you are," he said matter-of-factly, then followed the crowd.

"The first contest," Devham explained as the contestants gazed in awe at the rows and rows of banisters, with strips on either side just wide enough for a horse to run over it, "is the jousting tournament. You and a selected partner will get into spare sets of armor, grab a lance, and charge toward each other. The first to get knocked off their horse loses. Any questions?"

One hand rose.

"Yes?" the king called.

"Uh, what if somebody gets decapitated, but he doesn't fall off the horse, and his opponent does?"

"The one who's still alive is declared winner in that situation. Any other questions? Yes, you again?"

"Well, uh, what if they both slip at the same time?"

"Slip?"

"Accidentally fall of their horses, Your Highness."

"Then there will be a rematch. More questions?"

"Yes, Your Highness. For instance, what if—"

"One more word, and I'll have you executed."

"But...what if...with the lances—"

Devham nodded to a guard, who brandished his sword threateningly.

"Sheesh," the curious adventurer muttered. "Just asking a bloody logical question."

Cade's horse pawed at the ground, and Cade glared at his opponent. He could no longer feel the armor weighing down on him, the pads giving him a rash. All he could feel was anger at Bernard.

So the bastard thinks he'll crush me like a worm, does he? Cade thought. I'll show the brain-dead muscle head who's the worm. I'll win this contest using my wits, and wizardry!

If Cade didn't feel so angry, he would think he was insane. Obviously, success would spell certain doom for him, but right now, all that mattered was showing up that bastard Bernard. It was time to play rough, Cade decided for the first time in his life.

His opponent sneered at him through the helmet

visor, and Cade sneered back. Already he was pushing electrons back and forth, manipulating the straps on his opponent's saddle. As soon as he so much as tapped the contestant with his lance, he would go flying off the horse.

"Begin!" King Devham shouted. Cade kicked his horse to get it running, then hefted his lance, preparing to hit his opponent. He saw his opponent's lance coming for his face, and ducked to the side, thrusting his lance forward at the same time. It hit his opponent in the arm, knocking his lance away, and toppling him over, but Cade didn't see that.

He didn't see that because his saddle had been adjusted too loosely. He was currently sitting on a saddle that had flipped under the belly of the horse. His head was dragging on the ground.

And the horse wouldn't stop.

Milo's feet wouldn't touch the stirrups, so he sat with his feet dangling over the sides of the horse, holding his lance with both hands, and struggling to keep it upright. The king shouted to begin, and Milo gulped, looking at his opponent's lance. There had been no armor that fit the thief, so if he got hit with that thing, he'd end up being skewered like an shish-kabob. He'd have to dodge it, and quickly.

Dodge it, he thought slyly. *That gives me an idea.*

His opponent was already charging. Milo gripped the reins and urged the horse forward. The horse snorted without looking up, and didn't move. Milo muttered something no horse should ever have to hear, and watching his opponent approach, timed his leap.

Milo jumped, and grabbed his opponent's helmet. His opponent gasped in surprise and began to flail. His horse began to panic too, and ran around in circles, disrupting several other jousting matches.

Cade's horse, still dragging the poor wizard along, galloped toward Milo and his opponent, and collided with the horse they were precariously perched on, sending the whole group flying. Hastily consulting the rule book and finding nothing about these things, King Devham reluctantly declared Milo and Cade victors.

Half of the contestants were eliminated in that contest, and when all the jousting equipment was cleared away, the reluctant adventurers from Fool's Tavern, plus Bernard, were victors.

"The next contest," the king announced, "will be a battle of strength, speed, and wits on an obstacle course. Ten people will compete at once, and only one will succeed. Since there are about two hundred and forty of you, this will continue until it is narrowed down to the top twelve. Any questions? Yes, you?"

"What if one of the victors has a cardiac arres—"

"Shut up! I'm sick of listening to you! Guards, seize him!"

Aust was judged as having the fastest time for the obstacle course in his category, possibly because he was an elf, and elves are built for climbing and swinging through the forest quickly; Or possibly because his competition was a bunch of nitwits.

Cade once again used magic, and a little luck. It would be several days before most of his opponents could sit down without wincing.

Brottor bared his teeth angrily at his opponents, and knocked all of them unconscious with his axe. In spite of the grueling three hours it took him to get to the finish line, due to his bulkiness and height, he succeeded.

Ana too, knocked all of her opponents unconscious, then woke up the ones who had made sexist remarks, using a series of extremely painful wrestling pins, and knocked them unconscious again. She slung two of them over her shoulder, and crossed the finish line. It was declared a tie. She tried again, this time knocking them all unconscious, but not bothering to wake them or carry anybody over the finish line, assuming her point had already been made. It was considered a tie-breaking round.

Sir Bernard called upon the Holy Ruler and forced all his opponents to grovel, or be executed by royal order. Then he took his sweet time crossing the finish line, while all his opponents had their heads between their knees.

Milo, using his lack of height to his advantage, ran between the legs of each of his opponents one by one, tripping them in the process, then stomped on their heads until they blacked out. Another man was ahead of him, but when he saw Milo lunging for his ankles, he yelped and gave up first place.

"Now," King Devham declared after dozens of matches in which Bernard and the Fool's Tavern group used their basic strategies and succeeded every time, "twelve remain. Six of you will have the honor of fulfilling my quest. The most intense round of all is about to begin: the gladiator arena!"

This caused a loud gasp to run through the crowd. Devham smiled gleefully. "There are four ways to succeed: knock a person out of the arena using your weapon of choice; force them to yield; knock them unconscious, or...kill them."

"I'll split you up into six groups in six different rings. Let's see...uh, you, and you go together...and you two over there..."

Despite the odds, none of our heroes were paired up against each other.

Six pairs of competitors in six arenas walked slowly around each other, waiting for the right moment to strike. With bloodthirsty satisfaction, Devham sighed and leaned back into his throne as servants popped grapes into his mouth.

The would-be adventurers who had been eliminated from the tournament gambled on who would become an adventurer and who would end up sprinkled into the moat as alligator food. Faulty rationalization and disdain for wizards and women, made Ana and Cade safe bets for failure. Too, most people had a strong dislike of entertainers, elves, dwarves, and short people, and bet against Aust, Brottor, and Milo. Nearly everyone bet that Bernard would succeed.

A sweaty Cade stood motionless near the edge of his ring, watching his foe intently. His opponent was a skeletal figure sporting cheap armor and a toothless grin. He paced back and forth, waiting for Cade to move, then, realizing the wizard was paralyzed with mortal terror, screamed triumphantly as he charged the mage. Without thinking, Cade blasted him with a bolt of fire.

When the red spots left Cade's eyes, and the flames stopped roaring in his ears, Cade looked up, and saw his opponent, screaming and flailing through the air. Dazed, Cade wondered how much of a blast he had given the man.

Milo danced back and forth, dodging slashes and stabs, waiting for the moment to eliminate his opponent with a quick jab to a nerve. His opponent had turned out to be faster than he thought—stronger too—and now Milo was blocking and dodging, waiting for the moment to strike or the moment to run.

At that moment, a small meteorite landed on his opponent, slamming him into the ground and knocking him unconscious.

The meteorite, wearing charred armor and smoldering lightly, staggered to his feet, grinning drunkenly.

"Did I win?" he asked Milo, then fell forward and lost consciousness.

Bernard slashed and jabbed happily, calling out "Hiyah!" and "Take that, you fiend!" Finally, he knocked his opponent to the ground and pointed his sword at the man's throat.

"Do you yield?" he demanded menacingly.

"Yes! I yield! Don't kill me!"

Bernard thought about it for a little while. "Alright," he said. "Now, go fetch me a chair and some popcorn. I wish to watch the other fights."

His opponent, a servant of the king, nodded gratefully and ran into the castle.

"Do you yield?" Ana growled at her opponent, a pathetic man who was cowering on the ground. The tip of her blade was at his neck.

"I do not yield to women!" the man shouted, then covered his head with his hands.

"So you would rather die at the hands of a woman than simply give up the fight?"

"Yes, why do you ask?" The man sat back on his haunches and looked up at Ana.

"Well, you could give up now and track me down later and kill me later to prove yourself. If I kill you now, however, well, it would be an embarrassing way to die."

"I see your point," the man muttered. "Fine, I give up. But I'll be coming after you, some day!"

"Yeah, yeah," Ana muttered.

Brottor snarled at his opponent, who backed away nervously. Neither had so much as touched the other for two minutes. Battle axe hefted, Brottor looked extremely menacing, even for his diminutive height.

"Neither of us really want to be here, do we?" Brottor growled.

"N-no." Brottor's opponent shook his head nervously.

"No what?"

"No, sir."

"Good. It's stupid for me to just go ahead and kill you, isn't it?"

"Yes, sir."

"Good. Then we're in agreement so far. What should I do, do you think?"

"Dunno—"

"Why don't you just walk out of the arena and forfeit?"

"Uh—"

"NOW!"

"Yessir!" The man scuttled quickly out of the arena, stumbling along the way.

Aust leapt back and forth happily, thrusting his rapier in every direction and dodging blows from his opponent. "Hiyah!" he cried happily. "And hiyah! Take that, you clumsy little monkey-head!" His sword bounced off armor, and he opted to kick it in the stomach instead. A small "oof" came from the armor. Aust's opponent backed away slowly, stumbled, and fell. He struggled to get up, but the weight of his own armor was too much.

"Yield, slow-witted ugly-faced fiend!"

"I yield!" the armor shrieked. "I yield! Just please, for the love of the gods, shut up!"

King Devham read his parchment, muttering the lines over and over to himself, then looked down at six sweaty, disheveled people.

"The winners are," King Devham said, clearing his throat, "Sir Bernard!"

Sir Bernard laced his hands together in one tight fist, and pumped them from side to side, grinning confidently as the crowd burst into applause.

"Ana Anastacion!"

Ana raised her hands into the air, and grinned. Two or three different people clapped softly.

"Aust Galanodel!"

Aust twirled his rapier, thrust it forward, and bowed deeply. The crowd was silent.

"Brottor Balderk!"

Brottor growled menacingly at the crowd, and those closest to him stepped back.

"Milo Pennywise!"

The halfling had to jump as high as he could to make sure those in the back row, or even the third row, could see him. Devham could have sworn he had heard that name somewhere before, but let it slide.

"And Cade Welkland!"

Cade's mouth dropped. He rose to his feet slowly, feeling victory for one of the few times in his life. Then he actually thought about what being an adventurer entailed, and sunk back to the ground, head in his hands. "I'm doomed," he muttered.

A fish, hurled by a guard in the audience, narrowly missed his head.

The initiation ceremonies began in the dining hall. The six champions were lined up before the throne, standing stiffly as the formal occasion required.

"Six champions!" King Devham announced, standing in front of his throne. "Six will brave many perils to bring glory and victory to this kingdom. Your mettle will be put to the test in challenges, like nothing ever seen before!"

Oh joy, Cade thought.

"And now, for the royal quest!"

A trumpet section played a couple of bars. King Devham, holding a scroll, cleared his throat. "There is a great demon that lives west of this kingdom. This demon has a horde of unholy beasts that I have gotten word are planning to invade this fair nation. Adventurers, will you stand before the might of Kaos's army?"

"Yes!" Brottor and Bernard called, their excitement visible.

"As long as it makes for some good anecdotes," said Aust.

"What's the hourly rate?" Milo inquired.

"Now why would I do that?" Ana asked.

"Uh...yeah, sure, whatever you say," Cade whimpered, too meek to say otherwise. "Uh, Your Highness."

"Excellent!" Devham announced. "You will leave tomorrow at the crack of dawn! My servants will provide you with all the needed equipment. But first, there is one other matter I must attend to. You must all be knighted!"

The trumpeters repeated their two bars. The crowd gasped. King Devham drew his sword, and approached them, starting with Bernard.

"I, as King Devha—wait, you've already been knighted. Never mind. Moving on.

"As you say, m'lord."

"I, as king Devha—hold on a sec. You're a wizard, aren't you?"

"Yes, Your Highness," Cade replied. "I specialize in—"

"Can't. Sorry. Way too political. Moving on, I as king Dev—Oh jeez, an elf, huh?"

"I hope so. I've been acting under that assumption for my entire life."

"Well, humans only. Ah, where are the next two?"

"Down here!" Milo called.

"A halfling and a dwarf? That won't do. Oh, here's a human. I, king—Oh, a woman. Yeah. Well, uh, technically, we're not really allowed to knight women. I'm sure you understand, you know, you being inferior to us and all."

"Asshole," Ana muttered.

"Huh?"

"Nothing."

"You said something."

"No I didn't."

"Oh. Well...okay..."

King Devham turned and approached the throne. "Bad news, loyal citizens," he said. "Looks like none of these adventurers can be legally knighted. So, let's get them to their rooms, servants, chop chop! And meanwhile, speaking of chops, what's the kitchen working on for dinner tonight?"

As the group was led up to their rooms, Devham grabbed Milo by the arm.

"Just a moment," he said. "Do I know you from somewhere?"

"Uh, no," Milo said nervously.

"Are you sure?"

"Absolutely."

"You look familiar."

"Sorry, we've never met," Milo said, then rushed up the stairs.

"I've seen him before," Devham muttered to himself, then shrugged and left the room.

The six left in the morning, making their exit to the calls of a hasty goodbye. Many of those saying farewell thought the six were morons to go adventuring, and felt pity for them. The rest were filled with blinding rage that they hadn't been chosen.

So, after the ceremonies, the heroes were hustled outside the castle. They heard the moat roll up quickly behind them, the metal gate falling shut with a loud finality. They turned, sharing a moment's silence as they stared up at the castle.

As soon as the moat closed, Devham remembered where he had seen Milo. His eyes blurred and he staggered to his feet, guards and civilians looking on nervously. His eyes narrowed. "Guards," he muttered through his teeth. "I'm sure you all remember the attempted robbery of my crown?"

"Especially you," Devham added, nodding to Jeremiah, who hadn't been able to sit down ever since that incident.

Jeremiah grunted.

"Did you see that halfling who just left?"

The guards nodded. There was a long silence. "Does anybody recognize him?" Devham asked. All the guards shook their heads.

"Nobody happened to get a good look at him?"

Another shake.

"And nobody seems to understand what I'm getting at?"

Another shake of the head.

"He's the thief, you morons. Now somebody remind me what the hell I hired you people for!"

The guards gaped at him. Devham slumped back into his throne, sighed, and ran a hand through his hair. Nobody moved. "Well," Devham said irritably, "aren't you people going to go after him?" Then in a lower voice, drowned out by the noises of hasty scrambling toward the door, "morons. No pay raises this year."

The guards quickly lowered the bridge, and hurled themselves over it, falling on top of each other, clawing at the ground to move forward.

"Stop!" one of them yelped, seeing the heroes walking away. The six turned around.

"The halfling is under arrest for attempted thievery of the crown of our one true king!" another guard yelled, hands cupped around his mouth.

"Aw, shit," Milo muttered, and broke into a run. The guards stumbled over each other, pulling up clumps of dirt and grass.

Bernard drew his sword. "After him!" he yelled. Then he broke into a run after the halfling. He took two long strides, then paused, and turned.

"What are you people waiting for? After him!"

"Why?" Aust asked innocently.

"Because he attempted to steal the king's crown!"

"That was him?" Cade said with mild surprise. "Hmm. He did a pretty good job of it from what I heard. A little too theatrical, perhaps."

"Let's find him and kill him!" Bernard shouted.

"Kill him?" Cade's eyes widened. "Bernard, that's insane. Only a lunatic would—."

"Care to repeat that comment?" Bernard growled, point his sword in Cade's direction. His armor shuddered with rage and his face was twisted into an angry snarl.

"No," Cade said. "No, I honestly don't care to. How about I just go over there and wet myself?"

"Anybody else with me?" Bernard asked. He sheathed his sword.

"No," Ana said.

"Nope," Aust said.

"No," growled Brottor.

Now Bernard started to look like a child deprived of a favorite toy. "Oh, come on!" he cried. "The woman can stay behind, but you three have to! It's your duty!"

"Killing short people?" Aust raised his eyebrows. "I'll pass, thanks. I actually admire him, the little sneak."

"You would, Elf!" Bernard growled. "What about you, dwarf?" he asked. "You look like a real warrior."

"I don't run bloody errands for the likes of you, 'specially those that involve slaughtering innocents."

"Innocents? C'mon, people, he tried to steal the freakin' crown!"

The guards were starting to get to their feet.

"Uh, guys?" Cade said in a tinny voice from behind the rest. "We might have some trouble on their hands. Now I might be able to hold them back, but—"

"Do it," Ana said.

"But—"

"Just do it."

Cade grumbled something, then muttered a spell. Instantly, three enormous alligators leaped out of the moat, and lunged toward the six guards.

"What the hell do you think you're doing?" Bernard shrieked, and swung a gauntlet-plated fist at Cade. The wizard turned around to respond, and instantly doubled over, gasping for breath as the metal penetrated his chest.

"Look, Bernard..." Cade began, and received a kick in the stomach.

"That's Sir Bernard to you!" the knight shrieked.

"Look, we need the thief with us."

Bernard stopped in mid-kick.

"Explain," he demanded.

"It's the classic adventuring party," Cade muttered, blocking out the searing pain in his ribs. He was still curled in the fetal position on the ground. "We need a few fighters, a wizard, and a thief. Without the thief, there's no way we can scout out enemy positions or prepare a surprise attack. We need to make him a part of the party, then we can kill him when the mission is over."

Bernard thought about it for a moment. Then he sheathed his sword. "Fine," he said. "Since I am merciful, I will spare the thief for now. If he makes himself useful, he will live. If not, he will die. Come! Let us follow him, and welcome him back into the party."

With that, he strode off.

"He sure gave you a beating," Aust said as he and Ana helped Cade to his feet.

"I'm used to it." Cade could feel warm liquid trickling down into his lap, which either meant he was bleeding or he had wet himself. "Looks like those guards are still having trouble with the alligators," he said. "But they'll go after us. King Devham will make them chase us until either they or the thief go down."

Bernard, meanwhile, was far ahead of them, walking through the forest just beyond the castle, and searching through the dark for some sign of the diminutive thief he had wanted to kill.

"Don't move," he heard a voice say, and whirled around, unsheathing his sword. There was the glimmer of a hand crossbow from one of trees.

"I said don't move," the thief muttered. "I don't want anybody to die here. Just go away, and pretend you never saw me. I'm going to disappear."

"I found him!" Bernard shouted, undiscouraged.

"Shh!" Milo said nervously.

"He's over here!"

"Shut up!"

"Watch out, he has a crossbow!"

Milo heard the pitter-patter of footsteps, and angrily, fired his crossbow. One crossbow bolt bounced off of Bernard's armor.

"Over here!" Bernard said, gesturing to people beyond Milo's vision. Milo, frustrated, fired another bolt. It bounced off the armor again.

"Would you please stop that?" Bernard asked, waving his hand dismissively. Milo stopped.

Brottor, Aust, Ana, and Cade appeared.

"Milo!" Ana shouted, "we're your friends! We don't want to hurt you!"

"Ha!" Milo barked, and shot a bolt at Brottor. It bounced off his helmet.

"Don't do that," Brottor said. Defiantly, Milo loaded in another bolt.

"You have to trust us!" Aust shouted.

"Why?"

"Because the guards are coming! We can hold them off but not for long!"

Milo saw the guards stumbling toward them. Cade made a vague hand gesture in their direction, and a strong gust of wind blew them away.

"Alright," Milo said, after a moment's reflection. "I'll listen. But this had better be worthwhile. What do you want in return?"

"To join this quest you managed to qualify for!" Ana replied.

"What? Are you crazy?"

Cade shrugged. "Suit yourself," he muttered, and started to gesture in Milo's direction.

"Waitwaitwaitwait!" Milo screamed, stumbling back on the branch and covering his face. After a moment, he sighed. "Fine," he said reluctantly. "I'm screwed either way. At least this way I'll go out with some dignity." With that, he jumped nimbly from the branch, and turned toward the guards stumbling toward them. Hefting his crossbow, Milo fired a bolt at the nearest guard. It bounced off his armor.

"Ever try aiming it at their heads?" Cade asked.

"Uh...well, uh...." A guard readied his own crossbow and fired. It embedded itself in the tree Milo was standing beside. The halfling yelped.

"Run!" Ana shouted, and the six of them began running down the path, out-of-shape guards puffing after them, trying to aim their crossbows while in pursuit. After a while, they gave up and drew their swords.

Brottor, who was covering the rear, whirled around and snarled, swinging his axe. It put a nasty dent in one breastplate, and knocked the wind out of the guard wearing it, sending him to his knees. Brottor slammed the axe into the guard's helmet, knocking him unconscious.

There were five remaining guards now, all readying their crossbows. "Aim!" one shouted. "Ready!"

Cade turned around. He could see two trees on either side of the row of guards. With any luck, he could use some of the vines growing on them to disarm the knights.

"F—" the guard began, just as vines began to snap down on them like whips, splintering their crossbows. A few disappeared right out of the hands of the bewildered guards, the vines retreating instantly. The guards scrambled for their weapons, and the vines descended again, wrapping around the arms of Milo's pursuers. They were lifted up, high into the trees, screaming.

"As much as I hate to ask," Aust said, after a long pause. "what did you do to them?"

"They'll cut themselves loose eventually," Cade replied. "In the meantime, we'd better hurry."

"He's right," Ana said. "I think the noises have attracted some of the uglier creatures lurking in this forest. Let's go."

"What about him?" Bernard said, nodding toward the unconscious guard lying on the ground. "I'd hate to kill a servant of King Devham."

Milo shook his head. "Bad idea. What if he follows us? In the next city, we could find ourselves surrounded by guards."

Aust didn't seem as frightened by the idea. "Would I get my face on a poster?" he asked. "Because that would be great! I just hope they can capture my devilish good looks."

"I agree with Bernard," Ana said, ignoring Aust. "I doubt this guard could pose any further threat to us."

Milo glanced at Aust, then at Bernard. "Fine, let's get out of here," he muttered. "But somebody shut that stupid elf up."

CHAPTER
EIGHT
Our Heroes in the Hunter's Forest

Wilhelm's eyes snapped open and he struggled to his feet, running a gauntlet through the dent in his helmet. How long had he been out? Long enough, apparently. His foes were nowhere to be seen, and neither were the rest of the guards. *Probably dead*, he thought bitterly. *Killed while they were down by those traitorous bastards.*

"Mmmf!" somebody said, and Wilhelm looked up. High up in a nearby tree, his cohorts were strung up with vines, struggling wildly and trying to alert him through their gags.

Muttering to himself, Wilhelm struggled up the branches looming above him, sword at the ready.

"Let's get on a first-name basis," Aust suggested cheerfully as they walked through the forest. "I'm already well acquainted with my ol' pal Cade here, isn't that right Cade?" He slapped the wizard on the back, and Cade winced.

"Sure," Cade muttered, eyes watering from the rediscovered pain in his rib cage. Everybody looked at him expectantly. "Cade Welkland," he finally said.

"And Aust Galanodel, Master Bard!" the elf finished.

"Ana Anastacion."

"Brottor Balderk."

"Milo Pennywise, thief extraordinaire."

"Sir Knight Bernard, Champion of Irrellia. I also know Fool Welkland." There was a hint of malice in the knight's tone.

"Unfortunately," Cade murmured, too low for Bernard to hear, then, louder, "we went to boarding school together."

"Well," Bernard said. "As you can see, the better one of us became of the more successful, but here we are back together again, eh? Don't worry Cade, there's no danger of me stuffing you in the outhouse bowl now." He laughed in a way that chilled Cade to the bone.

"You went to school with that bas—" Milo froze, like a cat. "What was that noise?"

Not far away, Devham had heard it too, because he was reaching for his sword in its sheath, slowly. Ana had readied her longbow too, an arrow loaded into it. She saw a shadow flicker through the woods, close to the dirt path.

Too close.

"Shit," she hissed. "Lycanthropes. Werewolves."

"W-werewolves?" Aust's eyes widened, not in fear,

but in genuine surprise. "What a story this will make!" he cried.

"Shut up, or you won't live to tell it," Milo whispered irritably. He was pointing his crossbow all over the place, trying to get a fix on something he couldn't even see.

"Don't insult the great bard, shorty," Aust shot back sullenly.

A shadow flickered straight through the line the group was forming, and Brottor disappeared into the shadow with the clank of scale mail and a yelp of surprise. Ana fired her bow in the direction he had disappeared.

"You'll hit him!" Cade yelped.

"Trust me," Ana replied. Another arrow flew into the forest. "I won't. Cade, could we have a little light here?"

"I don't think that's such a good—"

"Just do it!"

"—idea."

Cade shrugged. "Your funeral," he said, then pointed one finger at a nearby tree. It burst into flames.

"I said some light, not a pyroclasm!" Ana shouted. "What kind of wizard are you?"

"The incompetent kind, and don't say I didn't warn you!"

The tree shuddered and fell over. Something beneath it started to shriek. Ana fired at it, and the shrieking stopped.

"Y-you killed it!" Cade stuttered in disbelief. Ana ignored him.

"I'm going to find this Brottor chap," Aust

announced, and before anybody could convince him otherwise, he leapt into the flames. Three seconds later, he came out, holding Brottor over his head like a prize trophy.

"Let go of me, you twig-legged pea-brained sonuvanelf!"

Aust shrugged, and set him carefully down on the dirt path.

"Is that the only one, then?" Aust asked mildly. "I mean, the one that got a log blanket and an arrow sandwich?"

Cade shuddered.

"No," Bernard said quietly. He pointed to Milo and Aust. "You two," he said. "I'll bet you're both good climbers. Go up those two trees over there, and scout out the area."

"Right!" Aust said, and saluted. He and Milo scrambled up the trees. Exactly eight seconds later, Milo called down.

"There is a very large werewolf over here!"

"Where?" Ana called back.

"Right here!"

"You mean near the tree!"

"No! I mean there is a werewolf, at the top of the tree, gripping me by the face, with a claw from the other hand at my throat, dangling me off the tree! Don't try and shoot it! You'll probably hit me, but if you hit it, I'll end up dropping!"

"Right!" Ana said, lowering her longbow.

"I think," Milo said, "what would be best, is if we all were just perfectly silent and still. Maybe, then—"

Milo paused, surprised by the sudden appearance

of an arrow in the side of his attacker's head. It had come from the tree across.

"You pointy-eared imbecile!" Milo screamed. "What'd you do—"

The werewolf's grip slackened, and Milo dropped, howling the whole way. Surprisingly, not five feet down, he hit a rather wide branch, and stayed there for a minute, waiting for the pain in his back to subside.

"Never," he called, "do that again." Then he groaned, and forced himself into a sitting position. He looked down, over the forest. "Uh, Aust?" he called. "Your tree's on fire."

"Oh. Oh, dear."

"Aust, get down!" Ana yelled. "Hurry!"

"Uh, 'fraid that's not possible at the moment. See, if I tried right now, it could potentially and fatally singe my hat feather."

"How high up are you?"

"About…uh…very, very, high up."

"Perfect. Cade, use some wind to steady and slow Aust when he jumps."

"What?" Cade shrieked.

"What?" Aust echoed. "I am not jumping out of this tree!"

"Suit yourself," Bernard said. He was in the middle of fending off the first werewolf. "Cade, blow him down."

"Uh, I'm not sure that's such a good idea."

The werewolf knocked Bernard over, and the knight swung at its head with one of his gauntlets.

"Blow the freakin' elf down!"

"Uh, yes sir." There was no arguing with a knight that could swing his fist hard enough to send a werewolf flying across the forest headfirst. He looked up, trying to find Aust in the tangle of branches, and swallowed.

"Don't hold it against me," he muttered to himself and the rest of the group, though they ignored him. Taking in a deep breath, Cade held his hands toward the flaming tree.

"Look out!" Ana shouted, and the spell disappeared in a harmless gust, no stronger than a harsh exhale. Cade was flying, his back racked with pain from an extremely powerful impact. A werewolf was gripping the back of his shirt, and an arrow was chasing after the werewolf. For a moment, it actually seemed possible for the beast to outrun an arrow, and Cade knew it was extremely likely he would suffer for it rather than his attacker.

The arrow entered the werewolf's skull, and it collapsed, glassy eyes staring down at Cade. Cade tried to move, then shrieked as if it was the first day of boarding school all over again.

He was trapped under a werewolf corpse.

Ana heard the scream, and broke into a run.

"Where are you going?" Bernard called after her, absentmindedly cutting off a werewolf's arm. "Oh, right, that girl over there. Probably just fainted or something."

"That's not what it sounded like," Ana muttered, and moved forward.

"Help!" she heard somebody cry. Cade. "I'm

trapped! And there are two more werewolves moving in on me! Help!"

"Stay perfectly still!" Ana called. "I'm coming to get you. Don't move or you'll provoke them!"

Ana readied her bow and took one more step forward. She saw in the dim light an animal corpse nearby. And under it, one silently quivering human form. Sighing irritably, Ana fired her bow, ignoring the quickly approaching scream.

"AaaaaaaaaaaaaaaaaaaaaaaahhhhhhhhHHHHHHHHHHHHHHHHHH. Woomph!"

It was Aust. His flaming tree made a loud snapping sound as it fell in between Cade's attacker and the arrow meant for it, a prison of flame for the helpless wizard.

"Urgh!" Aust burbled to himself, straightening out his back as he leapt to his feet. "Well, that wasn't SO bad, was it! Nothing at all, really. Good thing we elves know how to land just right. Like cats!"

"Or apes. Look, Cade's trapped on the other side of that log. We have to get to him, and kill the two werewolves with him."

"You mean there's more? Yeesh! Go ask Milo, I'm going back to fight with Bernard. At least he does all the work."

Grumbling, he walked away.

"Milo!" Ana called out.

"Yeah?"

"Can you see Cade from up there?"

"Yes!"

"Good! Is there any way to reach him and get him out of danger?"

"Er, a bit late for that!"

"What happened?"

"He's getting hauled away in a cage!"

"Werewolves aren't bright enough to make cages!"

"It's the Hunter !" Aust exclaimed happily. "All this time, I thought he was a legend! This should prove extremely interesting."

"The Hunter?" Milo looked down at him quizzically, and Aust broke into song:

"There is a man who lives on the land,
far away from the torments of civilization.
All who enter his forest shall die,
the last thing they hear will be his war cry.
His black mansion hidden in the woods,
host to thousands of terrible broods,
home of werewolves, dragons, and other such beasts,
the heads of his enemies on the door in a bloody wreath.
All who face him are doomed to die...
At the hands of the cunning, mighty Hunter!"

"That's enough, Aust," Ana said, wincing at every nasal note. "If there's a second verse, I'm sending you up another tree just so I can push you off it."

"Philistine," Aust muttered. "Anyway, the point is, the Hunter is this deranged hermit who lives in a black mansion, collecting a zoo of animals he finds interesting, especially if they're deadly. Any humanoids who enter his territory get captured and killed, one by one. Pretty interesting, huh?"

"So we have to get to the mansion before they kill the wizard," Brottor growled. "Jeez, why did I let Loki talk me into joining that cursed contest?"

Aust became a blur, and was instantly alongside Brottor. The poor dwarf was lifted up by the neck and slammed into the nearest tree trunk. "Who did you just call Loki?" Aust demanded.

"Let me down, you idiot!"

"Who is Loki?"

"I only met him a week or so ago. He and I were both traveling to Irrellia, so we teamed up. Not very safe to be alone in the woods after all. I haven't seen him since that night in the tavern. You must remember him. He talked you into joining the contest."

"Elf!" Bernard called, stepping gingerly over werewolf corpses. "Of what significance is this finding?"

Aust dropped Brottor and turned. "Loki is one of the lesser gods, not very well-known. But I know him. Loki is the human god of mischief. His appearance varies, but he's always in human form, usually in the form that he thinks will most easily manipulate whoever he wants. And his eyes are always yellow."

Everybody with the exception of Bernard gaped at Aust.

"You're telling me that I spent a week traveling with a god," Brottor mouthed, "and I never even noticed it?"

"That's exactly what I'm saying, and I hope you see the implications of this."

"You mean," Ana said, "that we didn't actually win any contest at all. It had nothing to do with skill, or even luck. The gods had already chosen us for this task."

"I couldn't help but overhear that little exchange," Milo said as he scrambled down a tree, "and the fact that I've been chosen by a god should probably make me feel better, but it doesn't."

There was a long, awkward silence. Finally, Milo cleared his throat.

"Uh, shouldn't we be looking for that wizard guy?"

The "wizard guy" was currently inside a brass cage on wheels, being dragged along by a rapidly moving werewolf harnessed to the cage. Cade was bewildered by the fact that he had been shoved into a cage by a werewolf, which then managed to handle the complex straps and get itself in a harness. He noted the ornate decorations carved into the bars of his prison, the speed of the werewolf, and the intricate carvings on the harness the werewolf was strapped to. This was all orchestrated by someone with far too much money and time.

The werewolf ground to a halt, and Cade was thrown to one side of the cage, banging his head on a bar. He looked up and saw an enormous black mansion looming ahead. Now the werewolf was plodding along on a dirt path, nearing a stable. The stable doors swung open, and a man on horseback rode out. Cade could see that the horse was powerful and well-bred, jet-black and with an angry gleam in its eyes. The rider skillfully dismounted, an old man with a pale yellow beard, dressed in the formal hunting clothes of nobility: a black, flowing cape, a short sword in a decorous sheath, and expensive black boots. He was carrying a crop, which he gripped with both hands, and was smiling menacingly.

"What's this?" he murmured, removing the harness from the werewolf. The werewolf purred loudly, and the old man stroked it with one hand, pointing to the stable with the other. The werewolf slunk in.

"Sir," Cade announced, "I believe there's been a horrible misunderstanding. I was just passing through here with my friends, and we were attacked by a herd of lycanthropes. I was apparently mistaken for food, caged, and brought back as some kind of offering. Now, I'm sure my friends are worried about me—"

"Yes," the old man said, and the tone of his voice chilled Cade. "I'm sure they are." He slammed his crop against the bars of the cage,.

"Nobody enters the Hunter's Forest and leaves in one piece," the old man snarled. "You have violated my territory, and for that dishonor you and your friends will pay dearly. If they are not already dead, they will come here looking for you, and then I will eliminate them."

The old man turned, and snapped, "Riptooth! Bloodfur!" Two werewolves appeared, growling viciously.

"Please escort our 'friend' to the dungeons, and provide him with a larger cage. Do not hurt him if unprovoked, but if he attempts to escape, kill him."

With that, the Hunter unlocked the door to the cage, and Cade crawled out. When he did, the two werewolves dragged him into the mansion.

"What are you looking at?" the Hunter demanded menacingly. Cade continued to stare at him thoughtfully. They were sitting in a dank hallway deep beneath the first floor. It was humid, cold, and dark. The floor was dirt, and the walls slick stone. Dusty gray light streamed in through a single window. Cade and the Hunter were separated by steel bars. The Hunter was pacing back and forth, and Cade was sitting at one end on an uncomfortable cot.

"Well?" the Hunter demanded once again.

"I'm just thinking," Cade finally said.

"Well it's starting to bother me."

"How long have you lived here?" Cade said, if you don't mind my asking…"

"Thirty years."

"Where did you live before then?"

"Raven Haven."

"And, if you, uh, don't mind my asking, why did you move out here? You must have certainly had a pleasant life in Raven Haven."

"What makes you say that?"

"You seem like a man who appreciates the arts, and I don't mean to be rude, but, um, you do seem to have quite a lot of money. Raven Haven favors people like you."

The Hunter sat perfectly still for a while. "The smog," he said finally.

"Er…pardon me?"

"It's everywhere. It was strangling me. I couldn't escape it. I felt like I was being smothered under a horrible-smelling pillow night and day. I couldn't stand it. So I moved out here."

"But that's not the only reason, is it? Why are there no servants? Not even a single picture of somebody?"

"You have a good eye, boy." The Hunter sighed. "I just hate people. That's why I try to kill anybody who enters this forest."

"Why do you hate people?"

"People caused the smog, and they continue to cause it. People never learn. My only friends now are the animals."

"Tell me about your parents."

"Excuse me?"

"Uh…if it's not too much trouble, could you, uh, well, tell me about your parents?"

"Why would I do that?"

"I'm just curious. If you don't want to tell me, fine. I'm just trying to help you."

"Alright, my parents—hey! What are you doing?"

Cade had whipped out a small leather journal, and a piece of charcoal. "Just taking notes," he said. "Is that okay with you?"

The Hunter thought about it, then sighed. "Fine," he muttered.

Nightfall. Milo peered out from within the underbrush, eyes glimmering. "There it is, folks," he whispered. "It would have been harder to track a hurricane, with the mess that werewolf was making. Shit, look at that place! I'll bet I could rob a fortune from there!"

"Not now!" Ana hissed. "We're going in, getting Cade, then getting out of this forest as fast as humanly possible. I really don't like this place, and from the looks of those werewolves we encountered, lingering is probably not a good idea."

"Fine," Milo said sullenly. "But it's not my fault if a few golden candlesticks accidentally fall into my backpack while we're escaping."

Ana started to say something, then sighed. "Fair enough."

"We should attack now," Bernard announced. "Under the cover of nightfall. I can take the lead, and you knaves can take leftovers."

"Oh no, you don't," Milo shot back. "You would just make things worse. Ana, Aust, and I should sneak in, grab Cade, then get out. But first I'll need blueprints of the mansion, and—"

"No, no, no," Bernard said. "I'd trust a thief less than I can throw him, though judging by your height and weight that's probably pretty far."

"Why, you self-righteous, overgrown—"

"Shut up!" Brottor shouted, just low enough not to alert any slumbering beasts. "There is only one way we can do this. We do not have the resources to get inside completely unnoticed, so that is out of the question, but I'll be damned if I let Bernard steal all the glory and make too much noise. Alright, now listen carefully. We sneak in as quietly as possible. Milo will be in the front for disarming traps and picking locks. Bernard and I will be up front to absorb any head-on charges, and Aust will be in the back to report hind strikes."

"Sounds good," Ana said. "What about me?"

"Uh…being a woman, you're required to stay back at the base, and cook a celebratory meal for the men."

Ana whacked Brottor on the top of the helmet so hard that it took all his strength to pry it back into its normal position on his forehead, allowing him to see again. "Alright, Alright," he said, massaging the bridge of his nose. "Take up the rear with Aust. But if I hear any feminine shrieks back there from either of ye, then you're both receiving dishonorable discharges!"

Cade listened to the Hunter, nodded sympathetically, then ripped out a blank page from his journal, and spilled a little ink on it.

"What does this look like to you?" he asked, holding it up.

The Hunter stared at it for a little while. "A cloud of smog," he finally said.

Cade nodded, and scribbled down some notes.

"Done," Milo whispered confidently. He swung the large studded front door open slowly, and picked up his torch from the front porch. Then he turned around and gestured to the rest of the party, ushering them in.

"Cade's definitely in the basement," Aust whispered.

"What makes you say that?" Brottor replied.

"You think the Hunter's going to put a dungeon right next to his bedroom? No, it's definitely beneath us."

"Shh!" Milo hissed. He handed his torch to Bernard, then flopped down and pressed his ear to the floor. Faintly, he could make out two voices.

"Aust's right," he whispered. "I can hear Cade down there. Let's go." He got to his feet, and accepted his torch back. "No, let's—wait!" He began to creep toward the living room, heading for the coffee table in the center of it. "One gold-plated ashtray," he pleaded to the rest of the party. "That's all I ask. Then we can continue rescuing Cade." Then, not waiting for an answer, he scampered over to the table, picked up the ashtray, and stuffed it in his backpack. Almost instantly, he heard a small click.

The sound of a trap being activated.

"Uh-oh," the halfling said, and before anybody else had a chance to react, a crossbow bolt shot out of a small, nearly invisible hole in the far wall. Luckily, Milo was too short to be hit. Unfortunately, Bernard wasn't. Luckily, Bernard's knightly plate mail was more than enough to protect him from a single crossbow bolt. Unfortunately, it exploded.

A flash of light filled the room, and everybody staggered back, covering their eyes and ears. The room seemed to shake with the sound of the explosion ringing against Bernard's armor. When the spots cleared from their eyes, and the ringing from their ears, everybody looked to Bernard.

"You okay?" Milo asked. "That explosion didn't look too powerful, but the noise and the flash were—"

"I-I can't see," Bernard exclaimed, waving his hands around. "I'm blind!"

As if on cue, hordes of snarling werewolves surrounded the group.

"When this is over, I'm going to throttle you until your head pops off like a cork," Ana muttered to Milo.

"And I'll let you," the thief replied.

"What was that?" The Hunter's head snapped in the direction of the sound, his body stiffening like that of a cat on the prowl. He shot Cade a feral smile. "Must be your friends," he purred. "Well, why don't I go greet them?"

He got up to leave.

"Wait!" Cade shouted. "We just had a breakthrough! We can't stop now!"

"Screw your breakthrough! I want to be there to watch my pets kill them!"

"But-but, the inkblot test—"

The Hunter sighed. "Alright. "My pets'll eat them anyway. Now, tell me again, what does my fear of communication have to do with my mother?"

"Get the wizard!" Bernard snarled. "I'll hold them off!"

"But, you're, uh, how do I put this…blind!" Aust shot back.

"I'll help him," Brottor said. "With his fighting skills, we should be able to fend them off together."

Milo, not being much of a combatant, was already bounding down the spiral staircase that went down to the dungeon.

"It's true," the Hunter sobbed. "Everything you said. About my mother, about the smog, about my communication difficulties, it's all true!" He got to his feet. "Mr. Welkland, I feel like a new man. All these things bottled up inside me for all these years! Maybe I shall spare you and your friends…what's left of them, anyway. I'll just go—"

"Freeze!"

The Hunter and Cade whirled around to see Milo, his crossbow pointed at the Hunter's head. Aust and Ana were standing on either side of him, their own weapons at the ready as well.

The Hunter, rather than going for his short sword as they expected, put his hands up and began to whimper.

"Well," Milo said, slightly bewildered, "that was, uh, easy. Aust, get some keys off the Hunter, and open that cage!"

Aust nodded and began to search the Hunter.

"What are you doing here?" Cade demanded angrily.

"What does it look like?" Ana said, starting to match Milo in bewilderment. "Saving your life!"

"And you just had to interrupt a session?"

"Uh...session?" Milo echoed.

"That's right! This man's a sensitive humanoid being, just like any of us, not some malevolent beast!"

"Cade?" said Ana. "He tried to kill us, then when that didn't work, he threw you into his dungeon as bait for the rest of us."

"He's had a rough life," Cade said as he swung open the barred door to the cage. "Haven't you, Hunter?"

Hunter nodded meekly. "I've changed," he said. "I swear."

"Well...alright," Milo said finally. "And here's your ashtray back." He reached into his backpack and held it out to the Hunter.

"Keep it," the Hunter replied. "I never smoke, anyhow. Cigar smoke is too much like smog for my liking. I just use the ashtray for a trap trigger."

"Okay…" Milo shrugged, and stuffed it back into his pack.

"Now…" the Hunter was slowly backing up against the wall, "let's just let bygones be—"

He never finished his sentence. Instead, he pulled a lever against the far wall, and began to laugh.

"Another trap!" Milo muttered. "Crap, this place must be full of them." He whirled around at the sound of a door slamming, and that was as much time as the Hunter needed. He leaped across the room and instantly disarmed Milo and Ana.

"I like your bow," he said to Ana as he threw it across the room. "Maybe I'll hold onto it as a trophy from my most challenging prey yet."

Cade shrugged helplessly to Milo, Ana, and Aust. "So much for psychotherapy," he said.

Bernard and Brottor heard the door slamming too, and whirled around. Bernard's eyes, having fully recovered after the initial flash of the flare bolt, turned toward the closed door, and uttered an expression of joy as he batted away another werewolf. "They're as good as dead. Brottor, the quest must continue. That door is magically locked, and we'll never get through. Come!"

Brottor looked confused. "You're just ditching them?"

"They didn't deserve such a quest anyway. They were fools, all of them. Come on!"

"I'm not leaving without them."

"You fool!" Bernard's shoulders slumped. "Alright, then," he said. "If I have no choice...I will continue on my own." Absently, he decapitated a werewolf that had been about to leap on him from behind.

"That's not what a real knight would do," Brottor muttered.

"And what would you know of knights, dwarf?" Bernard howled. With one gauntlet, he reach out and crushed a werewolf's throat. "You have no respect for chivalry, no honor!"

"Don't talk to me about honor when you're about to turn your tail on three people in trouble."

"I am not fleeing, I am leaving them to the fate they deserve!" Bernard was starting to froth with rage.

Brottor backed up and stared at him. "You're insane," he whispered. Bernard kicked him in the stomach hard enough to send the dwarf hurling across the room, then turned and ran, killing any werewolf along the way that blocked his path to the door.

"Get into that cell," the Hunter snapped. "All of you. Go!"

Nervously, Ana, Aust, Milo, and Cade shuffled into the one cell in the room.

"Against the wall!"

The heroes flattened themselves against the wall. Hunter stepped forward and locked the door.

"Now, if you'll excuse me...."The Hunter turned, and ran up the stairs. He shouted a word in elvish (the word, as only Aust knew, happened to be "daisies," of all things), and the door magically opened. The Hunter disappeared.

"What a mess," Milo muttered. "We're chosen by a god to go on an epic quest, and we're probably not going to last two freakin' days."

"Chosen by the gods?" Cade looked at him quizzically. "We were chosen by a king."

Milo sighed, and explained the whole thing. "That's Aust's theory, anyway," he added at the end, trying to emphasize that he was extremely skeptical of it. Cade continued to look at him with puzzlement as Milo spoke.

"No," Cade finally said. "Coincidence. I don't believe in the gods, or fate, or anything like that."

"Then what do you believe?" Ana asked.

"I believe we're all screwed, and I believe that the instant Bernard realized that, he decided he was just going to go merrily along and complete the quest on his own."

"Don't be so cynical," Aust said. "Bernard's a perfectly good fellow, and I'm sure he'll at least try to get us out. Besides, don't knights have rules about that?"

"Bernard follows his own rules," Cade replied glumly. "And they're for his benefit only."

Aust was about to reply when the dungeon door opened.

"Look who I found!" the Hunter cried gleefully. "More food for my babies tomorrow!"

He slowly descended the spiral staircase, leading Brottor at crossbow-point.

"Where's Bernard?" Milo asked,. He secretly hoped that Brottor would turn, grin, and say: Why, he's bringing the cavalry to save us, of course.

"He left," Brottor muttered as he was shoved into the cell. Cade hammered his own knee in frustration. The Hunter's laughter trailed up the stairs.

"I knew it!" the wizard muttered angrily. "He hasn't changed at all." He looked around the cell. "Don't you get it? He's crazy. We're lucky, like this. If we had hung around with him long enough, he would have eventually slaughtered us, then say we got overwhelmed by orcs, or something like that. And dammit, he'd still end up being the hero!"

"Cade," Ana said, "do you think you could break open this door?"

"And how would I do that?" Cade had his head in his hands now.

"What about using your magical abilities?"

Cade snorted. "I always wanted to learn the subtle side of magic," he said. "How to manipulate, evolve, alter, and so on. My first real experiment with magic, I was an apprentice to a wizard by the name of Devis Greenbottle. He told me to create an invisibility potion. The cauldron exploded, and the entire town was on fire and invisible at the same time for about three weeks. I'm not a wizard, I'm a time bomb. Sure I could melt those bars away using a few fire spells, but I could also melt them until the bubbling magma destroys us from the ankles down."

"Well, we're going to die anyway. Give it a try."

Cade sighed. "Alright. Step back, everybody. We're confined, but if anything explodes, I'll try to keep as small a blast range as I can."

He stepped forward, put his hands against the bars, and squeezed his eyes shut. "Focus. Focus. Focus."

Almost instantly, the bars began to turn red.

"It's working!" Aust said gleefully. "What a sight! Have you ever thought of joining a circus—"

"Shut up!" Brottor snapped. "He's trying to concentrate."

The two bars Cade was concentrated on were now entirely red. Steam rose between Cade's hands. The wizard mumbled a small prayer, not to any deity, but simply to his own unpredictable talents, and pulled the bars apart. When he drew his hands back, the bars were black again, only slightly warm to the touch, and there was a dent in between them just large enough for a person to squeeze through.

"Well," he said to himself, "that was actually pretty easy." Then he put one foot through the bars, and screamed. His hair stood on end, and his entire body began to twitch. This lasted for a few seconds, then he staggered back into the cage and collapsed to the ground.

"Another magical trap," he muttered. "He knew we'd find some way to get through. So he set up another surprise for us." He put his head in his hands again. "We're doomed."

CHAPTER
NINE
The Feeding Pit, and Meeting with the Gods

"Wake up everybody!" the Hunter called gleefully as he bounced down the stairs. "My pets are getting hungry, and there's no way I'm going to keep them waiting for breakfast!"

As light streamed through the windows and the adventurers rubbed sleep from their eyes, the Hunter escorted them out the cell in single file, holding up the rear with a crossbow pointed at the back of Aust's neck.

"Great," Cade said drowsily, "more werewolves."

"Not werewolves this time, young man," the Hunter informed him. "I've prepared something a little special for today."

"Oh, yippee."

The heroes were led to the back of the house where, much to their surprise, there was nothing more than a large chalk circle on the ground, big enough to fill up the entire backyard.

"All of you, stand in the center, and don't move," the Hunter said. "If any of you try to leave the circle, I'll kill you. Oh, and by the way, here are your weapons." He tossed Brottor his axe and Aust his rapier.

"I'm holding on to your crossbow," the Hunter told Milo, "because that's all that's keeping you in the circle at the moment. And as for you, my dear," he said, gesturing toward Ana, "I'm afraid that your longbow is simply too precious to be shredded by my pets. However, as I am not completely unfair, you may take these from my own personal collection."

He tossed two long swords into the circle, then turned to Cade.

"As for you, I can tell you are a mage. Therefore, you already have a weapon, a very interesting one at that. You had a slight handicap from those bruised ribs of yours, but wanting this to be harsh but fair, I used a few healing potions to mend you while you were asleep. Elven-made potions, quality stuff. You should be flattered. Now, if you'll excuse me…"

The Hunter backed up, and pulled a lever at the side of the house. The floor disappeared, and the adventurers fell into a circular pit, six-feet deep. The Hunter then pressed a false brick beneath the lever to reveal a few switches. Chuckling, the Hunter went to stand over the pit, a looming shadow.

"There's an energy field separating us," he mentioned. "Don't try to injure me with any of your tricks, as it will only ricochet and harm you. Don't try climbing up the walls. They're perfectly slick, and the energy field would hurt you anyway. Be right back."

He walked over to the control pad, and flipped a switch. Four holes appeared in the walls of the pit. Each one held a cage. In each cage was an enormous bear with two snarling, slobbering heads.

"They are my own creation," the Hunter said. "A special potion in the wombs of mother grizzly bears, and you get my 'Two Headed War Bears.' Pretty interesting, eh?"

"These are a crime against nature," Ana whispered.

The Hunter's eyes bulged madly. "And what do you know of nature? I am the one who has spent my life in service to it! I am the will of nature embodied! I am eliminator of the weak and vile! I am the Hunter!"

Ana shook her head. "You're a serial killer, plain and simple. You're nothing special, but of course, all psychotics of your ilk believe they are."

"Enough!" The Hunter flicked another switch and the caves began to open slowly. "I've had enough of you, and your insults. It is time for you to die."

The four bears began to approach slowly, eight sets of jaw gnashing, preparing for humanoid muscle and humanoid bone. The Hunter giggled, then ran into the house.

"Good thing we have our secret weapon," Ana said confidently. The others didn't seem quite so confident. "Cade, blast 'em."

Cade looked at her, confused, and then shrank. "Uh..."

"Blast 'em! Fry the bastards!"

"You don't understand. I'm a wizard, and I need to prepare new spells the night before I cast them. I don't have my spell book with me," Cade whined. "I must have left it at Irrellia. I could get a new one at Raven Haven if we survive this ordeal."

"Oh, we'll survive it all right," Brottor growled. "When we have the might of a god to back us up!"

The bears slowly moved in. The heroes shrunk against the wall.

"I repeat, we have the might of a god to back us up!"

Much to everyone's surprise, a great beam of light shot down from the heavens before Brottor, and there was his short-time traveling companion, Loki. "Do it yourself," he said. "If you can't take care of a few very large bears with two heads, then I don't know what I signed you guys on for."

The beam of light, along with the god, disappeared. The heroes were left scratching their heads at the encounter.

"That wasn't exactly the deus ex machina I was hoping for," Cade commented. "So much for being chosen by the gods. If anybody needs me, I'll be over in that corner, whimpering."

"I agree," Aust said. "Seems like the best course of action. Of course, we could always join an apocalyptic cult that worships gerbils."

Instantly, the beam of light shot down again, and Loki appeared.

"Alright, alright," he muttered. "You've got my attention."

"Good. Now kill those bears, or I renounce...uh, Loki-ism!"

Loki sighed audibly, then snapped his fingers. The bears disappeared.

"Hope you're happy," a heavenly voice boomed as the beam of light disappeared into a cluster of clouds. "You just interrupted my date with the goddess of beauty."

"Well, my pets," the Hunter said, walking out of the house. "How was the feast? Gory?" He walked to the edge of the pit, and shrieked.

"My pets!" he cried. "Where are they?" He ran to the control panel and flicked a switch. There was a low hum as the protective energy field dissipated. The Hunter jumped into the pit, drawing his sword and a dagger from his leg sheath. Throwing back his cloak, he got into a fighting stance. "You bastards!" he shouted.

"You really think you can fight all five of us?" Aust asked.

"As a matter of fact, I think I can kill all five of you. Observe."

The first person he moved for was Brottor. The dwarf growled and hefted his battle axe, but the Hunter was too fast. Brottor was sent flying and hit the far wall. Milo hopped on the Hunter's back, and started beating him on the head with his fists. The Hunter growled and threw Milo off, whirling around and thrusting his sword forward. Aust dodged out of the way, and received an elbow jab in the stomach. He doubled over, gasping. The Hunter turned to face him, and as he did, Ana smashed his jaw with one powerful punch. The Hunter hit the ground.

"Now," Ana said, wiping the blood off her fist, "let's get our crap and get the hell out of here. Milo, I'll boost you out. Hit the switch that will raise this platform."

"Which switch is that?" Milo asked.

"Just…just hit one."

"Right," Milo muttered. He was about to make a snide remark when Ana grabbed him around the middle and tossed him out of the pit. Milo staggered to his feet and ran to the switch box.

"It's no use!" he called. "I can't reach it!"

Ana cursed. "Find a chair in the house."

"What if it's trapped? I could combust."

"Oh, for the love of—You're a thief! Look for traps!"

Milo ran into the house, and a few minutes later there was an extremely loud crashing sound. Milo came out with the chair, scurried on top of it, then flicked a switch, and the circle sprang back up to ground level. The speed at which it rose threw Ana, Cade, Aust, and Brottor to the ground.

"Pendulum trap," Milo explained as they staggered to their feet. "They didn't screw it in tightly enough. Flew across the room and caved in the fireplace." He shrugged. "Hey, what's with Cade?"

Cade was vomiting near the edge of the circle. He glanced at the unconscious Hunter, then bent over and vomited again.

"Great," he muttered to himself. "One day on the job and I've already blacked out while lying under a corpse, started hyperventilating, had a vomiting fit, and I think I'm getting an ulcer."

Ana helped him to his feet, and the heroes walked into the house. After much searching, they found their other supplies in a large room behind a hidden panel.

"How did you find this place?" Cade asked Milo. Milo smiled confidently. He was now wearing a dark cloak, which would make him nearly invisible in dark places.

"I'm a thief," he replied. "I know all about secret panels."

The room had more than just their supplies. It was full of valuable items, and after much inspecting, Milo finally determined that these did not have magic traps, and it wouldn't hurt if he pocketed a few exquisite, gem-encrusted gold items. Ana's bow was there, and Milo's crossbow.

"My spell book!" Cade cried, searching through his backpack. "Guess I didn't leave it at Irrellia."

"Take this." Ana put a sheath with a short sword in Cade's hand. The sheath was finely made black leather, and when Cade looked at the sword itself, he could see his reflection. He felt like he was holding moonlight in his hand.

"I found it over there," Ana told him, gesturing to a weapons rack near the back of the room. "If you find a situation where you don't have time to cast a spell, or it's too dangerous, or you just don't have one ready...you might need this. Keep it near you. At all times."

"Thanks," Cade said.

The next day was, surprisingly, uneventful. Milo and Aust, both artistes, and both on the wrong side of the law a little too often, got along famously. Brottor got along well with Aust too, admitting he was a "remarkably intelligent fellow...for an elf."

Meanwhile, Ana was trying to learn a little more about Cade, feeling as she did a little pity for him. He seemed to have set up a wall around the subject of his past, though, and he wasn't going to let anybody get through.

The next day featured completely surreal experience. It started after breakfast, when they began the last long stretch of their hike to Raven Haven. After walking for an hour or so, they saw a bright beam of light appear before them, and they halted.

"Loki," Brottor said, and the deity himself appeared before them.

"Greetings, adventurers! The other gods have asked me to provide some information on your true quest."

"True quest?" Aust asked.

"That's right! So, if you'd just follow me..."

A blinding beam of light shot down from the sky and surrounded the adventurers. Then Milo and Cade began to scream, as the five were hurled upward into oblivion.

Cade gasped, and looked around. He, Ana, Milo, Aust, and Brottor, were all seated in comfortable armchairs, facing Loki, who was standing in the air with his arms folded. When Cade observed his surroundings more closely, he noticed the armchairs were resting on a storm cloud, hundreds of thousands of feet above the earth. He yelped, and gripped the armrests, then began hyperventilating. Loki glanced at him disdainfully.

"I have this phobia about heights," Cade explained breathlessly. "Sorry to bother you." He pulled his legs up onto the chair, and huddled there in the fetal position, trying not to look down.

"Would you feel better if I selected a different location for our little meeting?" Loki suggested.

"Much better," Cade replied in a nervous, high-pitched voice. Instantly, the chairs disappeared.

"Uh-oh," Aust said, and Cade began screaming loudly again as they plummeted out of the sky.

"Better?" Loki asked. They were standing in an enormous underground cave, lit by hovering balls of flame. The god of mischief was sitting on a gargantuan black throne.

"Where are we?" Milo asked, getting to his feet.

"We're at the underground fortress of the god of necromancy," Loki explained. "Okay," he said, clapping his hands together. "Everybody conscious and alive? Good."

Ana, Brottor, and Aust staggered to their feet. "Now, I'm sure you all know what this 'quest thing' is supposedly about, right?"

"Something about killing a demon named Kaos, if I'm correct," Cade said.

"Right. At least, that's the official story."

"Official story?" Ana raised her eyebrows.

"Well, it was half right. You have to kill Kaos, but he's not a demon."

"Well that's a relief," Cade muttered.

"He's a god."

"*What?*"

Loki sighed, and leaned back on his throne. "Where do I begin…" he murmured. "Kaos is a lesser god, offspring of the god of nightmares, and a demonic red dragon by the name of Delilah."

"Delilah?" Milo repeated.

"I know, doesn't sound very draconic, does it? Kaos was half-mortal, half-god, and ridiculously powerful. But he was also part demon. Remember how I mentioned 'Mommy' was half-demon? Well, somewhere in her ancestry lay the head demon himself—Morbius. Aust, you're a bard. I assume you know about Morbius?"

"Lived for three thousand years," Aust said quickly. "Commanded an army that took over half of the greater continent. Was killed only by the great wizard, Ledroc the Wise, and even he had to sacrifice his own life in order to save the world."

"Right. So, now you know where Kaos inherited his ability to breath fire, his scaly red complexion, his deep growling voice, his godly abilities, and his dark powers. And now you know why he must be destroyed at all costs."

"So you're sending us in," Milo muttered. "Not that it's my place to question the judgment of a god, especially one that could kill me by snapping his fingers."

Loki chuckled. "The thing is," he said, "the gods cannot get involved in this. We have no way of physically contacting his fortress. The gods actually have a very small degree of power in terms of interacting with the physical realm. We can transport people back and forth, but if a half-god is set loose on the mortal plane, then there is nothing we can do besides send mortals after him."

"So you're sending the five most incompetent adventurers in the world to take care of this," Milo said with a smirk. "Smart. No, wait—six—counting Bernard. There was a sixth one, and he snapped! Now he's probably out to kill us, too!"

"Bernard was a wild card," Loki replied. "I didn't choose him. I never directly interacted with him at all."

"Wait," Cade broke in. "You never interacted with me either!"

Loki shrugged. "Another wild card."

Cade's mouth dropped. "You mean...I wasn't chosen at all? There's no reason I should have gotten involved in this? Am I the next to go?"

"You're not the next to go. You simply have made this decision for yourself."

"No I didn't! For the love of the gods, I was completely hammered!"

Aust nodded. "He was. I was there."

"I can't believe it," the wizard muttered, running a hand through his hair. "What the hell am I here for?"

"You're here," Loki said, "because now that I have made direct contact with you, you are bound to the quest."

"Why did Kaos choose to enter the mortal realm?" Ana asked.

"An evil god desires power more than anything else. He wishes to create his own plane out of the mortal realm, to shape and bend to his dark will. He is building on the fringes of this nation, on his own mountain on the island of Risunbir, building for a siege on this planet."

"Then what can we do?" Milo said. "Five failures cannot mount an assault on the most powerful monster in the world while he's sitting in a heavily guarded fortress!"

"Yes you can," Loki said. "And you will. I will guide you, adventurers. Now, it is time for you to enter the city of Raven Haven. I am afraid more trials await there. But these are not of the body, but of the mind. Cade!"

Cade looked up. He had been sitting cross-legged on the floor, head in his hands, listening quietly.

"This trial is for you specifically," Loki said. "I can see a little while into certain possible futures, and I can see that you can succeed at this."

"How?" Cade sighed. "I'm not a good combatant, I practice magic but it's more dangerous to me than to my enemies, and I don't have people skills."

"You're too logical." Loki chuckled. "That is one of your many weaknesses, and it is also your greatest strength. Now, I must leave you. Goodbye."

Loki disappeared, and the area surrounding the heroes began to melt, fading into the Hunter's Forest again.

The Hunter's eyes snapped open, and he struggled out of the circle, looking around and gasping loudly.

"You there!" he heard somebody call, and he

turned. A bunch of guards, bearing the royal crest of Irrellia were approaching.

"What is it?" he snapped, spitting blood, and staggering to his feet.

"We are searching for six fugitives from our kingdom, one of them a halfling thief who tried to rob the king of his crown. They are one human female, one wizard, a dwarf, a—"

"I know them," the Hunter said shrewdly. "I am an expert tracker, gentlemen. If you wish, I will aid you in finding them."

But the smog! his mind screamed. *These men are acolytes of the smog, and their quest will bring you to Raven Haven!* The Hunter ignored these screams. He had to crush the fools who had hurt his dignity. He could always kill the guards later.

CHAPTER
TEN
Murder in Raven Haven

"Well, according to this map, it should be just over that hill," Ana said, looking up from a yellowed and curling piece of parchment at the lush green hill before them. Feeling more relaxed now that the dark woods were behind them, Aust nodded. Large clouds of smog appeared from beyond the hill, reaching up into the sky and turning it dark gray.

"Let's go, then," Brottor suggested gruffly. "It will be good to get a real bed to sleep on tonight, after the halfling sells his loot."

"My name's Milo, not 'the halfling,'" Milo muttered. "And you won't just have a real bed with all of this stuff, you'll have the best room at the inn!"

"Something to look forward to," Cade said absently, looking at the smoke-strangled sky.

"You okay?" Ana asked with genuine concern. Cade shook his head.

"I can't stop thinking about what Loki said," he replied. "It means I'm probably next. And he said there was a trial for me in that city. Maybe that's what will kill me."

"There it is!" Aust shouted. He was near the edge of the hill, jumping up and down. The rest of the party went to the edge alongside him, and gasped.

The city stretched out as far as the eye could see. A long merchant caravan was making its way through the enormous gates. Cade estimated that the gates were at least ten stories tall. And behind them, stood even larger towers, academies, museums, and all other kinds of buildings. Smoke stacks from factories puffed smoke into the air. Royal guards circled around and between the towers on giant Roc mounts. A wizard was testing out his newest invention, a rather noisy flying contraption. All of it blended together in gray, black, and the occasional vivid red or white. And in the center, was an enormous castle, bigger than King Devham's, and home of the mayor of the city.

"It's beautiful," Milo whispered. "One of those towers must have enough loot to fill three dragon's caves!"

Aust shot him a disdainful look, and began to walk down the path to Raven Haven.

"What?" Milo called after him, struggling to keep up. "What'd I say?"

The Roc Feather Inn was one of the taller buildings in the area. Once Milo had pawned his assorted loot from the Hunter's mansion, the group decided that they had enough silver to spend for a few small luxuries, and their search for those luxuries led them here, where, according to the sign at the front door, nobles from the wealthiest and most elite families like to stay.

Milo managed to bribe the manager enough to get the entire party suites on one of the floors closest to the top. Cade objected strongly to this, due to his fear of heights, but he was quickly overruled.

"By the way," the manager said, as they were about to begin the long walk up to their rooms, "there's a party going on at the top floor in the ballroom when the clock tower in the center of town tolls nine. Perhaps you would like to join our other visitors and patrons this evening.

"We'll think about it," Aust grunted as he pulled open the heavy wooden door to the staircase.

They trudged to their rooms, and all closed the doors. Cade poked his head out a window, shrieked, and quickly closed the curtains. Aust began tuning his harp. Milo threw pieces of silver in the air, and rolled around in the large pile. Brottor sharpened his axe, and made a fire in the fireplace in his room. Ana cleared out the furniture in one part of the room, and began practicing her martial arts.

The clock tower tolled nine, and Cade jumped back in his seat, startled awake. He felt wet ink on his face, and realized he had fallen asleep while writing in his spell book. Sleepily, he went into the bathroom, and washed his face.

He walked back to his spell book, and continued writing by the candlelight. He had never really liked parties.

An hour later, Aust walked in, dressed in ill-fitting

formal wear and gulping down a glass of champagne. "C'mon," he suggested heartily to Cade. "Join the party! You need to loosen up!"

"Where'd you get those clothes?"

"Whu . . ? Oh, this. Milo bought it for me with all the dough he racked up. C'mon!"

"No thanks," Cade said. "Some other time, maybe."

"Humans," Aust muttered. "Suit yourself." He staggered out of the room, emptying his glass.

Another half hour went by. Cade spent that half hour staring at his spell book, having nothing more to write. He couldn't go to sleep, though. He considered going to the party. No, he thought. I'll stay down here, and see if they have any good books on the shelf in this room.

Still, he couldn't read. He could hear the laughing, toasting, and music from upstairs.

As he was about to open *A History of Runes*, he was startled as the door to his room burst open, and Ana stormed in.

"There's been a murder," she explained.

Cade slammed the book shut. "Ex—excuse me?"

"Somebody's been killed!"

Cade opened the book again. "Are the royal guards on their way?"

"Look, Cade, remember what Loki said?"

Cade looked up. "I'm not a police officer!" he cried. "I wouldn't know where to begin!"

"I think we both know that's not true."

The curtains on one window parted, and a beam of light shot through it. Loki appeared, gave Cade a sharp smack on the back of the head, then leaped out the window and disappeared again.

"Alright, Alright, I'm going," Cade muttered, rubbing the back of his head.

Cade was pleased to see it was a poisoning. He knew that if it had been a brutal, bloody death, he would have fainted on the spot. He knelt beside the body, and examined it.

"Has the body been moved?" he asked the crowd gathered around him. Everybody shook their heads.

"Good," Cade murmured. "Aust, could you go and get my alchemy bag? It's on the table in my room."

Aust nodded and hurried off. Cade looked back to the body.

He was a human of about seventy, pale and gaping. Cade slowly moved to the other side so he could see his face, and yelped, jumping back a little, when he saw the wide, staring eyes.

"What is it?" an elderly woman from the crowd asked.

"The, uh, the eyes aren't clouded at all. The drug obviously wasn't any kind of narcotic, and he was probably in pain when he died. Who is this man, anyway?"

Somebody began to respond, and Cade silenced him.

"I'll find out during the interviews. Everybody should stay here. Nobody leaves the room until I'm done."

Aust returned with the bag, and Cade opened it, removing several kinds of flasks and bottles. He found some glass shards near the body, and sprinkled a little green powder on it. It bubbled angrily.

"As I expected," Cade said, putting the powder back in his bag. "There was a heavy dose of poison in that glass. Does anybody know what bottle this man was drinking from?"

The bartender brought forth a large half-empty bottle of champagne. Cade sniffed the cork delicately, then took out the power and sprinkled a small amount into the bottle. Nothing happened for a little while.

"The poison was administered the glass itself," Cade decided. "Which probably means that nobody else is at risk at the moment. I'm guessing a few dissolving pills were dropped into his drink while the man wasn't looking."

Cade poured a few more chemicals directly into the corpse's mouth, and it began to foam purple foam. "Ah," he said weakly, putting a handkerchief to his nose. The group of onlookers backed away slowly. "It's powder from the plant mortisweed. Very common plant, but only an experienced wizard knows how to mix it properly to create the poison, and it requires chemicals from many other plants. Aust, could you get me my spell book? It's on the desk in my room."

"I'm not the bloody butler," Aust muttered, but went for it. When he returned, he was carrying Cade's short sword, all his bags, and a handkerchief as well as the spell book.

"Because I'm not going down anymore," Aust explained, and dropped them all in front of Cade.

Cade, wrapped in his own thoughts, ignored the sarcastic elf, and reached for his spell book. He flipped to one of the first pages, chanted a few arcane words, and looked around.

"That's it?" Milo asked.

"Not quite," Cade said. "That was a detect magic spell. Now I know who has recently come in contact with a magical aura that has apparently rubbed off on them. One of these people is the murderer. Now, I need everybody to stand where they were at the time of death."

He moved his bags out of the way, and was about to stuff his short sword into one of them, when he remembered what Ana had said.

Keep it near you. At all times.

He fumbled briefly with the sheath, then attached it to his belt, and whirled around. Everybody was in position.

"Excellent," Cade said. "So, from the way this man, whoever he is, fell over, he must have been facing that way. There are three people behind with magical auras that could have snuck in the poison while he was looking the other way. I'll have to question all of them."

He selected the three of them, and led them away from the rest of the group. Then, he approached the first one.

"Name."

"Delvick Selman." He was a young man with a mess of straw-like hair and a reptilian look in his eyes. "I'm a cadet from the Knights of Irrellia, on leave in my home city. I was on leave because I was brutally injured by a rampaging ogre, and was sent here to be healed by a mage. That's why I have this aura." Cade noted the white powder on his hands, and moved to the next one.

"I'm Verne Messings, a wizard's apprentice," the slightly older boy with the slowly changing eye color said. "I have a magical aura because, well, I work with a wizard all the time, and my eyes are changing color like this from the temporary effects of a botched prisma-beast summoning."

"You realize that unless you have a warrant, summoning a beast that powerful is illegal in Irrellia?"

"Oh, we have a warrant, all right. My master has it. She's your third suspect, I think."

The wizard was a white-haired woman of about fifty, with stern gray eyes and thin lips of vivid red.

"I'm Vera Dragonwing. That's my apprentice you were just interviewing."

"Do you have a warrant for prisma-beast summoning?"

Vera looked surprised. "Why yes, yes I do. It's right here. Why do you ask?"

Cade examined it. "Do you always carry around federal warrants with you, Miss Dragonwing?"

"I had just gotten back from a government meeting when I went to this party."

"A meeting that ended at around nine-thirty."

"No, more around ten. I just got here. The meeting is very hush-hush, so I can't give you any details."

"Was your apprentice with you?"

"No, of course not! He was at the lab. I picked him up, and brought him here. We were supposed to meet a customer. That poor man you were inspecting on the floor."

Cade nodded. Then he turned to the party.

"I know who did it," he said. Everybody stared at him.

"But you don't even know who the body is!" somebody shouted.

"Doesn't matter. One of these people has a gaping hole in their alibi. And I know who it is." He turned to his three suspects. "Mr. Messing, you're under arrest for the murder of…well, you're under arrest for murder."

Everybody gasped. "If you'll please just sit down a remain quiet, somebody else can go call for a royal guard, and this will all be settled—"

"No!"

Cade saw what was going to happen. Verne Messing, a bit more apt a wizard than expected even by his master, hurled a force bolt—a distortion of energy in a small concentrated ball—at the crowd. Cade jumped in front of it, and took the full brunt, flying back several feet.

"Magical resistance," he explained to the stunned crowd a second later as he clamored to his feet. "No self-destructive wizard would ever survive without it."

A window shattered, and Verne leapt out, landing on an outdoor balcony.

"I can take him," Ana said, stepping forward and raising her fists.

"No," Cade replied. "This is my test. I have to do it alone."

"You're going to get killed!"

"Maybe, but cowards die a thousand deaths." He

grinned shrewdly. "I'd just have nine hundred ninety-nine to go after that."

Then he leapt onto the balcony. Verne had already leapt to the building across.

"Here goes," Cade muttered, and ran toward the ledge. At the ledge, he screeched to a halt, and yelped. Struggling to regain his balance, he fell off the building.

His wind spell caught him just before he reached the ground, slowing him down, then propelling him upward toward the building Verne was standing on.

"Guess he's gone," Verne muttered happily, clinging to a chimney. He stood, seeking cover from the strengthening wind, when Cade landed on top of him.

"There's one thing I don't understand, Messings," Cade gasped after knocking the wind from them both. "What was the motive? The one thing missing."

"Tell me how you knew I did it, then maybe I'll tell you about the motive."

"Deal," Cade said, then felt what was left of his air get knocked out of him again, as he was thrown back across the rooftop by a bolt of pure magic.

"Not so fast," Cade said, but he was too late. Verne had hurled himself off the building, and this time, Cade could see he had magical help.

"Lucky for me I've been studying my spell book," Cade muttered, and ran toward the ledge, this time ignoring the heights and the queasy feeling in his stomach. When he was convinced he wouldn't make the leap, he gestured at the fence of the roof of the next building, hoping his magnetic abilities would give him the needed edge. The fence unfurled, and he struggled across to the top of the roof.

"Very good," Cade spluttered as he got to his feet and wiped his lip. "As for how I found you out, your rapidly changing eyes gave you away. That is a similar effect caused by a botched making of the poison caused by an inexperienced brewer, such as an apprentice."

"You're very good, detective, but what about my alibi?"

"Practically everything an apprentice does must be overseen by a master by law. If the experiment were botched, your master's eyes wouldn't have been a consistent gray."

"Ah. Excellent. And now I will tell you my alibi. You see, this man was not only a customer, but also my father. He is the one who sent me away to work with Master Dragonwing."

"Then why...?"

"I hate it! All we do is study all day long, and I know she loathes me! All these years I've dreamed of revenge for my father putting me in this hell!"

Cade drew his sword, and approached Verne. "Since I'm afraid I've used up most of my energy on trying to survive and keep up with you, I'll have to resort to more pedestrian methods for bringing you in."

"Never!" Verne shrieked savagely, and lunged at Cade. Cade yelped, and they both plunged off the side of the building.

Come on, come on, come on, come on, Cade thought

ferociously as he and his opponent plunged toward the street. *Just one more gust of wind, that's all I ask, enough to slow the fall. Please, work!*

Finally, as the fifth floor whizzed passed Cade and Verne, a strong gust of wind rose from the ground, strong enough to slow their fall. Cade grabbed a gargoyle two stories above the street. Verne yelped, and snatched at his ankle.

"So," the apprentice said, grinning wildly. "I guess this is the end of the road here. What's wrong, detective? Scared of heights?"

"You could say that." Cade was shivering wildly, his arms wrapped around the stone gargoyle. His voice trembled, and he refused to look down.

"Well then," Verne replied, "I trust you won't object if I make my swift departure. Good day."

A buggy went by, carrying behind a gigantic wagon of crushed ice for the hotel. Verne dropped into it, laughing and waving as it began to move again.

"Alright," Cade muttered to himself, "come on, you can do this. It's an extremely short fall. Come on, let's go."

But he couldn't move.

He glanced down at his hands, and willed them to move. Then he saw the blood from his split lip on one of them. His own blood. In what could be described as either good luck, or bad luck, the sight of the blood temporarily stunned him, causing his grip to loosen. Cade fell.

The freezing ice was what woke him up. He had landed in it, felt it crunching under him, then saw

Verne looming just beyond his vision, grinning, and holding Cade's sword.

"Th-that was a gift," Cade stated. "I'd appreciate it if you'd return it."

"Of course," Verne replied. "Would you prefer neck or chest?"

"Chest," Cade said, and pulled his legs up, pulling them into a brief fetal position, then kicking forward with all his might. Verne's eyes widened, and he flew backward against the wall, dropping the short sword, and causing the buggy to halt briefly. Verne and Cade froze, remaining completely silent, and the buggy started again.

Verne lunged forward, trying to reach for the short sword he had dropped, and Cade kicked him in the chest again. Verne fell over, and Cade snatched up his dagger, staggering to his feet. Verne punched him in the stomach, and Cade backed against the wall. Then Verne reached down, grabbed Cade's ankles, and flipped him headfirst out of the ice box.

Cade felt his head slam into the cobblestones, and time stopped for him.

Cade's eyes snapped open. He was in his hotel room, lying on the bed. He wondered briefly and dazedly if that surreal chase with the wizard's apprentice had been a dream. Then he felt his head throbbing, and the thick gauze wrapped around his forehead. Cade put on a miraculously intact pair of glasses on his bedside table, and got up. When he looked in the mirror, he was surprised to find that the sight of his own blood on the gauze nauseated him only slightly.

I'm getting better at this, he thought, and walked out of the bedroom.

Ana was reading a book in the living room when he entered. Aust was there as well, plucking his harp.

"Where are Milo and Brottor?" Cade asked, and they both glanced up.

"Milo is out on the street picking pockets, and Brottor is at a weapons shop," Ana replied, caught off guard by Cade's unexpected entrance. There was a long silence, until Cade finally asked another question.

"How long have I been out?"

"About fifteen hours."

"Crap."

"What happened?"

"I got thrown out of a moving vehicle headfirst," Cade replied. He rubbed the back of his head. "Did they catch Verne?"

"Who?"

"The Royal Guard. Did they?"

Ana fell silent.

"Did they?" Cade repeated patiently.

"His whereabouts are still unknown."

"Hm," Cade replied, dissatisfied. "I'm going to go get changed. Where's my sword?"

"It's on your desk. Why?"

"I've got to start looking for this guy. Ever minute he could be getting farther and farther away."

"You're badly injured, and he's probably not even in Raven Haven anymore!"

"I'm going to finish what I started, Ana. I have to do this alone. And I know where to start, too."

"Where?"

"Master Dragonwing," Cade replied. "She's hiding that boy. I'd bet the farm on it, if I had one."

With that, he walked into his room and shut the door.

"This man," Wilhelm said, pointing to a poster of Milo's face. "A halfling. Recognize him?"

The innkeeper of the Roc Feather Inn nodded.

"Ah yes, that short fellow. I remember him well. He purchased five rooms, for his friends and himself."

"He must have used the money he got from selling my treasure," the Hunter hissed through gritted teeth. "Where are these rooms?"

The innkeeper told him. "Will you require the spare keys as well?"

"That won't be necessary," Wilhelm replied. "It's thief-smashing time."

Cade was halfway down the stairs when he heard the clinking of armor, sounds of several knights struggling upward. He froze, and began to listen.

"Ohh, my head," one voice moaned. "I think I'm dehydrating."

"Shut up!" a familiar voice snapped. "We're already halfway there. Now get up!"

"The Hunter," Cade muttered, and ran back up the stairs.

"You really think he's going to survive another encounter with his murderer?" Ana asked Aust, as he continued to pluck at his harp.

"Probably not," he replied.

"Then why didn't you do something to stop him?"

"Because, who knows? Anyway, nothing I say would do any difference, and he knows what he's in for. He's not stupid, head damage or not. And it's his quest. Can't really argue with the word of a god."

"I still don't like it," Ana muttered.

"Psssh," Aust replied. "You're treating him like you're his mother."

Before Ana had a chance to respond, Cade slammed open the door, and staggered inside, gasping for breath.

"You really shouldn't be exerting yourself, Cade," Aust reprimanded good-naturedly. "You've got a bump on the noggin the size of this hotel, and running around won't help it heal."

"The Hunter's here," Cade gasped. "With friends. The guys that ran Milo out of Irrellia."

"Oh shit," Ana replied, and opened the door a crack, peeking around the corner. She could see the Hunter striding toward their room. Then he turned, seeing the open door, and made eye contact with her, his cold gray eyes shooting darts of ice at her.

"They know we're here!" he shouted. "Attack!"

Ana slammed the door, picked up a chair and smashed the window with it.

"Time to go now," she informed Cade and Aust.

"Can't," Cade said. "Afraid of heights. And besides, I'm not leaving my spell book with these morons."

Ana ran into his room, reappeared with the spell book, threw it into his hands, then yanked him out the window by the collar. The door was starting to splinter now, apparently from some guard kicking it. Finally, it crashed open, and they were inside just in time to see Aust's green hat with the red feather in it disappear through the window.

The Hunter ran to the window and poked his head outside, scanning the drop to the sidewalk.

"I can't see them!" he called, and then he heard Cade's rapid hyperventilating. He smiled to himself. "Wait a second," he called to the guards, then poked his head out to window again, slowly lowering his body, until he came face-to-face with the people standing on the ledge under the window, flattened against the brick wall.

"Hello again," he said, grinning. Not even thinking, Cade hit him in the face with a spell book. There was a snap as the Hunter's nose broke, and he shrieked. His grip slid and he plunged right past the adventurers, screaming until he hit the street below with a wet thudding sound.

"Oh gods," Cade said, looking down. "I just killed somebody." His eyeballs rolled up in his head, and his knees went limp. Not knowing what else to do, Ana slapped him across the face, and forced him to face her eye-to-eye.

"There's plenty of time for that later," she snapped. "We need to get off of here, now!"

Slowly, they crept across the ledge, trying not to look down.

"Alright, show's over!" Cade shouted, bursting through the door to Master Dragonwing's lab. "We've had fun, lady's and gentlemen, but now we're starting to get a bit tired." He grabbed Vera by the collar, and shoved her against the wall. "Where is he?"

"What happened to your head?"

"WHERE IS HE?"

Dragonwing was unimpressed. Cade slammed her against the wall once more for good measure, then began to open and close all the doors leading to different rooms in the lab. Ana and Aust stood in the entrance to the lab, arms folded.

"He wasn't ever really like this before, was he?" Aust inquired mildly. Ana shook her head.

"I think killing the Hunter changed him," she replied.

"He should try anger management."

Another door swung open, and Dragonwing shouted out a "no!" Cade ignored it, and looked inside.

It was a walk-in supply closet. And inside lay the corpse of none other than...Vera Dragonwing.

"I tried to warn you," Dragonwing said, her features shifting and rippling like a melting jigsaw puzzle. "We both wouldn't like what you saw behind that door."

Cade wasn't listening. His eyes were fixed on the knife in the back, the blood the body seemed to be drowning in. It swallowed up his vision, and his mind.

Verne was now standing behind him, grinning, standing where Vera Dragonwing had been only a moment before.

"A potion of transformation," he explained to a distant Cade Welkland. "I hoped it would give me time to destroy you before you discovered the truth.

I knew you'd come here, and this costume seemed the perfect ploy. And now, die!"

Cade still wasn't listening as Verne cast his lethal spell. He continued to stare and gape, until Ana shouted his name.

Cade whirled around and unsheathed his short sword. He was at a disadvantage because he had no spells prepared at all.

Oh well, he thought to himself. *Guess I'll have to rely on my wits and my combat prowess. Oh dear lords, I'm screwed.*

A force bolt hit him in the chest, and he flipped onto his back, gasping for breath. He was up again in a second, staggering forward. He received another one for his effort, but this time tried to shift his weight forward.

"Magic resistance," he gasped, taking another hit in the chest. "No self-destructive wizard would ever survive without it."

He grabbed Verne by the neck, and inserted his sword into it. The apprentice screamed just before he died.

CHAPTER
ELEVEN
GROMMP

They left Raven Haven with claps on the backs from the entire RHPD. Fortunately, the Royal Guard was not allowed to touch them for at least one day, and probably not ever again if the paperwork they needed to fill out to keep hunting our heroes slowed them down long enough.

Still, Cade was silent through the entire thing, looking distant, and depressed. He couldn't get the fact that he had killed two people in one day out of his mind. He had become a murderer, and was being congratulated for it! This was not the life he had expected to live. Cade Welkland had wanted to lead a life of pacifism.

They continued for a few days, everybody trying to cheer Cade up, or at least get him to say something, until they finally reached a signpost.

AUST, it read.

THAT NAME HAS ALREADY BEEN SELECTED

   YOU HAVE BEEN ASSIGNED THE SCREEN NAME "MASTER_BARD"

          PASSWORD: *****

Aust stared at it, scratching his head.

"What the devil?" he muttered. "I've never heard of anything like this in all my travels…"

Shrugging, he lead the group past the sign. They noticed that stretching across the dirt path from the sign to a tree at the other end was a yellow line of chalk. As they stepped over it, they were surprised by several gigantic letters floating overhead:

PLEASE WAIT…

"For what?" Aust muttered to himself, and the words disappeared. Replacing them was a small village full of bustling townspeople.

MASTER_BARD: What the hell is going on here?

When he spoke, he noticed that instead of hearing himself, a text display showing what he said appeared in the corner of his eye. He didn't even feel his lips move. More text appeared whenever anybody else spoke.

ANA: And what are those two little bars in the corner of my vision? And why the hell are we talking like this?

CADE: You see two? I see three.

It was the first time Cade had spoken in a while, and everybody was thrown off guard by it.

ANA: Cade! You're—

CADE: This is neither the time nor place to discuss this. Yeah, I'm fine now that I've had some time to think, but what we really need to focus on is, figuring out what [message too long or complex].

ANA: What did you just say?

CADE: What the [expletive deleted]?

BROTTOR: [Expletive deleted]! [Expletive deleted]ing [expletive deleted]holes!

MILO: What the [expletive deleted]ing is going on here?

AUST: Now, now, we won't have the kind of language here.

CADE: Who are you?

MASTER_BARD: You stole my name, you [expletive deleted]!

Standing before the group was a strikingly handsome and rugged man, wearing a sash with pockets full of holy water and wooden stakes, a belt full of daggers, an ornately carved long sword sheath, and some light leather armor.

AUST: Calm down, I was here first! First come, first served! But I haven't introduced myself. I'm Aust, the undead Hunter around here. Pleased to meetcha. :-)

MILO: What the [expletive deleted] was all that [expletive deleted]?

AUST: What?

MILO: That colon, followed by a dash, and a parenthesis. And why the [expletive deleted] are we talking like this?

AUST: You must be new here. This is the village of GROMMP, a magical place where mighty heroes perform wondrous deeds, and evil villains threaten constantly.

MILO: What?

AUST: Lol!

MILO: Huh?

AUST: Lol means "laugh out loud." Never mind, it's geek humor. Anyway, I guess you all want to know what's going on here.

BROTTOR: [Expletive deleted] right!

AUST: You'll notice that when you talk, you see text messages instead of hearing voices. That's the way people communicate around here.

CADE: How? Why?

AUST: You see, this place doesn't operate like reality. It's really it's own self-contained universe where the laws are altered or simplified. The village of GROMMP is an MMORPG. It involves another dimension even stranger than this one, and takes a long time to explain. All I'll say in the meantime, is that you've entered another reality. You see those bars in the upper left hand corner?

MILO: Yeah…

AUST: The red one is HEALTH and the green one is STAMINA. Whenever you run or do anything strenuous, the STAMINA bar goes down. You'll have to rest before you can get it up again. The HEALTH bar tells you how far from death you are. When the HEALTH bar goes all the way down, you die.

CADE: What about the blue bar? And what does that zero in the upper right hand corner mean?

AUST: CADE, you're the only wizard in your group. You have a MANA bar, which shows how much energy you have to cast magic. You can cast all the spells you have currently, until your MANA bar runs out.

CADE: But that's not how—

AUST: The zero up there is your XP BAR (XP is short for experience). That shows how many experience points you have currently. You get experience by completing quests or killing monsters. When you get enough XP, you gain a level, and become more powerful.

CADE: That kind of makes sense…

AUST: Also, by a mental command, you can access your inventory and look inside. You can also switch weapons and armor at will. Here, I just added some magic items to your inventory. Try switching them around

MASTER_BARD focused on the new armor in his inventory (surprisingly, his backpack seemed to weigh nothing), and tried to make the switch. He looked down, and much to his surprise, a gleaming full plate appeared on him.

AUST: Pretty kewl, huh?

MASTER_BARD: Whuh?

AUST: Kewl. It's—never mind. You figure it out. Anyway, I'm glad you've come. There's trouble in the dungeons near this town.

CADE: Why are there dungeons so near to a quiet hamlet like this?

AUST: Because…uh…well, you can't expect us to travel for days just to find a good monster killing spot, can you? It's for the sake of convenience.

ANA: You put this town near a dungeon for the sake of convenience?

AUST: Of course! This world is nothing if there aren't enough monsters to satisfy the millions of heroes who log on each day!

ANA: Log on?

AUST: Uh…show up here. In this world, we do good deeds and complete quests because it's fun, and we get rewards such as XP and GP (gold pieces).

CADE: You kill things for fun?

AUST: Well, technically, they're not alive anyway. Look, I'm tired of explaining; we have a red dragon down there with a horde of skeletons and zombies, and we need to kill them!

CADE: Since when do red dragons control hordes of undead?

AUST: Party pooper. Anyway, I can see you're getting distracted by the text format here. Would you like me to switch to voice activation?

CADE didn't know what that meant, but he assumed it was the "normal" form of speech.

CADE: Would you? This is getting really distracting." He looked around, and smiled. "Hey, I can hear myself again!"

"Most of the people here have headsets," Aust explained, "so this shouldn't be much of a problem. Now come on, we need to go to that dungeon so you can level up. But first, let's buy some potions."

The streets were full of heavily muscled and heavily armored warriors, powerful-looking mages with ancient staffs, and thieves shifting their eyes back and forth and skulking through the alleys. Finally, they arrived at a shop that read: YE OLDE POTIONS. One powerful and heavily-armored knight walked through. Aust gestured, and the group followed him inside.

When they entered the cramped shop, the knight that had just entered was nowhere to be seen. MASTER_BARD shook his head dazedly. "Weird place," he muttered.

"How can I help you?" an elderly man at the front counter asked. Instantly, a floating list appeared beside him, naming products, with the prices next to them.

"Twenty three potions, and a scroll of resurrect," Aust said. The man nodded, and everybody in the party felt something drop into their belt pouches.

"Whenever you're down on health, drink one of those potions," Aust told them.

"Hey, I only got three!" Cade shouted.

"And a scroll of resurrect," Aust replied. "Since you're the only magic practitioner here, your job will be to use that if anybody dies."

"What will that do?"

"Bring him or her back to life."

"Oh. But that's imposs—"

"Now, come on," Aust said, marching toward some wrought-iron gates that presumably led out of the town. "There is not much time. Time moves quickly over here, and we don't want to be caught in the dark out in those woods. Follow me."

Cade had peered over Aust's shoulder and seen that he had been reading a map showing which direction the dungeon was in. The woods looked a lot larger on the map than they did when you were actually walking through them.

When they entered the cave, Cade shuddered. Aust looked at him questioningly.

"I'm just slightly claustrophobic," Cade explained. "And afraid of the dark. They're just these tiny phobias of mine." Aust turned again, and drew his sword. MASTER_BARD did the same. Ana readied her bow, Brottor his axe, Milo his crossbow. Cade unsheathed his blade, and felt it quaking in his sweaty hands.

The first room in the cave was a gigantic structure, stalactites dangling like an upside-down bed of spikes that could crash down at any minute. Bats fluttered back and forth, and Cade giggled nervously, shielding his face from them.

"He doesn't go adventuring much, does he?" Aust muttered to Ana. Ana rolled her eyes.

"He's not much of an outdoorsy person," she replied.

"Hey, Cade!" MASTER_BARD shouted. "Give us some light here!"

"I'm not sure that's such a good idea—"

"Oh, come on! You managed to catch that Verne guy, didn't you?"

"That was completely—"

"Besides, there can't be any skeletons or zombies this close to the tunnel entrance. According to most of the lore, they tend to stay deeper inside the caves. And there's nothing flammable in here for you to worry about either!"

"We're flammable!" Cade pointed out. Then he ran a nervous hand through his hair. "Oh…all right." Sighing, he pointed his finger into the air. A cloud of flame rose, illuminating the area.

"Good man," MASTER_BARD muttered, and they marched farther downward.

"Wait!" Milo hissed. They were in a narrow corridor, single file, with the thief in front "for trap detecting," Aust explained, unaware of the thief's track record when it came to finding traps. He edged toward a line that only his trained eyes could see, then turned to Aust.

"Give me one of those wooden stakes," he demanded. Aust handed it over. The halfling prodded at the line, and several jagged blades shot from the walls on either side of the line up to the door, whirling around randomly, and humming madly. Finally, they stopped, and retracted.

"Alright," Aust said. "Looks like there's a slight stalling period with this trap, so if I set it off, then we run through when it's over, we should be good." He prodded it again, and waited for the blades to stop whirring. When they did, he ran through, followed by Aust, then Ana, then MASTER_BARD, then Cade, then Brottor. As Brottor was about to run toward the door, the traps started again, skewering him in several places and tossing him up and down, blood spurting everywhere in a display of morbid fireworks. Finally, it stopped, and Brottor got to his feet, his wounds seeming to heal.

"That should have killed you!" Cade exclaimed, eyes wide.

"Yeah, well, it dealt fifteen points of damage to him," Aust said solemnly. "Heavy. He'd better drink one of his potions."

"Like hell I should," the dwarf grumbled, but swallowed one down anyway. It tasted like a bizarre combination of garlic and cinnamon, and he had to resist the urge to make a face at the taste of it.

"We should hurry now," Aust suggested. "Setting off that trap might have alerted some of our undead hosts."

"Oh boy," Ana replied, her eyes gleaming. "I can't wait for the fun to start."

Cade swallowed. "I was never much of a party person," he said timidly. Aust grunted, pushed open the door at the end of the hallway, and they all walked inside.

"Oh, crap!" Cade screamed, and the sound off his voice bounced off the cavernous walls, echoing down into the deepest chambers, where vile creatures began to stir.

They were looking down at a long staircase with no railings, spiraling down and seeming never to end.

"Shh!" Ana replied, and Cade nodded meekly. But it was too late. They heard some rattling far below.

"What was that?" Milo whimpered. The rattling began to grow louder.

"It's bones," MASTER_BARD replied. "And they're drawing closer."

Brottor hefted his axe. "Let them come!" he growled. "Wizard! Send some light farther down the stairs, so we may see our enemies more clearly!"

"I thought dwarves could see in complete darkness," Cade replied as he shot flashes of flame down the stairs.

"Well...we can. It's just...shut up!"

"Brottor! Aust!" Aust shouted. "We will lead the main attack force. Rogues, and wizards have lower hit points, so get behind us!"

"What about me?" Ana demanded.

"Well…you're a woman, so I just kind of assumed—"

"I fight alongside you as an equal, or I fight against you as the superior."

Aust looked down at Brottor questioning him silently.

"She has proven herself in battle more than once," the dwarf admitted.

"Alright," Aust finally relented. "Get in front. But you'll need something besides that bow."

"You're right. Does anybody have a quarterstaff?"

"There's one in my pack," MASTER_BARD said. "It's over by the entrance to this room. Is THAT going to be your weapon?"

"You'd better believe it," Ana muttered, and went to retrieve it. As she did, the first skeletons approached. Brottor roared, and lunged. The two Austs followed.

"Well, this is exciting, isn't it?" MASTER_BARD commented, beheading three skeletons with his rapier. "Just like in the poems of lore!"

"It gets better," Aust commented.

BROTTOR HAS REACHED LVL2!

"See?"

"Well I'll be damned," Brottor said. "Suddenly this is a little easier. Almost kind of relaxing."

"Yeah, skeletons aren't very challenging."

Brottor was starting to doze off, when Ana leapt

over his head, and smashed a skeleton skull in with MASTER_BARD's staff. Brottor would refuse to admit it later, but he had yelped.

Milo began firing crossbow bolts, and Cade shot bolts of pure energy at the skeletons, causing them to crash backward into their comrades.

"You know," Cade said mildly. "This is even easy for me."

"It's all a lot easier in computer games," Aust replied.

"In what-whats?"

"Never mind. Just forget you heard that."

"Done."

They fought for a few hours, then finally realized what was happening.

"We're not moving!" MASTER_BARD complained.

"Aust's right!" Aust said. "Gentlemen…and, ahem, ladies…press forward!"

Slowly but surely, they began to move forward, pressing against the endless hordes of undead.

"I'm all out of bolts," Milo said. "I'll just…whoa!" He slipped on a rock, and fell on his backside, bruising it badly.

"Are you okay?" Cade asked.

"I'm fine," the thief replied, not noticing the cracks growing around where he had landed. "Just a little…hey, what are you looking at? GHAAAAAaaaaaaa…"

The surface he had been sitting on broke away from the rest of the staircase, and he plummeted into the abyss.

"No!" Cade shouted, and lunged forward, trying to

catch him. Brottor grabbed him as he fought, trying to steady the wizard, but a four-foot-tall fighter, even a Dwarven one, only weighs so much, and he ended up being dragged along for the ride.

"Aw, shit!" Ana cried, smashing a skeleton to pieces with her quarterstaff. The cries of her party members distracted her, and she barely evaded a heavy blow from a skeleton, stumbling into both Austs in the process. All three plummeted off the sides of the staircase.

"Wizard!"

Cade looked up, and saw the rest of the part above him plummeting to the ground. It looked like a long way down, and Cade judged he'd be powdered when he hit the bottom.

"Wizard!"

It was Aust.

"What?" Cade called, then louder, "WHAT? Want me to teleport us to the ground unharmed? Or how 'bout I just turn us all into feathers, and let us float to the bottom?"

"You can save us!"

"Like hell I can!"

"Of course you can," MASTER_BARD said. "According to witnesses, that's what you did in Raven Haven."

"But that...that was just me. Six people! No, it wouldn't work."

"Well, better make up your mind, young wizard," Aust replied. "Would you rather die fighting for others to live...or die wallowing in despair and self pity?"

Cade sighed, and closed his eyes. "Hold on to your hats," he called.

"Done," MASTER_BARD gestured at his curled-up fist, from which a cheerful red feather protruded.

Floating deep in his own consciousness, Cade saw nothing but blackness, and felt nothing, not even the rapid falling . He drifted about, trying to focus, until a spell began to form in his mind. But this was something new…it smelled of previously undiscovered magic. Cade reached forward to touch it, feeling its volatile energy pulsate through him. It was a glowing ball of energy, resembling a faraway star, but this was close, and heat and pure static energy were emanating from it.

"Cade!" Ana called from the outside world, and the wizard sighed to himself.

"Oh what the hell," he muttered, and grabbed the ball of light with both hands. His eyes snapped open, his consciousness returned to the real world like a demon thrown from a giant slingshot. Red, searing pain ripped through him, and there was a flash of white light, consuming everything. The ground was approaching faster and faster, they were nearly there now, and then it stopped.

Everything stopped.

Cade groaned, staggering to his feet, and looked around.

"Is everybody okay?" he called. A few others stirred, and got to their feet.

"Hey," Milo said, dazedly. "Where did all the skeletons go?"

Brottor, now on his feet, lumbered over to the stairs and ran his hand through the white powder at the foot of the stairs. His eyes widened, as he crumbled it in between his thumb and forefinger.

"What the hell did you do?" he asked Cade, turning to him. "They're disintegrated!"

"I wasn't ready for the spell," Cade explained. "It was too powerful for me to control. It's a simple teleportation spell, one that will take you from anywhere to the nearest safe location. It's a new spell, one I just discovered. It's new to me, anyway. So, it caused extreme pain to the inexperienced user, and I think I nearly lost all of you people in the nether world, but the resulting psychokinetic blast took effect just as we were in between jumps, in the nether world, and thus we were unaffected by something so powerful and destructive that it appears to have destroyed every bit of living (or once living) tissue in the area."

"Whoa," Milo muttered. "That must mean it's pretty powerful, huh?"

Cade smiled wearily. "Yeah," he said. "Something like that." He stumbled forward, and put a hand to his head. "Whoa," he said.

"What is it?" Ana asked.

"Nothing. Just a little dizzy. Must have been that spell." He took a step back, and managed, miraculously, to keep his balance. His head was throbbing, and his vision was getting cloudy. Clumsily, he sat back on the ground. His arms and legs felt like jelly.

"Are you alright?" Ana asked again. Cade nodded slightly.

"I'll just rest here. You people go on without me. I'll be alright in a few minutes."

"W-we can't just leave you here!" MASTER_BARD spluttered. "More skeletons could be on the way!"

Cade pointed to a stream of powder coming from the steps, and the empty armor and weapons surrounding it.

"There goes the cavalry," he joked weakly. "Go on ahead. I'll be fine. I'm only going to slow you down like this."

"Aust, don't you have some kind of potion that will get him back on his feet?"

"Well…" the undead hunter began, then took a vial out of one of the pouches on his belt and poured it into Cade's cloudy eyes.

"GHAAH! That burns!" Cade jumped to his feet, rubbing his eyes. furiously

"What was that?" Milo asked.

"Holy water," Aust replied with a smile. "I generally use it on vampires and such, but a little bit in the eyes will pretty much do the trick for anybody."

"Is he going to be okay?"

Aust studied Cade for a few seconds. Cade was doing a bizarre dance of pain, "Probably," he said. They waited a few more minutes, until Cade was done screaming, and then the rest of the group quietly led him into the next room.

In the center of the room was a treasure chest, gleaming with gold studs running along the sides. Cautiously, Milo approached it.

"No kind of devices connected to it I can see," he said, and gingerly lifted it up. Nothing happened. He set it back down, and took out his lock pick set. He began to hum as he worked, and in seconds, the lock had opened with a satisfying click.

"Ah," the thief said as he pushed the lid back and looked inside. It was filled to the brim with glittering gold in perfectly shaped little wafers. Milo yelped with happiness, and dug his hands into it, throwing it into the air.

"Woohoo!" he shouted. "Who knew this adventuring thing was so…so profitable!"

Two rotting gray arms shot out of the pile of gold and grabbed his shoulders, yanking him inside. Nobody who was watching saw the gray arms, and when MASTER_BARD saw the halfling disappear into the treasure chest, his eyes widened with surprised.

"Wow," he said dazedly. "The little guy sure likes gold."

"Greedy little halfling," Brottor muttered with little sincerity. "They're all money-grubbers, and cowards too. Well, might as well drag him out, pack as much gold as we can carry, and move to the next room."

"Amen," Aust replied, and they both stuck their arms into the gold, looking for Milo. Both screamed as two sets of arms latched on to their shoulders, and pulled them in.

"Wait a second," Cade muttered, his eyes still stinging from his painful wake-up call. "Something's not right here. Did anybody else see those gray things on either side of them?"

MASTER_BARD and Ana both shook their heads.

"I think that something is pulling them in. And from

the looks of it, that treasure chest goes deeper down than you'd expect."

"Right," Ana said. "And there's only one way to find out what's inside." She ran toward the chest, ignoring Cade's cry of surprise and dismay. Cold, moldy flesh pulled her inside the chest, and she was surrounded by blinding gold, glittering everywhere she looked.

Cade and Aust Galanodel looked at each other, cursed, and ran toward the treasure chest.

Milo struggled vainly, coughing up gold and feeling it poke at his flesh. Drowning in gold, he reflected, wasn't as fun as he thought it would be. He felt something move beneath him, and prayed that it was a trap door. As it turned out, it was a hatch. He landed in a pile of coins, and struggled to get to his feet as more continued to pile on. He managed finally to stand up, when Brottor and Aust landed on him. Then he was up again, but only temporarily, because this time Ana landed on his neck, and Cade and MASTER_BARD on either side of her.

"That was incredibly stupid. Where are we, anyway?" Milo muttered, spitting out gold as he spoke.

Aust heard a grunting noise, and looked up. At least a dozen zombies were surrounding the group. "Very deep trouble," he replied.

"Oh. Shit," Milo glanced around. He drew his hand crossbow, and swiveled it around slowly. "Alright," he growled, "which one of you wants it first?"

"I'm afraid that won't do any good," Aust said. "Zombies can only be destroyed if they are burned, disintegrated, or just hacked down until there's nothing left."

"So then we're in trouble, aren't we," MASTER_BARD muttered. "Deep trouble."

"I have some holy water with me," Aust announced. He took a small jar, and turning to the closest zombie, hurled it at its head. The beast's face began to sizzle, and an inhuman howl filled the air as the beast fell over, turning to dust. Cade swallowed, and took a cautious step.

"Go!" Aust repeated, and dipping his blade in another jar, quickly took a swing at one of the undead with it.

Cade went, and the rest of the party followed. They heard an all-too-human scream behind them, but nobody turned to see what it was. Instead, they pressed on.

The next room was an enormous dome, seeming to stretch higher than any of the skyscrapers in Raven Haven. In the center of the room lay a gargantuan dragon sleeping on a pile of gold.

"Holy crap," Milo muttered. "They expect us to kill that thing?"

"I think that's the gist of it, yeah," Cade replied weakly. "I'm not sure if I'm up to casting more spells, though, and I don't think any blade made by just a normal blacksmith could pierce that armor."

"Actually, you're right," a familiar voice said. The group whirled around. Aust was standing there, grinning madly. "Her Armor class is through the roof."

"A-aust?" Cade spluttered.

"What?" MASTER_BARD asked in reply. "Oh, you mean other Aust. Right. Carry on."

"It was a simple matter to fake my death," Aust said, smiling. "You wouldn't, after all, turn around to see the gory details. Now, Delilah and I will simply kill you five, and collect the reward from Lord Kaos!"

"Delilah?" MASTER_BARD shouted in surprise. "You mean...Kaos's ol' mummy?"

"Don't call me that," a low voice snorted from behind them. Everybody but Aust turned and screamed. The dragon was several inches away from Cade's face, and was blowing hot steam from her nostrils. Cade, mercifully, fainted right away.

"That's starting to happen way too frequently," Ana muttered, and nudged him roughly in the ribs. Slowly, his eyes slid open.

"Look," Ana told him. "There is a very large dragon looming over us, and in a second we're going to have to run for our lives, so please don't black out again, because them I'm going to end up carrying you out of here, which will slow us down significantly, and end up in us both getting killed. Think you can handle that?"

"Okay," Cade whimpered, and got to his feet. When he saw the dragon, he began to faint again, and Ana stepped on his toe.

"Ow!" he muttered. "Alright, alright, I'm going, I'm going! Yeesh!"

Then everybody screamed once again, and ran.

"Aust, master PKer does it again!" Aust screamed triumphantly.

"Anybody know what a PKer is?" Milo asked as they ran.

Delilah reared up on her hind legs and roared, blasting flames. The party began to run a little faster, and squeezed in the narrow corridor leading to safety just in time. They leaned against the wall, breathing hard and sighing with relief.

"Hey, where's Aust?" Milo finally asked.

"They're in here!" Aust shouted from behind them. "Kill them!"

"Aw, crap," Milo replied. He turned to run down the rest of the narrow corridor, and saw that the zombies that Aust had supposedly killed to save them were ambling down from the other end.

"He was controlling the zombies all along," Cade muttered. "Oh crap."

Delilah opened her mouth again, and more flames spewed out. Cade shoved Brottor to the floor, and MASTER_BARD did the same with Milo. Ana ducked, and dragged Cade and MASTER_BARD down with her. Flames spewed over head, taking the oxygen out of the corridor. They were there for several seconds, singing the backs of our heroes. Then, when they thought they couldn't stand it anymore, the flames were gone.

Cade turned around, and saw the zombies, flaming as if somebody had doused them in napalm, but still moving forward.

"Bad news, people," he said, but Ana was already dragging him onto his feet, and the rest of the party was running back into the large room. Aust was now riding on top of Delilah's head.

"Hello again," he said mildly. "I see you didn't get fried to a crisp just now. Lucky you."

Cade summoned up all his courage, and then shouted out his cry of indignation in retaliation.

"Damn you!" he shouted.

"Excuse me?" Aust muttered.

"I said, damn you, and that overgrown lizard you're hiding behind!"

"Overgrown lizard?" Delilah snapped, her eyes glowing red.

"Yeah! You know what the funny thing is? Even if you kill us, you're still stuck here! Why? Because you can't fit through the exit! Hah!"

"Cade, what are you doing?" Ana hissed lowly.

"Provoking an attack. You might want to get ready to run."

"I'll have you know," Delilah said, her temper barely contained, "that I could leave here anytime I want."

"Prove it!"

"Alright," Delilah muttered, "you asked for it." She lifted her gigantic tail off the ground, and swung it at the side of the cave. Chunks of rock flew everywhere, and in its place was an enormous hole to the outside world.

"Run!" Cade shouted. Aust yelped in anger, and jumped off Delilah's head, sliding down her spine, and leaping to the floor. Delilah was enraged as well, and flew through the opening she had created, whirling around and blasting fire at the adventurers as they ran.

"Dammit!" Milo cried when he saw what was before

them—a vertical drop along a rocky wall into a river far, far below them. A rock tumbled down, and they never heard it hit the bottom. The heroes turned around, and saw Aust approaching them, grinning madly.

"This is going to hurt me more than it hurts you," Ana muttered, the stepped forward, and in one fluid motion, punched Aust in the face, grabbed him by the neck, and hurled him out of the cave.

"Why does every single day have to end up with us killing somebody?" Cade moaned as he picked himself up.

They ducked out of the way of a blast of flame, and Ana picked up another rock and threw it down. Halfway down, as Cade could see using his magically magnifying glasses, the air seemed to ripple, and the rock disappeared.

"Fascinating," he murmured. "We'll have to—uh, Ana? Hey, where'd she go?"

He saw Ana diving downward. "Oh, shit." MASTER_BARD looked at him, shrugged, and jumped down too, dragging the hapless wizard along with him.

Milo glanced at Brottor, snatched up a piece of treasure from the pile Delilah had been sitting on, then they both shut their eyes and leapt.

"Fascinating," Cade murmured, looking around. He, Aust Galanodel, and Ana were standing in the field where GROMMP had been not too long before. The sign that had before said PLEASE WAIT...now read CLICK HERE TO LOG OFF. As Cade spoke, Milo and Brottor hit the ground with soft thuds. "It appears we leapt through some kind of portal that stopped our rapid falling, moved us back to our plane of existence, then dropped us down where the town used to be."

"Where's that other Aust, anyway?" Aust wondered aloud. As if in response to his question, Aust, Master PKer and Undead Slayer, lurched to his feet and drew his sword, raising it above his head, and aiming it at Aust's neck.

"Look out!" Ana yelled, and Aust ducked. Aust's sword missed the bard by a couple of inches, and Ana leapt over him, kicking the Master PKer in the face. Cade began to prepare a spell while the man was down, but Ana held up a hand to stop him.

"No spells," she commanded. "He's mine."

Aust roared and struck out with his sword. Ana sidestepped it neatly, and chopped the side of her hand down on his wrist, loosening his grip. In the same movement, she brought her knee up, connecting with his chin with a satisfying crack. He bounced off of it, breaking his nose in the process, and fell to the ground.

"Well, that takes care of that," Brottor said gruffly. "Nice work, for a human female."

"I agree, three cheers and all that," Aust concurred. "But what happened to Kaos's mum?"

As if to answer his question, a gigantic red snout appeared from portal overhead, and breathed flame at the party. They all dodged out of the way, and rows of grain were fragged by hot dragon's breath.

"Log out!" Cade shouted. "Somebody has to log us out!"

"And what is that supposed to do, exactly?" Brottor shouted as Delilah slowly began to snake out of the portal.

"It will close to portal! Somebody, hurry!"

"I'm on it!" Aust shouted, and ran. Delilah began to breath fire after him, but elves are too fast and lithe to be caught by an upside-down hovering dragon with a stiff neck. He lunged at the sign, and slammed his fist against it where it read CLICK HERE. Something made a small clicking sound. Delilah's eyes widened.

"Uh-oh," were her last words. The portal closed, leaving her body in one dimension, and her head in another. Her eyes widened, became glassy, and her severed head crashed to the ground, causing a mini-earthquake.

"Think of it as an interdimensional guillotine," Cade thought aloud. Then he looked out the blood spraying from the stump that had once been Delilah's neck. "Would anybody mind terribly if I blacked out again now?" he asked.

"I'd rather you didn't," Milo commented. "It's becoming a bit of a bad habit, and it's annoying as hell."

Cade sighed. "I guess you're right. Hey, wait a second. Look at the sun."

"What about it?" Ana asked.

"Well, it's in about the same position as when we entered GROMMP. At most, only an hour could have passed in there."

"But it felt a lot longer."

"Maybe it was all some kind of strange, mass tripped-up dream," Aust said philosophically. "Something the gods made up to screw with our heads."

"Then I wouldn't be carrying this," Cade replied, and held up his scroll of resurrection.

"Or this," Milo added, and digging into his backpack, brought out a small golden skull with rubies for eyes. "This thing must be worth a fortune," he boasted. "Milo Pennywise, master thief, does it again!"

"Oh, I'm not that valuable, you big flatterer, you!" the skull said.

What followed was a long, awkward silence, interrupted only by Milo's mindless gibbering.

TWELVE

The God of Nothing, Introducing Kaos, and Lich Joins the Group

When Milo was finished babbling, the skull spoke again, its lips not moving, but the sound being heard all the same.

"Hey, chief, could you put me down? Pretty please? I'm getting a cramp."

Milo nodded meekly, and let go. The skull hovered out of his reach, then turned to face the group.

"Let's start with introductions, people. I'm Lich."

"Please tell me that's just a name, and not a bad pun," Cade said faintly.

"Oh, aren't you clever!" Lich said, without a hint of sarcasm in its voice. "No, you have nothing to worry about. Not an evil bone in my body...wherever that is, anyway!"

The six adventurers forced themselves to laugh, fearing what would happen if they didn't.

"So anyway, what's your name, friend?" he asked

Milo. Milo said his name, looking a bit too pale, his eyes as glassy as Delilah's, and almost as large.

"Pennywise. Hmm. You wouldn't be related to Albus Pennywise the Sneaky, would you?"

"Not that I know of."

"Oh, right, I forgot! It's a little too far into the family trees to recognize anything from back where I come from."

"Where would that be, exactly?" Cade asked.

"You're Hal, right? You look like a Hal."

"Cade Welkland."

"Ah. Are you related to...no, never mind, probably not. Anyway, I'm about seven thousand years old."

"That's quite a life span."

"Well, I was never really alive, not in the sense you're thinking of. I can tell you're skeptical, so here, take a look." It swiveled around, and floated into Cade's hands. Cade examined the underside, which was sealed with gold where a spine should be. Written on the bottom, it said Made in Abelrothameemlach-popatooeyzazzazam.

"Abelrothameemlachpopatooeyzazzazam?" Cade exclaimed. "Where's that?"

"Nice coastal city. In the country of Bobblemockar-eemarangcloockclangfragglesnazz, but you've probably never heard of that place either. It's about seven thousand years before your time. Anyway, the country was wiped out by wandering Twipplefrappies that had been visiting from the dimension of Incompre-hensiblenameofanotherdimensionthatcompletelyignore-suseofspacesinspeechasaregularpractice."

"Twipplefrappies? The plane of incomp...incomp—"

"Never mind, don't even try. It's nearly completely incomprehensible when spoken aloud in the human tongue, unless you break it down into small pieces, which I don't really have the patience for. Anyway, Twipplefrappies are the ancestors of modern orcs, except they possess godlike intelligence, and great knowledge of arcane magic. They're extinct."

"How?"

"God of Control-alt-delete."

"Oh. So how'd you end up in GROMMP?"

"I got bored, so I hitched a ride with this dragon, and decided to follow her around until she wreaked havoc. I wanted to get a good look at the heroes, and offer to help them. I've been lying on that treasure horde for about three hundred years."

"So you're offering to help us?" Ana asked.

"But of course, my dear! You're a Kirsten, right? You look like a Kirsten."

"Ana."

"Right. I knew that. Anyway, it would be unfair of me to back out now. Besides, this sounds like fun. I've never been on a real epic quest before."

"Well, I've never talked to a floating skull of solid gold before," Cade said, "so that makes a first for both of us."

"Oh, goody! I'm going on an adventure! And with an elf, too! What's your name, fellow ageless one?"

"Uh…Aust. I'm sorry, 'ageless one'?"

"Oh, right! I just remembered, the rules have changed a bit! Now you only have about ten times the average human life span, which you place you around, a quarter of a millennia old. Am I right?"

"About," Aust grumbled.

"And you must be a dwarf! Are you a Redbeard? You look like a Redbeard."

"Brottor."

"Right! I love your race's skill with artifice. So loving and meticulous, yet full of power, and extremely durable! Like the dwarves themselves, I guess."

"You're too kind."

"Could you hold up your axe for me to take a look at? I'm a big fan of Dwarven weapons."

Brottor raised it as far as he could, so it glinted in the sunlight, and Lich swooped in to take a look at it.

"Marvelous," it said. "But it's missing something…Ah yes! Magic!"

Red light shot from its ruby eyes, and Brottor yelped, leaping back. The twin beams hit his axe, and it began to pulse with newfound life. It dropped into Brottor's arms, and he stared down at it, eyes wide."

"It will do a little extra fire damage now, too," Lich explained. "Have fun with it! Go ahead, cut some wheat stalks!"

Brottor did. The stumps were charred and smoking.

"Old one," Brottor proclaimed, "something tells me you and I are going to get along very well."

The island of Risunbir is home to a small fishing village that makes its money from trade with coastal areas. It also houses the darkest evil in all the land.

High above the town, on an obsidian tower, lies an isolated castle of stone as black as the heart of Kaos himself. Hot smoke and the sound of screaming rises from the castle, and the town fears it. Nobody ventures outside at night, and nobody ever gets near to the mountain.

Kaos wore his traditional suit of black armor, with spikes sticking out, and a slit that revealed glowing red eyes. A sword with a blade as wide as a dwarf was lying next to his gigantic throne of black, with gilded gold.

"M'lord," somebody said, and Kaos looked up. The thing that was once a man standing before him was dressed in a twisted mockery of the clothing of royal wizards, now ripped to tatters by centuries of wear and tear. Its face was gray and rotting, and its eyes were bulging sockets of glowing green. This thing that had once been a wizard, Yarthank the Vile, was now a lich, a hideous creature made immortal by powerful magic combined with deeply embedded evil.

"What is it, Yarthank?" Kaos demanded.

"We have just received word…those adventurers who you placed a bounty on…"

"Spit it out, fool!"

"Aust and your mother are both dead."

Kaos dismissively waved a hand covered by a spiked gauntlet. "They were weak," he said. "I will need to find somebody else to dispose of them later. The high bounty on their heads will attract many people. What of the other one, Sir Bernard?"

"His whereabouts are still unknown. But it is thought he may reach the castle before them."

"If he does, then he will surely die. Now bring forth one of the slaves. I require a sacrifice."

"Yes, m'lord."

Yarthank left, and a few minutes later, he was back, with a nervous-looking man with a long, tangled mess of a beard and dressed in tatters.

"Here is your sacrifice, m'lord," Yarthank announced.

"He's skinny," Kaos replied disdainfully as he surveyed the slave. "There was nobody meatier?"

"Shall I take him away and bring you another one?"

"No, never mind. I shall make do with him, at the moment. He looks like he will be a good snack."

"As m'lord wishes."

Yarthank bowed, and backed out of the throne room. Kaos smiled beneath his horned helmet, and beckoned for the slave to come closer.

"Y'know, I'm not really a slave here," the slave mentioned as he neared. "If I were you, I wouldn't eat me. You don't know where I've been."

"No disease can harm me."

"But don't you think you'd be better off with a juicy, nutrient-rich slave? I'm full of sugars, and fats, and calories, and whatnot."

"I will rip your flesh off and feast on your soul."

"Mmm. Sounds delightful. All the same, though, think of the economical risk!"

"What do you mean?"

"How many slaves do you consume a year?"

"Three hundred and sixty-five."

"Hmm. And how many do you acquire each year, on average?"

"About three hundred."

"Ah. I see slave shortage problems arriving."

"What do you mean?"

"The slave trade is a tough market, Kasey."

"Don't call me that."

"Right. Anyway, as I was saying, it's only going to get worse. I'd recommend you invest in something else, like livestock."

"I prefer my victims to be intellectually aware of the pain I'm inflicting on them."

"Alright then, how 'bout monkeys?"

"Monkeys?"

"Yep. There's a buncha them in the southern lands, they're pretty bright, and all you need to fatten them up is a buncha bananas."

"Bananas?"

"Yep. Might wanna try having some of them yourself. Rich in calcium. A warrior like you needs strong bones."

"I have the bones of a dragon."

"I don't know much about dragon bones, but I do know this: it's very possible you're not getting your recommended amount of calcium."

"Recommended by whom?"

"Uh…Yarthank!"

"Really?"

"Yep! I heard him talking just back down there in the hall about how you're going to lose your next war unless you get more calcium in your system!"

"You are…very knowledgeable when it comes to a healthy diet."

"And the economy."

"Yes, that as well. If I let you live, would you advise me?"

"Sure, sure, but then there's the matter of a fee."

"A fee?"

"Right. You're signing me on as a nutritionist, a trainer, and an economist. That's gonna rack up quite a price."

"Fine, fine. You get a nice room, and you get out of the slave pit."

"Who'll cook for me, and do my laundry?"

"You'll be provided with a small kitchen, and washing basin."

"Oh no, that won't do at all."

"Then I suppose you'd prefer it if I just devoured you right now?"

"Waitwaitwaitwait! Hold on just a second! Oh, by the way, I don't know if I mentioned this earlier, but if I'm going to be your nutritionist, I need to see you out of that armor."

"What?"

"Yep. Get the royal seamstress, or one of the slaves, or something, to sew you up a nice pair of gym shorts. And while we're at it, the metal boots probably won't work too well when we're running track."

"Nobody has seen the great Kaos outside of his armor. Nobody living, anyway."

"Well then we have a problem. Can you do a pull-up in that thing?"

"A pull-up?"

"It's where you take a metal bar, and…never mind. You have much to learn. What's your weight?"

"I do not know."

"I suspect you're growing a bit of a gut under that

armor. We really need to work on your deltoids, glucoids and biceps and such."

"I do not understand what you're saying."

"Alright, fatty! Get down on the ground, and give me fifty!"

"Fifty what?"

"Push-ups, chunky!"

"Nobody talks to the great Lord Kaos like that, and lives to tell of it!"

"Look, do you want to get in shape or not?"

"… fine. But if I don't see results soon, then you're fired. And I'll kill you."

"Guaranteed, three weeks or less."

Kaos considered killing the slave, then thought better of it, got on the ground, and began doing push-ups, his new trainer berating him the whole time.

The group traveled for another few days, Lich grudgingly allowing himself to be carried in Milo's backpack, until they reached a monastery. There was nothing particularly special about this monastery, except that it was in the center of a large, desolate field.

"Monks!" Aust exclaimed. "This should be an educational experience!"

"Yeah, but monks are dirt poor!" Milo whined. "Who am I supposed to rob in this trash heap?"

"You'll think of something."

A monk greeted them at the front gates. His head was shaved, and he was dressed in flowing, brown robes. "Welcome to the monastery where we study the teachings of the God of Nothing."

"What is the name of this monastery?" Aust asked.

"It has no name."

"Hmm. And what is the name of the God of Nothing?" he asked again, taking out a sheet of parchment, and removing the feather from his hat to write this down.

"He has no name."

"Huh?"

"He's the God of Nothing."

"Oh, I get it now. Clever. So what's his job, basically?"

"He does absolutely nothing. He serves no function other than to be the very essence of nothing."

"So there has been nothing at all recorded about him," Cade added.

"Right."

"So how do you know he exists?"

"Because we have no evidence at all."

"So he's nonexistent."

"Not necessarily."

"Yes necessarily! Nothing, by definition, fails to exist."

"He doesn't fail to exist. He never tried to exist."

"So he doesn't exist."

"Right."

"So he's nonexistent."

"Incorrect."

"How can he be neither existent nor nonexistent?"

"You're thinking in terms of mortal definitions of existence."

"So, in immortal terms, he does exist?"

"Nope."

Cade ran a hand through his hair, his eyes narrowed with frustration.

"Ow, my brain," Milo moaned.

"Never mind them," Brottor grumbled. "We need rest and sustenance. Can you, oh good servants of the God of Nothing, provide us with this?"

The monk smiled pleasantly. "But of course," he said. "Please, follow me. We have about a dozen guest rooms, and they're rarely filled. Come along now. Supper will be around eight-thirty, and breakfast will be early in the morning, around five-ish..."

The group gathered together in Aust's room a few hours later, to discuss their course of action. It was a surprisingly large room, but sparsely furnished, with only a bed, a bureau, and a single window.

"I say we rest here for a while," Brottor put in. "Even if their beer is substandard, this place is fairly safe, and I think we all need a good rest."

"I agree," Ana concurred. "Besides which, the monks seem harmless enough. What could go wrong in a well-protected monastery full of pacifist hermits?"

"I don't think they're pacifists or hermits," Lich replied.

"What?" Cade turned and looked at him quizzically.

"You have a good instinct for human nature, young wizard. You sensed it too, but maybe you repressed it." The gold skull tilted upward, and the light streaming through the room's single window caught on the rubies in its eye sockets, causing it to strangely.

"Evil," Lich muttered. "It is near."

"Oh, crap!" Cade cried, and kicked the bureau.

"Uh, are you okay?" Milo asked, backing away a step or two.

Cade looked up. "Lich is right. I hate to say it, but Lich is right! Oh, why is it that whenever we go somewhere that seems nice enough, it's always infested with horrors beyond imagining?" He kicked the bureau again for effect. Then, once again, he turned to the group, and answered the question lingering in everybody's mind. "You don't think it was a bit too convenient? A monastery in the middle of nowhere, when the map says that there's nothing out there for miles? And it didn't occur to any of you that if Delilah and Aust failed, there might be a price on our heads? None of us thought that Kaos might have a backup plan?"

He sat down at the foot of the bed, and put his head in his hands. "There was something wrong with these monks the moment we walked in here. The idea of a god that they wouldn't have to work into existing mythology to make plausible. And the monastery seems to have been made recently. Look at the ceiling, the walls. No cobwebs? No dust on the furniture? No cracks, water marks, or dents?"

"You're both completely out of your mind," Aust said. "These monks are a perfectly nice bunch of fellows. You people just aren't used to having to think in an adventurer's frame of mind. Now if you'll excuse me, I'm going down to the kitchen to sample whatever they're making."

He strode out the door.

"That sounds good to me," Milo said.

"Here, here," Brottor concurred. "And while I'm down there, I might as well have a little more beer."

"Wait!" Cade called after them. Milo and Brottor turned.

"The food could be poisoned," Cade explained. "So make sure Aust has some before you try it."

Milo stared at him.

"You don't have a very high opinion of Aust, do you?" the thief commented.

"Elves are immune to poison, but they can still identify the taste of it. So if there is poison, he'll be able to warn you."

Brottor and Milo shrugged.

"Fine," Brottor muttered, and they both walked out the door.

"You two are really serious, aren't you," Ana said, once Brottor and Milo had left. Cade nodded, and Lich bobbed up and down in a gesture similar to nodding.

"Dead serious," the immortal replied.

"Well, sorry, but I'm going to have to side with Aust on this one. You're both paranoid."

"But that doesn't mean they're not out to get us," Cade shot back as Ana left the room.

At dinner, the group sat together at the end of the table. After the blessings for food, Aust dug in. Milo and Brottor were about to, but Cade elbowed Brottor sharply and kicked Milo in the shin. Reluctantly, they put down the food, and waited for Aust to sample everything on the table.

"Mmph, this is delicious!" he cried between gulps

of food. "Why aren't you guys eating at all? Well, whatever it is, your loss."

Reluctantly, Cade picked up a drumstick of chicken, and nibbled at it. Then he nodded at Brottor and Milo, and they began to scarf down the food.

"I don't understand it," Lich sighed after the group had recounted the story to him. Not being able to eat, he had been up in Milo's room, and the monks still didn't know he existed. "If they wanted to get rid of you, why didn't they just poison the food?"

"Because they don't want to get rid of us?" Ana suggested.

"Because," Cade explained. "They knew ahead of time there was an elf in the group, and decided to avoid using anything that would set of alarms due to an elf's heightened senses. Instead, it could be anything. A dagger in our sleep, smothering, strangling, beheading…"

"You're doing well, young wizard," Lich muttered. "Very clever. Maybe I should guard the hallway, see if anybody tries to get into your rooms tonight. I'm small enough to remain unnoticed, and I never sleep."

"Fine," Ana sighed. "If you two will shut up about it already."

"Yeah," Milo said. "You're even starting to make me edgy."

"I thought thieves were supposed to be paranoid," Cade muttered, as he got up to go to his own room.

"Only when they're hoarding stolen valuables," Milo replied.

"You are," Lich pointed out. "Me."

Nightfall. Lich hovered in a corner of the ceiling, watching with gleaming ruby eyes, waiting for something to move. His rubies were enchanted with the ability to see in pitch black, so clearly identifying a potential assassin wouldn't be a problem.

As he was watching, a man clothed in black robes and wearing a mask of the same color crept into Brottor's room, clutching a short blade whose curve gleamed dangerously through the infrared vision.

Lich quickly moved through the open door to observe. The assassin raised his knife over the slumbering dwarf, and slammed into the back of the assassin's head. The assassin's eyes clouded, and he fell over. Then Lich looked at Brottor, and sent a psychic signal toward the dwarf.

Brottor...wake up!

Brottor jumped out of the covers, yelping. Lich would later say that you haven't seen true hilarity until you've seen a pajama-clad dwarf jump half out of his own skin.

With a thud, Brottor hit the floor, and staggered to his feet. He lit a candle, glanced at Lich, yelped again, then glanced at the assassin lying on the floor.

"Still breathing," Lich said.

"I'll take care of that," Brottor replied, and reached for his axe.

"No, wait. Tie him to the bed, and question him, first. I'm going to go wake the others."

Brottor nodded, and Lich moved out.

In the next room, Aust's, another assassin had been just about to stab him when he had been startled by the yelp. Elves happen to be notoriously light sleepers, so it took only one glance from Lich to see he had it under control. But that meant that the others might already be dead.

Lich raced into the next room to save as much of the group as he could. The next room belonged to Milo. The assassin within seemed confused by the absence of a body in the bed. When he turned around to search, Milo slammed a candlestick into his knees. The assassin yelped, and fell. Milo smashed him on the back of the head, and turned to Lich.

"Guess you and Cade were right," he said, catching his breath. "I was going to wait until nightfall before looting this place for whatever valuables it had, and I heard somebody creeping toward my room. I hid in the shadows, hoping that I could pick the pocket of whoever it was. When I saw it was an assassin, I gave him a good thwack on the back of the head with this."

He looked around, and grinned. "Well, I guess that's that, then. What about the others, by the way?"

Lich raced over to Ana's room. Inside, a groaning assassin was lying on the ground, pinned there by the bureau. Lich was amazed that whatever had gone on in there hadn't made a sound.

"Your paranoia and Cade's paranoia were starting to wear off on me," she explained. "I never went to sleep, and just waited for something to happen. How's everybody else doing?"

Lich, once again, didn't answer, and went to Cade's room, knowing that this was the one he wouldn't be able to save, a bright young man, but not cut out for adventuring, and certainly an easy target for assassins.

Much to his surprise, Cade was still fast asleep, and his would-be assassin was trapped in a cage made of electricity. The hapless assassin seemed to be trying to wiggle in between the bars, and each time he did, he'd get a painful shock, and be thrown back inside the cage. When Lich woke him up, Cade watched the assassin with little surprise on his face.

"It's good to be paranoid," he commented. "I knew those magical traps I set up would come in handy."

The assassin groaned in agreement, sizzling from under his robes.

The group gathered in Milo's room, the room with the only guard that wasn't groaning in pain or misery. They agreed that they did have a problem, a very big one at that: they could hold one assassin for interrogation, but what should they do with the rest?

"I say we kill them," Brottor growled. "After all, they tried to kill us. In the dwarven kingdoms, that gets the death penalty!"

"There will be no killing of the unarmed or defenseless," Ana replied. "They were trying to do exactly that, and if we acted the same way, how better would we be than them?"

"They started it," the dwarf replied sullenly.

"What about sending them back with a message?" Aust suggested. "Let them know we're to be feared, and that one of them is in captivity."

"Then they'd bring in an even greater challenge, and we might not live through that," Cade replied.

"Oh, where's your sense of adventure, human?"

"I left it back in Raven Haven."

This was greeted with a long, awkward silence.

"I know!" Lich finally said, and everybody looked at him. "Cade remember how you caught that assassin in the lightning cage?"

"Yeah…"

"I could cast a spell to make a cage large enough to fit all of them in there! Then, we could escape!"

"How would they get out after we left? You can't let them be stuck in there forever."

"I'll set a timer for the spell to dissipate after one full day. How's that sound?"

"Perfect!" Milo said. "We'll get them all in here, except for Brottor's assassin, who's already tied to the bed for interrogation. While they're stuck in here, we can squeeze as much information as possible out of Brottor's captive, and make our swift exit!"

Everybody went to work, bringing their captives into Milo's room.

"Wake up."

The assassin slowly came to, and as his eyes focused, he tried to scream . The bed sheet was an efficient makeshift gag, and even the appearance of a gold skull a few inches from his face, with piercing red rubies for eyes, only provoked a few muffled sounds.

"Talk," the skull said, and a woman who had been leaning against the wall and watching, moved forward and ripped the gag from his face. He looked around now that his head was unrestrained, and saw four others watching intently.

The assassin bit down on another scream, and leaned back, squeezing his eyes shut.

"Never." He tried to sound assertive, but his voice was barely above a whisper.

"Never say never," the skull replied, and sparks leapt from its ruby eyes. The assassin screamed as pain wracked his body, then he slumped against the bed.

"I assume you work for Kaos," the skull snarled.

"Indirectly, but yes," the assassin replied, gasping for breath.

"Indirectly?"

The assassin turned, and saw an elf leaning against the bureau with his arms folded.

"I work for an assassin's guild," the assassin explained. "Based in Gorgal. The guild was promised a large amount of money and power by Kaos for bringing in your heads."

"What sort of power?" somebody murmured.

By the light of a single dim candle flickering in the room, the assassin could see the gleam of a pair of glasses, shining like a sliver of moonlight in the shadows. "He would let us rule the city. He would crush all the other guilds, and we would rule supreme!"

"What is the name of your guild?" the skull demanded.

The assassin didn't want the pain to return again, so he cried out the name, over and over again, until he was plunged back into the darkness, a vague memory of eyes made of ruby lingering in his mind.

"He'll sleep now," Lich said, moving away from the unconscious figure on the bed. "When he wakes up, he won't remember anything about this interrogation."

"The Bladed Hand," Aust murmured. "What an incredibly poetic name for an assassin's guild. I have to write this down before I forget it. And in Gorgal, of all places. I had forgotten we had been traveling this far west. I've been there, once or twice, you know."

"Where is Gorgal?" Cade asked.

"Just east of here, according to the map," Ana replied. She had been sitting in the corner, looking it over.

"Not a pretty place to visit," Aust continued. "It has the highest crime rate of any city in Irrellia. Full of thugs, mercenaries, muggers, thieves, blackmailers, gangs, mobsters, smugglers, peddlers, con artists, and…assassins."

"Well," Cade replied quietly, "it can't be worse than any of the places we've been recently."

Aust shook his head. "Trust me, it can."

"I'd prefer going there than sitting in this room and waiting for somebody to come and kill us," Ana said, and tossed Brottor his backpack. "Gather up your things, everybody, and hurry. We should leave before the monks suspect anything."

"The faux-monks," Cade corrected, then left to get his things.

The next morning, the Guild of the Bladed Hand discovered the cage, the assassin tied to the bed, and a note on Aust's bed.

Dear Guild of the Something-something Hand,

Never send a rookie to do an elf's job. How dumb did you really think we are? Well, we're off now, far out of your reach, so phffffffft! to you!

Cheers,
Aust Galanodel and Co.

CHAPTER
THIRTEEN
Gorlal

"Hmm," Aust muttered disdainfully as he inhaled Gorlal's foul air. The party was trotting along the city's cobblestone path beneath unstable and twisting skyscrapers that seemed to encroach on the street, blotting out the sun. The group had been looking for a place to stay, and so far, none of them could really say they would feel particularly comfortable at the nearby inns.

Finally they settled on a place called the "Happy Gnome." The grimy, rapidly deteriorating building didn't look very happy at all.

"I performed here once," Aust said, and then pulled his hat down over his brow.

"Let's hope nobody here remembers you," Cade muttered.

"Five rooms," Ana announced to a sleepy looking innkeeper. He took out a greasy journal, scratched some things into it, then pointed to the stairs in the back of the place. As they walked up the stairs, the man grabbed Aust's elbow.

"Hey," he muttered. "Do I know you from somewhere?"

"No," Aust replied quickly. "Whatmakesyouthinkthat? Neverbeenhereinmylife!"

The man looked at him closely, then let go of his elbow.

"Whatever you say," he muttered.

"How much longer are we going to go through this?" Cade muttered wearily to Ana as they walked up the stairs.

"Through what?"

"This quest. I'm starting to get very tired of it. One thing after another, and it always ends up in the same way."

"Well, let's see," Ana replied, removed the map from her belt pouch, and unfurled it. "From Gorlal, we're going to the Canyon of Doom, and the Mountains of Misery. Then we move on to the Sea of the Damned, and from there, we should be on the island of Risunbir, where the fortress of Kaos lies."

"Oh, crap," Cade muttered. "But first things first. We have to infiltrate an underworld infested with assassins, and eliminate the guild that's hunting us for a very high price."

"I didn't hear anybody say this would be easy."

"What about the Plains of Eternal Happiness, or whatever they were? Shouldn't we be going there too?"

"The Plains of Eternal Joy? Uh, let me see…nope, we already passed through there."

"The place with the faux-monks?"

"Yep."

"Guess it's not all it's cracked out to be."

"Guess not. Cade, look, we've gotten this far already, haven't we? We're more than halfway to our goal, and now his no time to quit on it. Just hang in there."

"What's in the Canyon of Doom, anyway? Any ideas?"

"I think there's a horde of cannibalistic goblins living there."

"You're kidding."

"Nope. Look."

She pointed to the map. Near the area marked "Canyon of Doom" was a small sign that said: CANNIBALISTIC GOBLIN ALERT: TRAVELERS, TRY NOT TO SMELL APPETIZING!

Cade raised an eyebrow, then glanced at the sweaty, dirty dwarf climbing up the stairs in front of him.

"Well, at least Brottor's safe," he murmured. Much to his surprise, Ana burst out laughing.

Night fell on Gorlal, and Milo glanced out the window before turning back to the other five members of the party, all who were sitting in his room and waiting for him to speak.

"Let's go over this again," he said. He had managed to obtain a map during the day from the local thief's guild, and now knew the exact location of the Guild of the Bladed Hand. He traced a circle around it with the thin branch he was holding.

"This building has two trained guards at the front door, according to my sources. The place is a front as a brothel, and that's where Ana comes in."

"This is ridiculous! I'm not going to—"

"Come on, Ana. We need you on this."

Ana's shoulders slumped. "I'll pretend I'm looking for work," she muttered.

"Good. And then what?"

"Then I kick their asses."

"Right. After which, the rest of the group will come out of hiding from behind the bushes, and I'll pick the lock. Ana will stay outside and wait for the rope to come down from the window, but more on that later. The men, minus Lich, who will still be tucked away in the bush, will wander about, pretending to be enjoying the show, until we reach the stairs leading to the employee's area on the floors above. Cade, what are you going to do?"

"I'm going to approach the guards, and complain about some drunks ruining the party. Then, I'll take care of them. How, exactly, am I supposed to do that, by the way?"

"Improvise. Just zap 'em. Whatever. So, then we go up the stairs. Lich, got that scroll of disguise ready?"

"Yep."

"Then we'll throw the rope down from one of the windows, and you and Ana can get up. When you get up there, you'll use this scroll, and we'll disguise ourselves as professional assassins. We'll report we have slain the adventurers from Irrellia, and request to speak to the Guildmaster. Then, when we get there, everybody will get to do their thing. Then we'll get rid of the Guildmaster, thus disbanding the Guild of the Bladed hand, and move on without a bunch of professional killers breathing down our necks."

"No," Cade said quietly.

"Pardon?"

"I'm not going to be involved in an assassination attempt."

"Look," Ana said, "Cade—"

"No, you look. You think this is going to change anything? There are other guilds, other killers. Kaos should have no trouble finding them. We have a lot to lose with this, and he has nothing to lose if we succeed. Besides which, I don't think I can stand killing another person. Self-defense is one thing, but actual premeditated murder? I won't have any part of it."

"You signed up for the contest! You put in the effort to win! We all did! Snap out of your silly, self-righteous delusions, and face facts!"

"Hey, don't be so hard on the newbie," Aust objected. "Being human, he has a shorter lifespan than us, and we're both much more experienced in the art of combat, so let's cut him a little slack, eh?"

"The art of combat? All I see you do is haul around that harp, and make us listen to horrendous and preachy poems about shitty heroes from centuries ago!"

"Is that so, 'shorty'? Well, I'll have you know—"

"Never, ever, insult somebody about their height!"

Brottor roared. In a fit of rage, he leapt on top of Aust, and began pummeling him with his bare fists. Aust calmly picked up the dwarf and threw him against the wall.

"STOP IT!"

Everybody froze, clutching their ears, and gritting their teeth. They turned to Lich, stunned. The gold skull gleamed angrily.

"Listen to me," he said, his tone softening from the psychic blast he had dished out a few seconds ago. "Arguing will get us nowhere. The sad truth is, Milo is right. We don't have much other choice beyond killing the Guildmaster. As for Cade...hey, where is Cade?"

"I'll go talk to him," Ana said, and left the room. Milo looked around, and folded his arms sullenly.

"The one time," he muttered. "The one time I come up with a plan, and that braniac has to steal the glory, yet again."

He noticed everybody was staring at him.

"What?" he demanded irritably.

Just as Ana expected, Cade was sitting at the bar, nursing a mug of beer.

"This reminds me of one day a couple weeks ago," he snorted as Ana drew up a stool. "Back in Fool's Tavern. That time, it was Aust giving me the lecture."

Ana observed him carefully. "Are you drunk already?"

"Completely inebriated," Cade replied. "Low tolerance for alcohol. I blame it on my mother's side of the family."

"Look, Cade—"

"If you're trying to convince me to kill again, you're wasting your breath. I don't even know why I'm in this group, anyway."

"You're thinking of quitting."

"Yep." He gulped down some beer, and slammed his half-empty mug on the table.

"You've already gotten this far, and you're going to give it up? Just like that?"

"Just like that. I may not have liked what I was doing before I got involved with this group, but at least it made sense. At least my life was logical. Now, I don't know what to think of this planet. It's certainly not the world I live in. I need to return there."

"Listen to what you're saying! You don't have any money, or even a home to go back to! That's what all of us have in common. That's what keeps us going. The promise of a home to return to."

Cade snorted. "I was under the impression you were doing this for the glory of it."

"I just want to be respected as an equal. You don't know what it's like to be a skilled combatant, but still be rejected in favor of those weaker than you, simply because they're men. On my first attempt to join the military, I was nearly arrested, simply for beating the guards that had been assigned to duel against me. My family was so ashamed that they kicked me out of the house, and tried to forget about me. That was six years ago."

"At least your life was reasonably enjoyable before then," Cade replied. "You had luxuries. I had three concussions on average before lunch period. Most of them, were in fact, inflicted by our noble deserter Sir Bernard. Once I was finished with school, I thought I'd be able to become better than him, finally, prove I was the superior one by becoming a successful instructor in the arcane arts. That didn't go so well, as you can probably tell."

"And you want to go back to that?"

"Hey, it might not have been much, but at least I was alive, and had the security of knowing I'd be alive the next day, too."

"It doesn't sound to me like you were alive at all."

"It's better than this! Adventuring is hell!"

"What about the people who are relying on us to make sure that Kaos doesn't destroy them?"

Cade looked at Ana with the eyes of a pathetic creature that's been beaten one too many times. "Ana, I have the utmost confidence in you and the rest of the party. You're all good adventurers, even Aust. You know what to do, and you're good at it. Me, I'm not cut out for adventuring. I'm just dead weight."

Ana's eyes caught a glimpse of Cade's short sword, sheathed by his side. Her arms moved quickly, and Cade's eyes widened as he saw the short sword fly from its sheath, into the air, and bury itself in the bar before him.

"The person who accepted this wouldn't say that," Ana said. "You're stronger than you think Cade. I think everybody in this party is. The difference is, you're not even giving yourself a chance to test your own strength. I'm not asking you to kill. But I'm asking you to take a good look at that blade, and the person you see in it. And if you see somebody who looks strong enough to do it, I want you to march right back up those stairs, and rejoin the party. Maybe Milo is wrong, but if he is, then you have to argue logically, and consistently, and show him what an ass he's being. So look, Cade. What do you see?"

Cade gazed into the short sword, and as he did, his eyes narrowed, and his features hardened. Before Ana's eyes, he seemed to transform temporarily, not into an eager, inexperienced adventurer, but one hardened by years of battle, who is returning to fight the good fight one last time.

He grabbed his blade, and re-sheathed it, then stood, and looked around.

"Thank you," he said to Ana, then marched back up the stairs.

"Hey!" the bartender called. "Aren't you gonna pay for that?" Cade ignored him. Ana sighed, and reaching into her belt, tossing a few silver pieces onto the bar. Then she followed Cade up the stairs.

"Well look who's back," Milo muttered as Cade barged back into the room. He yelped, and scuttled off the bed as Cade slammed a fist on it, and looked him straight in the eyes. Milo had seen few pairs of eyes looking so determined or ferocious, much less those of nerdy wizards.

"Listen to me," Cade growled, "you're looking at this the completely wrong way. First of all, we're attracting to much attention even by letting ourselves be seen on the brothel area. We need to get through the back window, here." He jabbed at the map. "Second, you can hold onto your precious scroll of disguise, or sell it back, because we can't use it. They've probably already gotten word of our escape. I suggest we shimmy down the skylight right here, and then simply get rid of the Guildmaster's bodyguards the messy way. Third, nobody is getting killed, because we can just as easily disband any assassin's guild by making the Guildmaster wet himself. Scare him a little, maybe rough him up, and let the other assassins see it. That will be the end of his career, and the end of the guild. Got it?"

Milo's mouth worked noiselessly for a little while, until he finally found it in him to say something.

"Got it," he whimpered meekly.

Bernard was running. He grabbed at the dirt at his feet, struggling to stay upright, but steadily slowing to an awkward stumble. He was running through the desert, red sand running into the cracks in his boots, ignoring the oppressive weight of his armor bearing down on him. His face was dirty, and drenched with sweat. His eyes had the sharp glimmer of a madman in them.

Cade had always had a theory about Bernard's pattern of behavior, and if he had looked into Bernard's eyes at that moment, he would have known instantly, that he was right. You see, they lived in a world where good and evil are clearly mapped out, and aren't just philosophical theories, but facts. At least, Cade lived in this world. Bernard had a dim awareness of this world, but he didn't really think or exist in it. His physical self was just there for a short stay.

You see, to Bernard, only one constant existed: himself. And all the ends justified the means, no matter how terrible those means were. Why was he a knight? Why did he go through all the trouble of defending his home, when others could have done it just as easily?

The answer was that the mask of righteousness is the most dangerous mask evil can ever don. And knighthood was simply means to an end. What end? Why, Bernard's glory, of course. So he could wallow in riches beyond his wildest imagination. And he already had the king wrapped around his ironclad finger.

So here Bernard was, setting out to destroy the greatest evil that ever lived, and it had nothing to do at all with a sense of responsibility to those who could be killed by Lord Kaos. It was out of a sense of responsibility to his own swelled ego.

Maybe Bernard wasn't ever really evil, but simply self serving. Maybe, deep down, all true bullies are like that, walking a thin line between insanity and evil. Maybe Bernard was never evil.

Until the night that he completely snapped.

Bernard continued to run for several hours, until he was slowed to a slightly fast stagger. Finally, as night fell, his eyes went cloudy, and he collapsed, a few miles from the Canyon of Doom.

And he dreamt.

Bernard, something hissed. Bernard was falling through a world made of a liquid dark purple color, and it seemed to be the color of evil itself. He was falling slowly, as if in a very viscous liquid, and the liquid seemed to be calling him.

Bernard...if you join with me, there will be riches beyond your imagination.

Bernard looked up, and he was lying on a plateau made of the same purple stuff, solidified. A black beam of light was pulsating in the center of the plateau, and Bernard scrabbled to his feet, and watched it. It was strangely seductive, beckoning for him to join it. Cautiously, he edged forward and touched it.

The black light exploded, and Bernard was thrown to the ground again. He looked up, and saw the light dissipating, replaced by a large man, an unnaturally large man, in black armor, with glowing red eyes. It was carrying a sword as wide as a dwarf, planting firmly in the ground, both hands resting on the hilt.

Join with me, Kaos commanded, and images of wondrous riches, and slaves, and power, filled Bernard's head. Eagerly, he grinned and nodded rapidly. Then he screamed, pain wracking his entire body.

He was still screaming when he woke up, and the pain was still there. He shut his eyes, trying to shut the pain out at the same time, but it wouldn't end. Eventually, it slowed to a dull ache.

The group began to leave the inn as night was beginning to fall, and the innkeeper stopped them.

"You can't!" he cried.

"We were just about to!" Aust replied.

"Are you sure I don't know you from somewhere?"

"Yes! Now, getouttaourway!"

"Don't you know what happens when you go out-side at nightfall?" the innkeeper shrieked.

The group eyed each other nervously, then shook their heads.

"You fools! The gargoyles rise!"

"Oh," Aust murmured shakily. Then he regained his composure. "Is that all? Then let us through!"

The innkeeper opened his mouth to respond, and Aust brushed him out of the way. Milo, being slightly more inquisitive, stopped the group, then walked up to the innkeeper, who was sniveling against the wall.

"What did you mean, the gargoyles rise up?"

"They're vile, winged beasts made of stone, with horns, and antlers, and—"

"Yeah, yeah, I know all that, but they tend to be static objects."

"Static?"

"Inanimate."

"Inanimate?"

"Not moving."

"Oh. Well, a curse was placed on the city a few years back. Some bard entered the city, and happened to piss off an evil wizard who was forced to listen to the bard's horrible singing voice as he plotted from his tower, as the irritatingly loud voice carried from this very inn throughout the city. So, he put curse, that anybody who ventured outside, thinking the bard would, would be marked for death by the cursed gargoyles of this cursed city of cursedness."

"C'mon, my singing- er, his singing, er, not that I would know that he was a he...I mean it! It was a he! I mean, not that I'd know that...so this elf, er bard, er human bard, er, bard of unknown origin, really pissed off that wizard, huh?"

The innkeeper stared at him in disbelief.

"Y-you're him!" he screamed. "Get out of my inn! To the gargoyles with you, scum!"

Then he shoved the party out the door, slammed, and bolted it.

"Uh, maybe we should try to sneak back inside," Cade suggested. "Then we could get down on our knees and plead for our life."

"Yeah," Brottor mumbled grumpily. "Maybe offer Aust as a sacrifice."

"Hey!" Aust cried. "I resent that! It wasn't my fault! I was just trying to let the audience in the back row hear!"

"Does that count as the back row?" Cade screamed, and pointed to an enormous ebony tower rising up in the center of town.

"Well, I could have amplified it a bit too much..." Aust considered.

"Look people, we have only two options," Ana said. "One, is to find another inn to stay at, and seeing as this was the best inn in town, and still a dump, that's not recommended. The other option is to go destroy the gargoyles and the evil wizard who controls them, thus gaining the favor of all the townspeople. The catch with that is, we'll be risking our lives...yet again."

The group thought about it.

"I still like the begging and pleading idea," Cade muttered. "And if that doesn't work, we can just find another inn."

"It's a bit late for that!" Milo shrieked. Everybody turned, and saw he was pointing up at an enormous gargoyle swooping down toward them.

"Holy!—" Cade began, and was cut off as Ana drove an elbow into his stomach as she charged forward, throwing them both out of the gargoyle's way, and knocking the wind out of Cade. Cade caught his glasses as they slipped from his head, and quickly readjusted them, still sitting on the ground, with one hand clutched to his stomach. No sooner had he regained his vision, when Ana yanked him up, and the group began to run for the tower.

"Maybe..." Milo panted, taking up the rear. With his short legs, he had to run twice as hard, and was still only just in front of Brottor, who had heavier armor. Aust and Ana both froze, jumped backward, and picked them up, Aust lifting up Brottor, Ana lifting up Milo. Lich said something muffled from Milo's backpack, and Ana opened it as they ran.

"I think Milo had something to say," Lich commented as he floated leisurely alongside the rapidly moving group.

"Maybe we could, y'know, use this to our advantage," Milo suggested. "Bait the gargoyles into entering the Bladed Hand's headquarters, then let them freak out the Guildmaster."

"That's an idea," Cade gasped, not being the fittest of the party. "I think the headquarters is somewhere near here."

"Right next to the tower in fact," Ana said.

"Just our luck," Cade grumbled, with little enthusiasm.

Behind them, a gargoyle went into a dive bomb. Milo who had been watching over Ana's shoulder, yelled for everybody to duck, and they all did, Cade going into a humorous dive, and screaming bloody murder. The gargoyle swooped over them, and looped around, zooming in for the kill. Lich put himself in its way, and it barreled right through him, chipping off one of its horns in the process, and sending the skull flying. Cursing, Ana grabbed the helmet off of Brottor's head, and as the gargoyle moved in, shoved it directly on to its snout. The gargoyle's glowing red eyes widened with surprise, and it landed, struggling with non-opposable thumbs on the ends of awkwardly large paws, struggling to pull the helmet off. It finally came off with a loud pop, and so did its head. Holding its severed head in its hands, the thing collapsed, and dissolved, leaving Brottor's helmet in a pile of gray dust. Brottor ambled over, picked it up, and snarled disapprovingly at Ana. She just shrugged sheepishly.

"Two more coming in!" Milo announced, and they began to run again, Lich tailing along, and shaking cobblestone fragments out of his eye sockets.

"I love adventuring," Cade panted under his breath. "Especially all the great feats of bravery."

"Shut up," Brottor replied sullenly, feeling his pride was injured enough by the fact that an elf was carrying him as if he were a baby.

" Y o u … "   A u s t   p u f f e d , "should…really…lose…some…some…weight!"

"Figures. All you Elves are grotesquely un-muscled twigs. What you need is some meat on those bones."

"I'm just thanking the Forest Gods we don't have those mangy beards you dwarves always drag through the mud."

"Pfah! These are signs of masculinity! You elves are all women!"

Ana glanced over her should at Brottor, and glared at him. He mumbled a hasty apology.

"Here it is!" Milo announced, and the group skidded to a halt, and took cover under the enormous marble steps that served as an entryway to the Guild of the Bladed Hand. The gargoyles passed over heard, scanning the terrain for their foes.

"Lucky for us it's a windy night," Milo said, unpacking his equipment. "They won't catch onto our scent for a while, but we'd still better hurry."

"What makes you think they can smell?" Aust asked. Milo looked up at him blankly.

"Well, they can see, can't they?"

"Good point. Hey, what's that?"

Milo unpacked a small rod, one with a single button on it, and grinned, until he remembered his "fool proof" plan to steal King Devham's crown.

"This, my friend," he announced, "is the most useful tool in the business. Besides lock picks, that is."

He pointed the rod at the roof, and pressed a button. Aust gasped as a thin rope shot from the rod, attached to the roof, and then carried him rapidly up to the top. He threw the rod back down, and Cade caught, then began examining it.

"Fascinating," he muttered.

"Hey, Geek Boy!" Milo called. "We have plenty of

time for that later! Right now, hurry up and get up here! Then throw it back down for the rest!"

"Uh…" Cade began, and judged how high up the roof was. Instantly, he felt dizzy.

"Oh, shit," Ana muttered, seeing the vacant look in Cade's eyes. "Hey, look, Cade, this is no time for a vertigo attack! Got it? Snap out of it, and get up there!"

"But it's so tall…"

"Deal with it!" Ana slammed the button on the rod, and the rope shot up to the ceiling. Cade had enough time to glance down at the rod in his hand, and his eyes widened in pure terror. He turned to Ana with a look of betrayal that it truly hurt to be the target of. Then, the rope tightened, and Cade shot upward, screaming all the way. Milo saw he was obviously shaken when he reached the top, and despite his clumsiness and general incompetence in all things stealthy, he couldn't help feel a little sorry for the guy.

"Toss it down," Milo instructed, and Cade blankly dropped it off the roof. Brottor caught it next, and accidentally pressed the button in the process, so he was completely taken by surprise when he rocketed skyward. He seemed a little shaken as well, but when Milo suggested it, Brottor tried to turn him to stone with his glare.

"I see them!" Cade called, watching the gargoyles with his magnifying spectacles. "Ana, take Lich, and hurry up!"

Ana grabbed for the skull, and it dodged out of the way.

"I can float up by myself, thank you very much,"

the skull replied primly, and rocked to the roof. Ana turned, and saw the gargoyle lunging at her. She slammed the button, and followed the skull, the gargoyle slamming into the wall behind her.

"That was close," Cade muttered as he helped her up, then turned around, and looked down.

"We're in luck, people," Milo announced, as Cade scrabbled nervously away from the skylight, saw the steep drop from the ledge, then scrabbled back, repeating the process like an extremely phobic pendulum. "The Guildmaster," Milo continued petulantly, trying to ignore Cade, "is - cut it out, already, you nitwit! Is currently in the throne room which is located directly beneath here. If we were to drop down, then the gargoyles would follow us inside.

"Wait, hold on a sec," Cade said. "Drop down?"

"Yep. About two stories."

"Two stories!"

"Probably farther."

"Well, er, you guys can go ahead. I'll guard the roof, here."

"Don't be stupid, human," Brottor said irritably. "You'd be killed by the gargoyles."

"It's less embarrassing than being killed by a marble floor."

"But stupider," Milo replied. He nodded to Ana. Ana gave him a look that said: Again?

Milo nodded.

But I scared him out of his wits last time! Ana mouthed.

Milo shrugged, and gestured toward the

approaching gargoyles. Ana shrugged back, and grabbed Cade's wrist.

"What the—" the wizard began. "Wait, oh no. You're not dragging me into another death trap!"

Ana kicked out a pane of glass in the skylight large enough for two people to fit through, then looked at Cade with a mixture of pity and exasperation as Milo pulled out his rod again. Ana slapped it in Cade's hand, pressed the button again, and then shoved him through the skylight the instant the rope went slack.

"Er," Milo began watching Cade scream his lungs out and go swinging across the room. "Maybe we shouldn't have sent him down first."

Cade stumbled to the ground, the rod shot back up to the ceiling. Instantly, several assassins surrounded him, and the Guildmaster, who had been sitting in a corner of the room on his throne, jumped up and down and yelled for them to kill him.

"Here goes," Ana muttered, fired the rod, and swung down toward the Guildmaster, a tall, skinny, bald man with a bewildered expression on his face. Ana kicked out as she let go of the rod, making direct contact with his face, and they were both slammed into the throne.

Milo went next, landing on one of the assassins beating Cade, and began whacking the trained killer over the head with his bare fists. Then went Brottor and Aust, doing the same.

Lich was the last one down, grabbing the rod in his teeth, and shaking it loose from the ceiling. He looked around, saw Cade, Aust, Brottor, and Milo disposing of the last of the guards, then looked at Ana, who had the terrified Guildmaster in a corner.

"That was unsettlingly easy," Milo commented as the last assassin fell. "Where'd the gargoyles go?"

Lich began to answer, but a gargoyle cut him off by diving through the skylight, shattering it instantly. Pieces flew everywhere, and it lunged for the smallest group first, Ana and the Guildmaster.

Cade yelped and ran at the gargoyle, trying to grab onto its tail and getting a swift slash across the face, sending him flying. Ana pulled the Guildmaster out of the way, and they both went sprawling to the floor. The gargoyle crashed into the throne, and was instantly reduced to powder.

"They may be aggressive," Aust said, "but they're certainly not very bright."

Ana shrugged, and turned to the Guildmaster. "You've been marked," she told him, grabbing his shirt and throwing him against the wall. "The gargoyles will stop at nothing to catch you now. You're going to get the bounty off of us, or they come back, and so do we."

She slammed the Guildmaster against the wall, and he moaned in terror, his head rolling to the side.

"Do we have an understanding?"

"Yes!"

"You're going to disband the Bladed Hand, then you're going to retire."

"I can't do that!"

Ana put a hand around his neck, and prepared to snap it.

"Oh yes you can."

"Alright! Alright!" The Guildmaster began waving his arms comically. "Whatever you say! Just let me go!"

Ana dropped him to the floor. "Remember," she said, "if we find another assassin on our trail, we're going to come back, and we're going to kill you."

The Guildmaster nodded meekly, still sprawled on the floor, and whimpered.

Milo pointed the rod at the ceiling and shot upward, then tossed it down for the others.

"All in favor of turning around and pretending this never happened?" Cade asked.

The rest of the group looked at him with irritation. Cade had been looking upward at the wizard's tower for a while now, terror in his eyes.

Without answering him, Milo shot his rod up toward the balcony at the very top of the tower, and reminded himself how thankful he was that he had gotten an extremely long rope extension in Raven Haven, while shopping with his newfound riches.

He rocketed skyward, watching the balcony get closer and closer...then, halfway up, he stopped.

"MILO!" the wizard shouted from ten stories below. "I think there's something jammed in the firing mechanism!"

"No shit, Cade! I'm going to have to climb up the rest of the way, then repair it when I'm at the top!"

A shadow appeared on the balcony, blotting out the full moon. Milo almost managed to touch the wall, then the howling wind pulled him back. Cade could now see that the shadow had wings.

"Gargoyle!" he shouted, and Milo glanced up, and yelped. The gargoyle roared, and dove off the balcony, looping around Milo. The thief kicked around helplessly, praying that one foot would connect with the gargoyle's head and send it spiraling toward the ground. He was about to smack it in the head, when snarling, it grabbed his ankle, and yanked him away from the rod.

"Stupid halfling," Brottor grumbled, and hefting his battle axe, ran toward the front door as the gargoyle disappeared through a window.

"What are you doing?" Cade shouted as Brottor hacked away at the wooden door.

"We're going through the only way we can!" Brottor replied. "The long, messy way!"

"You dare to invade my territory?" the wizard snarled, as he pushed Milo to the floor. They were standing in a cramped study, made even smaller by the number of bookshelves, gargoyles, and torture devices surrounding them.

"And during nightfall," he continued, brushing his flowing black robe aside. "You must be really stupid." He chuckled. Long black hair hung over his sunken face, completely white except for the dark rings under his eyes.

"Well you see—" Milo began.

"Silence! I don't want to hear any of your pathetic excuses!"

The wizard lifted Milo off the ground, and shoved him against the torture rack, buckling his wrists in. Milo used this opportunity to brace against it and kick out with both legs. The wizard, being very bony and lightweight, went flying. He soared back over his desk knocking over an ink bottle, a paperweight, and a box of charcoals, and landed on the chair behind it.

"You'll pay for that!" he yelled, staggering to his feet, and wiping blood from his lips.

"By the way," Milo said cheerily as he darted between gargoyles, "what's your name? I'm just curious, because I'd hate to just be murdered by some miscellaneous bad guy!"

"Viprilith the Immortal will destroy you!" the wizard screamed. He clumsily scrambled onto the back of a gargoyle, which crashed through the door, leaving a large dent on either side of a frame built for humans, and dove down the spiral staircase leading to the ground floor.

"Y'know," Aust said, "you'd figure this place would be full of traps and such. But it's basically one giant spiral staircase up to a tiny room."

They had been climbing the stairs for a long time, and they weren't getting any closer to the top.

"Y-y'know," Cade stammered behind them. "It oc-oc-occured to me we might be in the mid-middle of a giant illu-illu-illusion." The extreme height was causing his sudden case of stuttering.

"What do you mean?" Ana wheezed.

"Well, wha-what if the stairc-c-c-ase seems to be going on for-for-forever because of an enchant-enchantment designed to keep us continually wander-ing."

"That's an interesting idea," Lich commented. "I

had detected a strong magic aura, but I passed it off for the fact that a wizard's tower usually radiates one. But not one like this."

"I'm not really skilled in counter-count-counter-spells. Do you think you could dissip-dissipate th-this?"

"I could try."

Lich began to rock back and forth smoothly, words from an ancient language to float on the air. The world seemed to go dark, then slowly to change, shift. The stairs melted away, and Cade yelped, leaping back against the wall. That fell away too, and he fell to a stone floor. When it was over, the group looked around, and Ana groaned loudly. They were on the ground floor again.

Milo began to get the slightly sick feeling that many people get when they are running around in circles. As he ran, Viprilith dove straight down, gaining on him, pale hands clawing at the nape of his neck.

"You can't outrun me!" Viprilith screamed. "Give it up!"

An idea struck Milo, and he turned to face Viprilith. Then he gave him the finger.

Viprilith screamed in rage, and Milo grabbed the banister for support, grinding to a halt. Viprilith's inhuman scream turned into a gasp. There was not enough room for his gargoyle to stretch its wings and slow the fall and they smashed through the staircase, reducing the gargoyle's wings to powder.

"Did you hear something?" Aust asked. Everybody, including Lich, shook their heads.

"Doesn't surprise me," the elf replied. "It's very distant...well beyond human ears. I guess we'll encounter it on our way—"

"Wait," Ana muttered. "I do hear something."

"Me too," Cade said. "It sounds like...uh-oh. Everybody, get against the walls! Move!"

"What's this about?" Brottor grumbled.

"Unless you want to get crushed by one ton of clawed and fanged gargoyle, get out of the way!" Aust shrieked, and threw the dwarf against the wall, then ran for cover with Cade, Ana, and Lich.

Still screaming, Viprilith and his steed crashed into the ground, sending a shockwave throughout the building, and leaving a very large dent in the floor. Pieces of shrapnel flew everywhere, and one took Aust's hat off his head, nailing it to the wall.

"Hey!" somebody called from high above. The group glanced up, and saw Milo far in the distance, leaning over a staircase and waving his arms wildly.

"Hey!" he repeated. "The staircase is smashed up! Somebody give me a hand?"

Reluctantly, Lich floated up, and allowed Milo to grasp the sides of his head on the way down. As he did that, Aust gingerly plucked the stone nailing his hat to the wall away, brushed the dust of his hat (which, remarkably, had no ragged hole in the side), and put it back atop his head.

"So," Cade said on his way out of the building, "I guess that's the end of the gargoyles?"

"Guess so," Milo replied. "I assume once their leader gets smashed up that bad, they dissolve or something."

"Probably. I strongly suggest we pack our stuff and get out of here as quickly as possible. I never want to see this city again."

Aust sighed and looked toward the first rays of sunlight poking out over the horizon. "Amen," he muttered.

FOURTEEN
Mmm…Adventurers

The group hiked south for a few days, which were pleasantly uneventful, but unpleasantly dry.

"If we don't find a spring," Aust wheezed, "I think I'm going to shrivel up and die."

"We're almost to the Canyon of Doom," Ana pointed out. "Just a few miles away. I think there's an oasis near there."

"Oh boy," Milo grumbled. "You know it's not going to be a nice hike when the nearest landmark has 'Doom' in its name."

They hiked for a few more hours until they reached the edge of the Canyon of Doom.

"Let's set up camp," Aust suggested cheerfully, peering over the edge into the abyss below. He noted what appeared to be a complex network of naturally formed bridges and ledges in the canyon.

"Right," Cade said. "Over here." He was standing as far away from the edge as possible while still being near the other party members.

"Fine," Aust grumbled. "Wouldn't want somebody to roll over in their sleep and fall into the nether world, anyway."

So, they set up camp, and ate around the campfire, eating their rations and chatting about what they were going to do once the quest was over.

"If we live," Cade pointed out.

"I'm going to retire," Milo said, nibbling lightly at his share of pseudo-meat. "Well...maybe rob a few really big mansions, then retire."

"I'm going to go back to my tribe, and become one of the old warlords," said Brottor. "Ah, to sit around the fire, and tell stories of my conquests like those I listened to in my youth..."

"I'm going to donate myself to a museum," Lich murmured. "Maybe become a tour guide, or something like that. Great gimmick."

"I'm going to travel the world, singing the same old songs," Aust muttered dreamily. "Working hard for my own place in legend someday."

"I wonder how saving the world would look on my resume," Cade pondered. Everybody else chuckled. "I'd probably use that to become professor in a good school, maybe improve my own magical aptitude. Write a few books, then retire. What about you, Ana?"

Ana was staring at the fire, not touching her food. "I don't know," she said.

There was an awkward silence. Milo leapt to his feet.

"Hey, what's that?" he demanded, pointing. A small green creature, about his height, with pointed ears, an extremely large nose, and large, yellow eyes, wandered out from the underbrush.

"Calm down," Aust said, examining it as it made soft chirping sounds, and scuttled around. It had to be either a pet, or at least semi-intelligent, because it was dressed in tattered rags.

"Look at the little bugger," Aust sighed. Slowly, he got to his feet, and reached forward to pat the "Little Bugger" on the hand. "Little Bugger" promptly bared its large, sharp teeth, and bit Aust on the hand, spraying blood everywhere.

"Oh, crappitycrappitycrap!" Aust shrieked, and began to dance wildly around the fire, waving his hand in a desperate attempt to shake the creature off. Droplets of blood flew around him in concentric circles. Ana grabbed her backpack and began beating the creature over the head with it. At last its grip loosened, and it fell from Aust's hand.

"We'd better get that wrapped up," Ana muttered, kicking the creature to stop its twitching. Aust nodded.

"What was that thing anyway?"

"Well, I'd say we just saw our first cannibalistic Goblin. We should make for the mountains now. There's a bridge near here, and I don't think it would be wise to linger."

Watching the adventurers pack up their tents and move along the edge of the canyon were five small goblins hiding in the underbrush. Their names were Chitterbite, Sawhead, Bonescritch, Fleshnibbler, and Bob. For the reader's sake, their hushed and clandestine conversation is translated from Goblinoid into the Common Tongue.

"Who do you think they are?" Bonescritch pondered.

"Must be adventurers," Fleshnibbler pointed out. "Look at all the equipment they're hauling around.

"Mmmm…" Bob sighed, "Adventurers…"

"Quiet, idiot!" Sawhead hissed. "We don't want them to hear us! Come on, let's go tell the others."

"Wait a second," Chitterbite said. "Wasn't there another adventurer passing through here a few days ago?"

"Mmmm…" Bob sighed. "Advent—"

"Shut up!" Fleshnibbler muttered. "Yes, I think there was. A guy in big spiky armor, right?"

"Yeah, I think that's the one," Chitterbite replied. "Man, he could really use that sword! Maybe we should just let them pass through, I mean, what if they wipe out half the tribe? There're five times as many of them this time!"

"Yeah, but none of them look like real adventurers," Sawhead argued. "And that floating skull thing with them, well, I don't know what the heck's up with that."

"Mmmm…"

"Shut up, you moron!" Bonescritch yelled. Then he turned to the rest of the group. "Anyway," he said. "I say we tell the king. He'll know what to do."

Everybody nodded in agreement, except for Bob. Then they all scuttled on their way.

"Well, here's the bridge," Ana announced. It was an

extremely unstable thing made of wood and rope. There were no rails.

"Good," Cade muttered. "That's good. You guys can go on ahead, I'll stay here and keep lookout."

Ana sighed, rolled her eyes, and dragged him kicking and screaming across the bridge. Everybody else followed.

"Wait," Lich murmured as he floated across. He pointed to the network of naturally forming bridges below. "What's that?"

Milo raised his crossbow, and looked down as well. Ana dragged Cade to his feet, borrowed his glasses, and used them to zoom in on whatever was scuttling across.

"Looks like one of the little bastards," she said. Then she handed her glasses back to Cade.

"More than one," Aust replied. His improved Elven vision could make out a few more dotting the bridges, then more and more, their numbers growing like flies on flypaper. Soon, every single bridge was swarming with them. A few slipped, and dropped into the abyss beneath. Aust watched with wonderment, standing perfectly still, already on the other side of the canyon.

"Aust?" Milo asked. "What is it? Aust?"

Shakily, leaning on Ana slightly for support, Cade approached the canyon, and zoomed in. His mouth dropped open.

"I think...I think we should all run."

Far below, one tiny green hand reached up and grabbed the crevices in the side of the canyon. More hands joined it, and Goblins began quickly hoisting themselves up, scrambling toward their newest victims.

"Cade!" Ana shouted, starting to back away. "Set fire to the bridge! And run!"

Cade did as he was told, watching the bridge explode in a fiery burst, and then he began to sprint after the rest of the group. The Goblins were small but fast, and they were gaining on the group sooner than expected. One snapped hungrily at Cade's ankle, and he quickened his pace. Another one made the same attempt, and this time, latched on.

"Ah!" the wizard screamed. "One's got me!"

More creatures began to climb up his leg, and he felt warm blood trickle down. He fell over.

Hearing the dull thud, Aust whirled around. "Uh—" he began, but Ana was already running for the wizard, trying desperately to shake Goblins off as well.

"Ana!" a muffled voice yelped from beneath the pile of Goblins clamoring to get to their feast. "Run!"

"I'm not leaving a man behind!"

"Just stay back, and let me try something I've been saving for a tough moment like this..."

"The teleportation thing?"

"You guessed it!"

"Cade, you're being gnawed to death! And so am I," she added, realizing that going back to save him and then getting into a conversation was not such a good idea.

The churning lump under a pile of Goblins made a gesture resembling a shrug, and then there was a flash of light. Ana stumbled, temporarily blinded, and fell on her back. Now, the other adventurers were running to help her.

"Hmm..." Cade said. "Nothing happened. It must have had something to do with the dungeon in GROMMP amplifying my magical abilities. Well, I give in. We're screwed." His voice began to grow smaller and smaller as more blood was drained from his body. "You shouldn't have...come back for me..."

Brottor roared, and charged into the fray, hacking back and forth with his axe. Goblin bits sprayed everywhere, and the few not feasting, wisely retreated. Then Aust was there too, fighting with a style that was both comical and elegant; and Milo and Lich, who simply ran (or floated) back and forth, bashing whatever was in their way.

Slowly the goblins began to retreat. And the six adventurers were left lying in the sand, gasping for breath, nearly all of them bleeding a little, with the exception of Cade, who was bleeding profusely. His glasses, still intact, lay next to him on the ground. With one blood-caked hand, he shakily put them on, then tried to think of something clever to say, something to make light of the situation. Finally, he used the only phrase that came to mind.

"Ow," he muttered, then grayed out for a little while.

He came back a few seconds later, and found himself standing up, blinking sleepily at the sun

"Cade?" Ana asked. "Cade? Are you alright?"

"I think I'm bleeding to death," Cade replied. "You?"

"Cade, we can't stay here. We need to go someplace safer. I think if you can just hang in there until we reach the mountains, then we can...Cade?"

Cade grayed out again, and he remembered nothing of the hike to the Mountains of Misery.

"Cade, are you okay?" It was Ana speaking.

"Fine," Cade muttered, and got to his feet, look around the campsite, and then down at the makeshift bandage wrapped around his torso, arms, and legs. He could feel the pressure of gauze on his forehead. "Where are we?" he added.

"A few miles into the Mountains of Misery. I think there are some goblins behind us."

"That's not what I'm worried about," Cade replied. "What's ahead of us?"

"Orcs," Aust replied grimly. He was sitting on a log, and warming his hands against the fire. "Orcs, and in the snowier areas, the Sasquatch."

Orcs are closely related to goblins. Like goblins, they have green skin, and are stupid and ill-tempered. Unlike goblins, they are about six feet tall, have snouts rather than humanoid noses, and prefer cleaving through people or bashing them with clubs to nibbling them to pieces.

Sasquatch are large, hairy creatures that live in the cold, snowy areas of the world. Little else is known about them, except the reason why little else is known about them: anybody who's tried to find out anything else has been promptly eaten.

"Hmm," Cade replied. "Well, I guess it's not any

worse than what we'll be facing in the next two weeks or so."

"What's that?" Brottor asked, from where he was sitting.

"Well, after the Mountains of Misery," Ana announced, "according to this map, there's a small coastal village called Troutville. We can catch a ship from there to Risunbir…the home of Kaos's fortress."

Milo went pale at the thought.

"Orcs," Milo announced. He was kneeling next to a rather large footprint on the ground, one of several thousand,covering the snow-capped mountain the adventurers were looking at.

Milo touched the footprint with one finger, digging up dirt with it, then sniffed it lightly. He recoiled.

"Still fresh," he murmured. "Anybody have some soap? I just rubbed my hand in something an orc stepped in a few hours ago."

Aust handed him a bar of soap, and Milo began rubbing it vigorously over his hands.

"Anyway," he said, "what do we do next? I'm sure no one's exactly in the mood for seeking out an army of orcs."

"Well," Cade replied, "the footprints seem pretty far apart, meaning a long stride. If we keep at the speed we're traveling right now, and they keep at the speed they were going at when these were made, then we should always be behind them."

"I say we chase after them," Brottor grunted.

"I agree," Ana concurred. "They can't be up to any good."

The following conversation was spoken at an orcish campsite, inside one of the tents, shortly after midnight. It is translated from Orcish.

"Hey, Grog!"

"What?"

"Do you smell something?"

"Ibdiot! I'b gob a colb!"

"Well, I smell something. Smells like human flesh...no wait, there's definitely an elf, and...hey, I can smell something else too, probably a gnome. And...ugh! I can smell a dwarf, too."

Jarl waved a hand in front of his nose. "Pee-yooh!"

"Man, amb I glab I'b nob you!"

"Yeah, me too, or I might be an imbecile."

"Hey!"

"Stay here. I'm going to go alert Barlcrag. Maybe we can have a good ol' fashioned human flaying tonight."

"Oh, gooby."

Aust's ears perked up, but only Lich saw the telltale sign of trouble in the darkness that covered the mountains.

"What is it?" Lich demanded quietly.

"Do you here something?" Aust asked.

"We don't have elf ears, remember?" Milo chimed in.

"I think there's an encampment on the other side of this mountain."

His ears straightened up even more. "Yeah, sounds like orcs. And they've probably already smelled us, too. I think we should find a way around."

Ana looked at her map. "Well, according to this, we're at the edge of the Pass of Midrillon. There are two ways around it, and unless you have gills and are completely unappetizing to orca-sized polar piranhas, then we're in trouble.

"Elves have very small lung capacities," Cade pointed out, and gestured at Aust. "He wouldn't last long underwater."

"So…" Milo began. "We have three choices, two of which are impossible, one of which is extremely improbable. Decisions, decisions…"

"I say we meet the orc scum head on," Brottor grunted. "At least we can all die like men that way, rather than turning our tail and fleeing."

"If it's all the same to you, I'd rather turn my tail and flee the way a man would," Cade commented. "But the chances are still higher that we'd survive the orcs. I don't think we have much of a choice. Besides, there's always the chance that they're friendly."

"Then why are they yelling for everybody to get into battle formation?" Aust asked, his ears perking up again.

"Maybe they think we're hostile."

"We are. Unless you'd rather go peacefully, and be a snack rather than the main course."

"Out of the frying pan and into the fire," Ana commented. "I think we were better off when the flesh-eaters were shorter than us."

"Amen," Cade muttered. "But, we have little choice in the matter. I say one of us goes down, and tries to communicate peacefully with them. I still think there's a good chance they'll let us pass."

"That's a good idea," Milo said thoughtfully. "You can go."

Cade looked surprised. "Uh, I th-thought that was more Aust's thing."

"Orcs hate elves," Aust replied. "I think you're more qualified."

"Well, you're…I mean, you seem to be more charismatic than I am. Besides, I don't know Orcish. Wait, doesn't Lich know Orcish? I bet he knows a lot of languages."

"What do you think those orcs are going to think if a twenty karat talking hunk of bone goes down to meet them? Think they'll feel comfortable with that?"

"Hey!" Lich yelled. "I resent that." His voice dropped to a mutter. "Hunk of bone my nonexistent ass…"

"How 'bout Brottor?" Cade suggested desperately.

"Of course!" Brottor shouted. "I'll cleave all the bastards in half! Dirty green dirt bags…"

Cade looked down at the dwarf, eyes widening in despair.

"Fine," he finally muttered. "I'll go."

"Hey, there's one of them!" Torbreck yelped excitedly, from his post overlooking the encampment

"Yeah, you're right," Krawlkin muttered in reply. "Why's he alone, though? I thought Barlcrag said the witness had smelled at least four."

"Maybe the witness was exaggerating."

"By making it look like three more people? Not bloody likely."

"Fine, then. Piss all over my theory."

"Hey, he's waving at us."

"So he is. I wonder what he wants."

"Maybe he thinks we're going to spare him."

"Hah! Let's go alert Barlcrag. This'll be like taking organs from a human."

Cade was relieved to see the orcs on the tower waving back at him. So he approached, and when he reached the encampment, he stood nervously as orcs clustered around him.

"Excuse me," he called, "but do any of you speak the Common Tongue?"

The orcs looked at each other blankly. One stepped forward from the ring they were forming around Cade.

"I do," the orc said in perfect Common. "My name is Barlcrag, at your service. What brings you to our humble encampment?"

"I come from a part of si- of five," he said, realizing that Lich would not be kindly welcomed, and must be, once again, stashed away in Milo's backpack.

"And what is it that you wish, human?" Barlcrag asked, snapping Cade away from his thoughts.

"We wish to pass through. It would take only a minute, and then we would be out of your way. Please, grant us this one favor."

Barlcrag pretended to think it over. "Very well," he finally said. "As chieftain of this orcish tribe, I grant you and your party passage through our territory."

Cade looked relieved. "I'll go alert the others," he said. "Thank you." Then he turned, and ran back up the hill.

Barlcrag watched the human go, and chuckled softly to himself.

"You actually trusted an orc?" Brottor shrieked. "We can't go down there! Let's just make for the water!"

"They seemed very trustworthy!" Cade replied angrily. "They said they'd let us pass. I say we go!"

"Fine, then. You can go ahead! Somebody help me look for lumber to build a raft!"

"A raft?" Milo shouted back. Then he began to laugh shrilly. "We're in the middle of a freakin' desert!"

"I say we go with Cade," Aust announced.

"I agree," Ana replied. "It seems like the only choice we really have."

"All in favor?" Lich asked.

"Aye," Lich, Ana, Cade, Aust, and Milo said.

"Nay," Brottor grumbled. "But, what the devil am I going to do? I'm outvoted. Let's just get this over with." He picked up his axe, and got to his feet. "But I'm not lowering my weapon!"

"Fair enough," Cade sighed. "Just try to look less menacing."

"You're telling me that this situation doesn't make you the slightest bit nervous?" Ana muttered to Cade as they cautiously walked through the camp. Orcs peered out of their tents, eyes on the travelers, mouths tightened into thin lines, as if the urge to open their jaws and devour the humans was nearly unbearable.

"I'm the slightest bit nervous," Cade replied. "Only a bit, though. I mean, they seem fairly trustworthy."

"Well, we're not halfway through the encampment, yet," Brottor murmured, his axe raised defensively. "Let's see what happens then."

"Nothing will 'happen,' Brottor," Cade replied irritably.

Something did.

As they reached the center, Barlcrag roared something in Orcish. The group glanced around nervously.

"What was that?" Milo yelped.

"It means," a muffled voice from within Milo's backpack replied, "that he is telling the others to attack. I think they're going to surround us and kill us."

"What?" the rest of the group shrieked at once.

"Bu-bu-but there are hundreds of them!" Cade spluttered. "We'd never survive!"

"I thought you said they were trustworthy, Cade."

"Aw, shit," Ana observed, as the orcs formed a ring around the group, and began to close in slowly. "Oldest trick in the book. When an outnumbered enemy charges you, you part, and let their confidence build. If they're stupid, they'll try to pass through the opening. Then you just close over them again, and attack from all sides."

"That's bad."

"Very observant, Aust," Lich commented.

"Shut up, chrome dome."

"It happens to be gold, you pointy-eared little—"

"Uh, people?" It was Cade. "One of them just took a swipe at me. I think they're going to kill us now."

"Not if I can help it!" The group glanced up, and standing high up on a rocky ledge was a lone old man, bony and frail-looking, and clad in ragged furs. His scraggly white beard reached down to his waist, and his green eyes had a half-crazy glimmer to them. He was carrying only one very large saber, battered by the ages, much like the man himself.

"Oh, grachtlackchall," one of the orcs muttered, which, translated to the Common Tongue, means roughly: "Oh, shit."

"Whoa, creepy," Aust commented. "Who's he?"

"I have a very sick feeling in my stomach that tells me we're about to find out," Cade replied.

"My name is simply Hermit!" the old man cried.

"Turn back, Hermit!" Barlcrag called out. "I've already claimed them as my prey!"

"My understanding was that we weren't playing 'finders, keepers,' orc," the old man replied calmly. "More like 'survival of the fittest.'"

"If you try to fight us all, you will surely lose."

"That's probably true. Care to test it?"

"Bring it on, old man."

Hermit let out a piercing cry, and jumped off his ledge, saber raised. Orcs scattered, and he landed in the kneeling position, one hand at the ground, the one holding the saber at his side. His hair was in his face, and his breathing was perfectly steady.

"Fools!" Barlcrag snarled, "kill him!"

Orcs scrambled to obey their chieftain, and Hermit leapt to his feet, proceeding to cleave through them left and right.

Ana, Aust, Cade, Milo, and Brottor ran a short distance away from the carnage, and stopped for a breather. Brottor sat on a rock.

"Gangway!" somebody yelled, and Brottor looked up. He screamed, and jumped out of the way, rolling through the sand. Hermit landed nimbly on the rock Brottor had been sitting on.

"Jumpy little fella, isn't he?" Hermit said to the rest of the group, grinning a gap-toothed grin.

"I'm not little," Brottor growled, spitting sand out of his mouth and getting to his feet, but didn't say any more.

"I'm Hermit," Hermit announced, jumping into the air, and skipping across the sand toward the party. He bowed comically, and glanced up in mid-bow.

"All your little orcish friends over there are dead now," he commented.

Milo turned around to confirm that, and his mouth was hanging down to his collarbone as he turned back.

"You...y-you did all that?"

Hermit grinned modestly. "Hey, one hundred and twenty years of fencing, and you'll learn a thing or too. Barlcrag was an old enemy of mine, and I had been looking for an excuse to carve 'im for a while. You provided one."

"He's insane," Cade muttered to Ana. Ana glanced at Hermit, whose left eye was twitching, the other one staring like a deer caught in the path of a rampaging ogre.

"You're right," she observed. "The question is, what do we do about it?"

"I say we try to lose him," Aust suggested. "And keep heading for Troutville."

"I can take you to Troutville!" Hermit yelled, and

everybody jumped. He jumped up and down a few times for no real reason, then did a back flip and bowed.

"And," he said, eyes twinkling, "I can get a boat for you, free of charge."

The group folded in on itself to discuss the situation. Finally, they all decided to humor the old man. If he was telling the truth, then they were stuck with him, but he would aid them in their quest. If he was lying, then he didn't look quite subtle enough to manage to quietly assassinate them all. And besides which, he seemed just crazy enough to be harmless, despite what he had done to the orcs.

The group traveled for another day or so, until the area started to get snowy. Finally, Hermit allowed them all to stop for a rest, and build a small fire.

"We should stay on our guard, though," Hermit said, sniffing the air. "I smell Sasquatch nearby."

"That's ridiculous," Aust replied. "I'm an elf, and I don't smell anything."

"Cold impairs your senses, elf. I've been living in this harsh climate for sixty year."

And he continued to listen for an hour, while the rest of the group gathered around, and discussed their next course of action.

"Maybe we should let him know about Lich," Cade suggested.

"Maybe not!" Milo replied angrily. "He'd kill us if he knew we were carrying something like this."

"Besides which," Ana pointed out, "he seems a little unbala—"

"Sssh!" Hermit hissed, whirling around. He began to throw snow on the fire. "Sasquatch," he explained. "Coming from behind. We have to run for the path to Troutville. Run!"

The group stomped out the fire, then threw themselves into a run after the unnaturally quick old man.

Far away, a tribe of one dozen large, white-haired beasts with gray hands and dark, feral eyes, trudged forward. They were all about nine feet tall.

The leader sniffed the air, then grunted toward the others. They began to run.

"We've been running for an awfully long time now," Milo panted. His short legs were making him drop even behind Cade.

"Put some effort into it, coward," Brottor snarled, staggering forward.

"I did put some effort into it," Milo replied. "They must be far behind us now. I say we rest."

"No!" Hermit yelled. "You fool!"

But Milo was already slowing down. His muscles began to relax, and he nearly jumped out of his skin when a large fist wrapped itself around him, then lifted him off the ground effortlessly.

"Oy gevalt!" he yelped, trying to wriggle free. The rest of the group turned around, and drew their weapons. The beast gripping Milo slowly stepped forward, and eleven more appeared behind it.

"Next time, let's run faster," Cade suggested.

"Blast one of them," Ana ordered.

Deciding not to argue, the wizard blasted the beast

holding Milo with a fire bolt. The beast burst into flames. It hurled the halfling at the rest of the group, then began to roll around in the snow, screaming. The other beasts screamed loudly, and charged.

"The thief is becoming more trouble than he's worth," Brottor grumbled as he charged at the remaining eleven.

"Hey!" Milo replied indignantly. "You hairy old cod-sniffer!" He leapt at the nearest Sasquatch, and stabbed it in the shin with his dagger. It roared, and hurled him to the side, pressing forward regardless of the wound. Hermit ran at it next, jumping over a fist, and landing on its shoulders. He remained perched their for a moment, poised like a stalking tiger, then slit the beast's throat.

The Sasquatch Cade had burned was back on its feet, and it began to chase after the wizard. Cade shot another bolt at it, and the Sasquatch stumbled to the side, out of the way. An enormous hand reached out and grabbed Cade's ankle as he tried to flee. He yelped, and drew his sword, flailing it around helplessly.

Ana heard Cade's cry for help. She whirled around, drew an arrow, and aimed it at the beast's left eye.

Milo was up again, shaking snow out of his hair, and leaping at another Sasquatch. This one turned, and observed the little halfling casually. When Milo leapt, the Sasquatch swatted him out of the way. He collided with Ana, whose eyes widened with surprised as she accidentally released her arrow. It barely missed Cade, who cried out again, and wriggled around some more, his hands turning red from clawing at the snow.

"I'm getting sick of this," a muffled voice muttered from within Milo's backpack. "I'm helping too."

Before the halfling could respond, a large, ragged hole appeared in his backpack, and Lich was hurled outward, flying toward the Sasquatch clutching Cade.

There was a loud thudding noise, and the Sasquatch froze, his grip tightening for one painful moment. Then its eyes rolled up in its head, and it fell over.

"What did you do?" Cade asked, staggering to his feet.

"I head-butted him," Lich replied, then hurled himself at another Sasquatch.

"What the hell?" Hermit muttered, and Aust grinned at him nervously.

"Uh, there's another member of the party, that, er, we, er, well, it...it slipped our mind to mention it. Him. It. Uh...him."

Hermit grinned wildly, then turned to the ricocheting skull.

"Lich, you old rascal!" he exclaimed, then skewered a Sasquatch.

"So you two know each other?" Cade muttered. They were all sitting around the fire. Cade, wrapped up a blanket, was shivering uncontrollably. He glanced at Lich.

"Why didn't you tell us?" he demanded.

"Well," Lich replied mildly, "you had made your own decision at that point. Nobody really wanted to listen to my opinion. This isn't really my quest anyway. I'm just along for the ride."

"You could have mentioned that earlier," Aust grumbled.

"It was implied."

"Imply this, you little snot," Aust said, and made an intricate hand gesture elves usually reserve for special occasions. Lich's expressionless face peered back at the elf, then silently turned away.

"So, what've you been up to these past few centuries?" he asked Hermit.

"Uh, exactly how old are you?" Cade asked Hermit. "No offense or anything."

Hermit grinned cheerfully, but soon after, his face turned blank.

"Y'know," he muttered, scratching his head. "I honestly don't remember. But anyway, to answer Lich's question, I moved out of my old cave down near the beach, went to the courts of Irrellia, learned how to fence, became a knight for a while, and after everybody realized why I wouldn't just give up an' croak, I went to GROMMP, where nobody ages anyway. I slayed a few dragons, gained so many levels that the programmers asked me to become a system administrator…er, a 'god,' if that'll help you. I refused, and moved here."

"Uh-huh," Ana muttered skeptically. "Where do you get to the part about becoming ruler of the world?"

"Oh, that was a while ago," Hermit replied. "Lich, you remember that, don't you?"

"Oh yeah. That didn't last very long, the way I remember it."

"Well, you try to run a bloody planet."

"Maybe I will, someday."

"Just avoid those bloodless coups. They're even harder to get rid of than the messy ones."

"Will do, old friend."

"Uh, hate to interrupt this fascinating conversation," Cade announced, "but I think we should get some rest now, then pack up our stuff and head for Cod-ville—"

"Troutville."

"Thanks, Ana....as soon as possible."

"I agree," Hermit said, then fell over, fast asleep.

"What an eccentric old man," Aust observed, then rolled out his bedroll.

FIFTEEN

FASHISM: Pain and Suffering at an Affordable Price!

After a few days, the snow eventually faded back into desert, and the desert finally faded back into grasslands. Deer, rabbits, and other animals grazed tranquilly at small ponds near the dirt path to Troutville. The group's spirits were high, but a shadow loomed over them. They could feel themselves approaching the stronghold of Kaos.

After a few days, they came to a building on the road, standing in the center of the long, flowing fields, looming over them. It was simply a five-story cube made of sandstone with two large rocky pairs of double doors. One read ENTRANCE. The other one, NOT AN ENTRANCE.

"This is ominous," Cade said. "I think we should probably avoid anything that's not on the map."

"I think we should check it out anyway," Ana said. "It appears to be some kind of store, and we're running out of rations, so maybe we could get some extra ones here. Besides, this can't be much worse than some of the stuff on the map."

They voted, and Cade lost in a landslide. So, they approached the doors reading ENTRANCE.

Milo stepped forward. He was about to knock on the door, when without warning, it flew open. Milo squeaked, and leapt backward, stumbling over his own feet, and falling to the ground. The doors slammed shut again.

"Hm," Cade muttered, and slowly made his way to the spot where Milo had been standing. He winced as the doors flew open again. He took a step back. The doors shut. He took a step forward again. The doors opened.

Aust began to do the same.

"This is interesting," Cade murmured, but Aust ignored him, and began jumping back and forth, causing the doors to flutter open and closed very quickly. He was grinning. Eventually, he forgot about that, and decided just to charge through the now-closed doors. They didn't open, and he slammed headfirst into them, flopping backward. He ended up sitting on the grass, rubbing his nose.

Slowly, Cade stepped forward again, and the doors opened. He held up a hand, and a small flame began to float above it. Slowly, he stepped through the door, followed by the rest of the party. The doors slammed behind them.

Milo tripped over a lever, and yelped. The entire building became visible, the group shielding their eyes from the unexpected brightness. Cade snuffed out his flame, and gazed around, blinking.

"Where's all that light coming from?" he asked himself, then in response, glanced up at the ceiling. Large tubes of light were hanging from the ceiling by cobwebbed chains. The light seemed to be emanating from them.

Then, slowly, his eyes dropped downward, and he surveyed the rest of his surroundings.

The place was one large room, with many racks filled with clothing of all shapes and sizes, from unusually small shirts to grotesquely large and baggy pants made of denim. To the left of the party lay many large boxes with strange metallic devices bolted to them. Stamped across each box was the word FASHISM in stylized text. Behind each box was a skeleton, sprawled across the floor, cobwebs covering them from head to toe.

"Well, the place seems harmless enough," Ana said to Cade as she glanced around WOMEN'S OFFICE WEAR. "Looks like some kind of ancient clothing store. Strange tastes they had back then."

"There's something about this place that makes me nervous, though," the wizard said. "And it's not just that back then they named their clothing stores after a sadistic kind of government. Maybe I'm just being paranoid."

"You have good reason to be," Ana commented. "Everywhere we've been so far, we've been in constant danger. But I think this place is different." She examined a high heel quizzically. "What the hell is this? Are you actually supposed to walk in these things?"

"Why yes," a voice said, and Cade and Ana screamed. Peering down at them was a grotesque skeleton in a smock labeled FASHISM, maggots squirming inside its eyes sockets. "Would you like to try one on? What's your shoe size?"

Cade's mouth opened and shut nervously, and he finally said the only thing he could think of. "N-no thanks. We're just...er, browsing."

"You two seem like a nice couple. Getting married? Maybe looking for a bridal gown, or maybe a tuxedo? Well, you've come to the right place!"

"Er, no, not getting married," Ana stammered. "Just browsing. Now, if you'll excuse us..."

They turned, and slowly walked away, the skeleton standing there obediently.

"What the hell was that?" Cade shrieked, once they were in the CHILDREN'S department, and safely out of hearing range.

"I don't know," Ana muttered. "Seems like you were right. There is something seriously wrong with this place."

"But there's nothing wrong with our selection!"

Cade and Ana both screamed again. Another one.

"Select this!" Ana roared, kicking the skeleton's skull right off its shoulders.

"Select this?" Cade muttered, raising an eyebrow. Ana shrugged.

"Gimme a break, it's the best I could come up with on short notice."

The skeleton lumbered over to the skull, picked it up, then reattached it to its spine.

"You know," it said, "we're having a sale on swimwear this month."

Grimacing, Ana reached into the skeleton's ribcage, ripped the spine entirely from the body, causing the entire thing to collapse on itself, then carefully dismantled the spine piece by piece, and threw them in all directions across the room.

"Was that necessary?" Cade asked sickly.

"Probably," Ana replied, then watched as the pieces began to float toward the center of the room, slowly reforming the skeleton. "Or maybe it wasn't enough. Run!"

Ana turned, and Cade was about to follow when he heard another scream.

"That way," he directed, and he and Ana sprinted toward the scream.

It turned out to be Milo. He was in the COSMETICS department, men's cologne being shoved at him from all directions, a throng of skeletons, surrounding him and chattering amiably. Beside him, Aust was on the floor, his hat pulled down over his ears. He had a look of utter terror and agony on his face, and a skeleton was in the process of tying sneakers onto his feet.

"Go ahead," it chattered. "Try 'em out. You'll love 'em."

Cade leapt up behind it, pulled its skull off, then slammed it back down on its spine, sending the spine shattering in thousands of directions and letting everything else fall apart. He was roaring like a madman while he did it.

"Ouch," Ana winced. Cade blinked, and realized he was still holding the skull.

"Sorry," he said, breathing heavily, and dropped the skull. "Sometimes I just have to let it out. Some people think I have anger issues."

"Help me!" Milo yelped, and Cade blinked again. Then he turned around, and began to watch placidly as the skeletons smothered Milo in some cologne called "NECROPHILIA."

"Cade—" Ana began. Cade held up a hand to silence her.

"It's coming," he said cheerfully. "Just hold on a sec. I need to focus my energy…wait, here we go."

Flames sprouted from his eyes, and blazed through the throng of skeletons, throwing them to the floor in harmless piles of charred bone. Milo lay quivering in the center.

"Subtle," Ana muttered, watching the bones reassemble themselves.

"Thanks," Cade replied, and yanked Milo to his feet. "We should meet up with the others."

Brottor, Hermit, and Lich, were fighting off a crowd of watch salesmen. In the bloody battle that followed, they managed to finally escape, but not without some wounds.

"Too…many…watches…" Milo gasped, staggering around. Tied around his wrists, ankles and necks, were dozens of watches in all shapes and sizes. "Cutting off…circulation…to brain!"

He flopped face-forward, but was quickly on his feet again once the rest of the group helped remove the watches.

"So what do we know so far?" Lich pondered. "How do we get out is the real question, and we need to make a list of what we know in order to do it. A: This is a millennia-old clothing store."

"B," Brottor grumbled, "lotsa skeletons."

"C," Lich countered, "they appear to be trying to sell us stuff."

"D," Cade replied. "They just won't die."

"Ah!" Aust yelped, cutting off the conversation. "They're coming!"

The group turned, and before them stood an army of skeletons carrying all kinds of products. Belts, sneakers, underwear, pants, shirts, hats, umbrellas. Glasses. Ties. Cummerbunds. Cologne. They were all pushing forward, chattering at the top of their lungs in an attempt to sell their products.

Aust was the first to break down. "We'll take it all!" he screamed, tears running down his cheeks. He began throwing silver pieces at the skeletons. "We'll take all we can carry! Just, please, in the names of the gods, leave us alone!"

"You should have told them we were just browsing," Brottor muttered sullenly. The group was sitting outside FASHISM, shopping bags filled with clothing sprawled across the floor. Brottor was wearing a baggy pair of pants, a backward baseball cap for a team called THE ICELANDIC ERICKSENS, and a lot of gold jewelry.

"We tried that," Cade muttered, head in his hands. "They tried to sell Ana and me bridal supplies."

The stench of NECROPHILIA hung in the air around him.

"Please…" Milo begged, clawing feebly at the ground. "Get them off…" His hand was a pulsating purple, the blood vessels cut off by an extremely tight watch. Beside him, Aust lay unconscious on the floor, a very small Ankh bracelet tightened around his neck.

Lich was hitting his head against a tree, trying to shake off a pair of sunglasses.

Hermit was sitting in the corner, humming cheerfully. "It wasn't a complete waste," he chirped, tying his new sneakers. "I heard these things are endorsed by some sports guy. Don't know his name, and don't remember the sport, but it is endorsed, so it's gotta be good!"

CHAPTER

SIXTEEN
Misadventures in Navigation

"Welcome to Troutville," Hermit said, beaming proudly. The party was standing at the top of a rolling green hill that overlooked a small village at the edge of the water. Beyond, ships slowly moved back and forth. The city bustled with energy as townspeople built ships, sold fish, bought fish, cooked fish, and generally went about keeping their commerce going.

"Their whole way of living revolves around fish," Cade observed.

"Must be depressing as hell," Milo replied. "All that fish…your entire life, every single meal, all fish. You see any cows living down there? No! Only fish."

"Lighten up," Aust said cheerfully. "Thanks to our associate here, we now have access to a boat! So, where do we start?"

"I know an old ship yard down near the water," Hermit said. We should start there."

"Right!"

They went down to an old but large docking area called MEL'S USED BOATS: LOW PRICES, HIGH QUALITY! A rickety sign confirmed this. The group looked around uncomfortably, waiting for a salesperson to arrive.

"Hello!" somebody called, and they saw a slim, man in a business suit appear behind them. His hair was slicked back. He was grinning like a weasel.

"Hey, you're not from around here, are you?" he asked cheerfully.

"No, we're, uh, from out of town," Cade replied. "Way out of town." He adjusted his glasses.

"We need a boat," Ana explained. "A big one."

"Hey, is ol' Mel here?" Hermit asked.

"No...I'm his great-grandson."

"Great grandkids! Mel, the ol' rascal...so what's he up to now, anyway?"

"Er...he was dead long before I was born. Sorry."

"Oh."

There was a moment of uncomfortable silence. Hermit rubbed the back of his neck.

"Time flies, huh?" he muttered. The salesman shrugged helplessly.

"I don't normally do this," he said slyly, winking at the adventurers, "but I could get you a discount on one of the boats. What kind are you looking for?"

"Something sturdy," Brottor said. "Something that can stand up in battle."

"With big rooms," Milo added. "And nice furniture."

"Fast, and aerodynamic," Cade continued. "With a large food store. And a library, if possible."

"A library!" Brottor snorted. Cade glared at him.

"Uh…Alright," the salesman said. Now he was rubbing the back of his neck. "What kind of price range were you thinking of?"

"Well, we don't really have any money," Ana muttered. "We spent it all on a shopping spree a few days ago. But we were forced to. It's…a long story."

"I see. Well, there's a boat right over there that suits all your requirements, but…it's a lot."

He named the figure.

Milo and Cade both dropped their jaws at the same time.

"But there's another boat roughly in your price range," the salesman continued. "It's a bit of a fixer-upper, but think of it as…rustic."

"How rustic, exactly?" Ana asked, raising an eyebrow.

"Pretty rustic."

The salesman gestured vaguely to a boat near the end of the dock, a large, hideous monstrosity with rusty nails protruding everywhere, and covered in fungus.

"How much?" Milo asked.

The salesman named another figure.

"That's a ripoff!"

"I know. That's what we're paying people to take it off our hands."

"Oh."

"Will that thing hold?" Cade asked.

"Probably not."

"Are there any other boats that you'll pay us to take?"

"Well, there's one that's basically a hollowed-out log with some sails, cannons, and a snorkel."

"How long a snorkel?"

"Oh, I don't know...about ten feet."

"We'll take it," the group said.

An interesting thing to note about Uberwood is that it is not from the type of tree that is normally thought of as "large." "Large" generally refers to height rather than width, but this particular tree has plenty of both. A forest of about a dozen such trees is the size of a small village, and if hollowed out, can be inhabited by a dozen times more the amount of people in that village. Some people have cut down these trees, which is not recommended unless by magical means, since otherwise, it takes years, requires a very long, heavy saw, and almost always ends with the falling tree throwing the lumberjack miles away. Usually the tree is then processed into a whole century's worth of lumber, after which the lumberjack retires. Occasionally, the whole thing is hollowed out and made into something. This takes a few more years, is extremely expensive, and definitely not worth it. The boats this creates are slow, susceptible to flipping over, and the laughingstock of the entire nautical community. How the things stay afloat in the first place is a complete mystery.

But, as humans have learned throughout the years, if you're on a tight budget, you can swallow anything.

"I don't suppose anybody knows how to navigate a ship." Cade asked helplessly, gazing around the log.

"I know a little about it," Lich said. "But you need opposable thumbs for it. Two of them."

"There's no way you could get me up there, even if I did know," Brottor grumbled. He was curled up on the ground, clutching his stomach. His face was a sickly green.

"Dwarves are naturally afraid of water," Ana explained to the rest of the group.

"Not afraid!" Brottor snapped. "Just...uncomfortable."

"That explains why they're not too big on hygiene," Aust muttered. Brottor growled incoherently in reply, but didn't get up.

"Y'know," somebody said behind them, and everybody jumped. It was the salesman again. "I know how to pilot a boat. If you would bring me along for an extra fee, then I could bring you wherever you're going."

"What extra fee?" Cade asked suspiciously.

"The money I gave you to take this boat," the salesman replied.

The group huddled into a group, and discussed it in whispers for a while. Finally, the turned.

"Fine," Cade agreed reluctantly.

"And by the way," the salesman said, grinning slyly. "My name's Dave, and I'll be your captain for this voyage."

"I'm coming too!" Hermit called, and began to scramble onto the boat. Ana sighed, and leaned toward Lich.

"I thought we'd be rid of him after he took us to the shipyard," she muttered.

Lich bobbed in a way that looked a lot like a shrug. "He's been a friend of mine for some time, and I think he'll be of continuing use to us."

"Strange friends," Cade replied quietly. "Exactly when was his lobotomy?"

"Hmmm…hard to recall," Lich replied. "Must have been centuries ago."

Everyone's mouths dropped. Lich's teeth clucked together in what sounded like a chuckle.

"Just kidding," he said. "Yeesh. It's a wonder how you survived this long without a sense of humor."

The first few days were hell. Uncomfortable beds, incomprehensible maps of the ship (which was far too big for such a small crew), slop for food, and worst of all, work, work, work. The adventurers had to work in shifts to watch for any danger, adjust the masts, cook the food, steer the ship, and numerous other jobs. Dave leapt heartily into his new role as the motivational speaker everybody wants to kill. Even Hermit, Aust, and Lich seemed in uncharacteristically bad moods.

"Did you hear what he was calling himself today?" Milo muttered one night, as he shoveled food into his mouth. "Our supervisor. Our freakin' supervisor!"

"I'll supervise him!" Aust growled.

"Probably not a good idea, if you're suggesting what I think you're suggesting," Ana said. "As obnoxious as he is, we need him to run the ship. He's the only one who knows how to run this ship."

"And in exactly how many ways we're doing it wrong," Hermit responded. Ana didn't answer to that.

Cade had horrible stomach pains during the trip, but besides that, he was still able to function relatively well. Brottor, on the other hand, had horrible fear of water, and elected to cower in his cabin day and night. Despite the damning evidence, however, he refused to admit that he was even the slightest bit fearful of water."

"What kind of ship has a snorkel?" Cade cried excitedly at dinner one night. Dave was out tending to the ship. "Its mere presence probably means that whoever made this ship knew it was extremely likely to submerge!"

"Or they could have been just as paranoid as you," Ana commented.

"Every time I get nervous like this, you call it paranoia, and every single time I end up being right. Every single time!"

Lich (who insisted on taking meal breaks, despite the fact that he didn't eat) began to giggle. Everybody else stared at him.

"What the hell is so funny?" Milo demanded irritably.

"Nothing," Lich replied. "It just occured to me that I'm the only one here that doesn't require oxygen to survive."

"Oh," Cade said hollowly. "Funny."

The room shook. Cade and Milo yelped, the halfling falling off his chair and scrabbling toward the wall. The entire ship began to list to the side.

"What the hell's going on?" Ana shouted.

"Sure isn't a storm!" Cade called back. "The barometer didn't indicate it when I last checked it!"

Aust leapt at the stairs and sprinted toward the forward deck, and Dave. "What in the name of sanity is going on here?" he yelled.

Dave grinned at Aust nervously, a wisp of greasy black hair falling on his brow.

"Sorry for the trouble, folks," he said. "We're experiencing some slight turbulence—"

"Due to?" Cade yelled, coming up behind Aust.

"Pirates."

"What?" Cade and Aust both screamed.

"See for yourself. If you'll just direct your attention to the right of the—"

"Oh, shut up!" Aust commanded. Then he and Cade looked to the right.

Sure enough, a pirate ship was backing up, and preparing to ram itself into the ship again. Up above the crow's nest was a black flag with the skull and crossbones on it.

"What do you want with us?" Cade called, running up to get a better view of them. When he did, he could see the tallest pirate, presumably the captain, shaking a hook at him. He was dressed in traditional pirate captain garb, with a black eye patch, peg leg, and a black mustache.

And he saw canoes full of pirates from the pirate ship descending upon them.

For a long time, everybody below the deck listened to silence.

"That's probably a good thing," Ana said. "Means the pirates left."

"Not necessarily," Hermit muttered. "Something seems wrong. Very wrong."

"You're all paranoid," Ana grumbled, then turned toward the stairs leading up to the deck. "Aust, Cade!" she called. "Is everything okay up there?"

"Fine, Ana!" Cade called back down. "Don't come up!"

"Why not?"

"Well, er…no reason, everything's fine. Fine, fine, fine. Just, er, don't come up."

"You know," Ana said, "I'm starting to agree with you."

"Aust!" Milo called, "how many pirates are up there?"

"About sixty! Ow! Watch it! I mean…I don't know what you're talking about! Heheh. Pirates. The idea is…hey! Ow! What the hell was that for?"

"That's enough," Ana muttered. "We can take on sixty pirates. Ready your weapons, people."

"Sixty pirates?" Milo yelped. "We'd need a diversion just to get up there!"

"If we could contact Cade to get him to use some of his magic…" Lich pondered. "But how?" He paused a short while before realizing everybody was staring at him.

"Oh no," he muttered. "I know what you're all thinking. No. I'm not doing that."

Ana grabbed him, shoved the porthole open, and pitched Lich out.

Lich sighed and floated up to the deck, looking

around to make sure none of the pirates saw him. He wondered briefly what his "distraction" was going to be. He thought about it, deciding after a short while that a pyroclasmic blast on a boat with the rest of the party onboard probably wasn't smart. He finally decided on the only other thing he could do.

Lich yodeled.

"That's the signal," Ana whispered below deck.

"What signal?" Milo muttered. "Nobody said anything about a signal."

Ignoring him, Ana ran up the steps, and kicked the door open, disappearing into a cloud of pirates. Hermit followed. Milo sighed, looked around, then sprinted after them.

Below deck, Brottor cowered, completely unaware of what was going on above.

When Lich yodeled, all the pirates turned in his direction, and Cade took advantage of the opportunity. He waved his hand, and the crow's nest burst into flames. Then he and Aust began to fight, as Ana, Milo and Hermit charged up to support them.

"Looks like rain!" Cade shouted to Milo over the sounds of battle.

"We're outnumbered ten to one, and you wanna talk about the weather?" Milo yelled.

"I'm just sayin' 'cause the crow's nest is on fire."

Milo glanced up, and saw the flaming crow's nest, storm clouds hanging above it. A rumble of lightning rolled across the air.

"That was fast," Milo muttered, as the rain began to pour in buckets.

Everybody paused and looked upward. A few pirates nearby adventurers realized that everybody had paused and was looking up, and decided to knock the party unconscious, then drag them back aboard the boat.

The pirates then huddled beneath deck, not bothering to ransack the ship.

Because of that, they did not notice Brottor.

Brottor had to go to the bathroom.

The thing about a dwarf's metabolism is it moves very slowly. Thus, despite the amount of food they tend to consume, it takes a very long time for it to accumulate into something they can excrete. Thus, Brottor had not gone for five days.

He searched his room for a chamber pot, and when he realized there was none, he decided he would have to go up to the deck, and do his business off the side of the boat.

When he walked into the hallway, Brottor was surprised to find himself ankle deep in water. Apparently, there was a storm going on, a big one, which would explain why the boat was listing nearly to the point of being upside-down, and water was pouring into the living quarters. Hefting his axe cautiously, Brottor decided to investigate.

When he got up top, he felt the boat rocking even more strongly, and began being battered from side to side of the deck helplessly, wishing he could have stayed down below. The terror was all-consuming, and the thing that cleared his head was a loud cry from the mast.

Brottor staggered toward it, and found, standing near the mast, Dave yelling at him.

"The rest have been kidnapped!" he shouted. "Pirates!"

Brottor's spine turned to ice. But then he smiled. This was exactly the opportunity he had been waiting for to prove his bravery. To save the day. He would show them all. He may be half their height, but he didn't deserve only half their respect.

"Which way did the pirates go?" he yelled. Dave pointed wildly toward the east. Off in the distance, Brottor could still see another ship.

"Follow them!" he roared. Silently, Dave obeyed.

"Either there's been a drastic change in the seating arrangements, or we've boarded another ship," Cade muttered.

He, Ana, Aust, Milo, and Hermit were all sitting in a small cell in the center of a long, wooden hall. The gentle rocking of the hallway told them that they were still on a boat, but a very different one at that.

"Where are the other three?" Ana groaned.

"Who?"

"Lich, Dave, and Brottor. Where are they?"

"Well," Aust speculated, "they probably didn't find Brottor, the way he was cowering away in his chambers. Dave would probably still be on the boat too, as he obviously got out of the way when the fighting began. As for Lich...well, if they're holding him, the bars of this cell are too wide. He probably escaped, but if not, he's in some lockbox somewhere on this ship."

"That sounds about right," Milo muttered. "Question is, what do we do about it?"

"Probably nothing," Cade replied. "We're in a cage, remember? Maybe this is the end of the road for us."

"Hold on a sec," Ana replied. "I didn't get this far to be locked away in some cage and sold into slavery. There has to be a way out. There's always a way out. So stop feeling sorry for yourselves and help me."

"Well," Cade began, looking around, "there's no door around, and the bottom area seems cemented shut, which means we must have been lowered down. Meaning there should be a trap door right above us."

He looked up. The ceiling was made out of wood.

"Trapdoor," Cade muttered, pointing at the ceiling. "Probably what they used to drop us down here in the first place."

"Milo," Ana said. "I'm going to boost you up. Press up on the ceiling."

"Fine," Milo muttered. "Just keep it steady."

He hopped onto Ana's hand, and the warrior shoved him upward. Milo yelped, and flew at the ceiling. He crashed through it, the trap door flying open, and landed beside it, hacking up dust.

"Sorry about that!" Ana called, and winked at the rest of the group. "You're a little lighter than I thought. What do you see up there?"

"Er...another big room. Completely empty."

"Doors, windows, anything?" Cade shouted.

"No...there's a treasure chest."

"Good, that's a start. Open it."

"Okay...damn, it's locked. My lockpick set is on the other ship."

"Great," Aust muttered, sliding against the bars. "Where do we go from here?"

"Wait!" Milo yelled down. "I have a knife, hidden in my boot. Hold on a sec."

He slipped a small blade out of his boot, and began to prod the lock with it, slowly fiddling with the tumblers, waiting for them to give.

"There," he decided aloud. "That wasn't so hard."

He opened the chest. A bright light flooded the room. Beneath, the rest of the party heard a scream, which slowly faded away, then became louder again. Hermit, startled awake by the noise, peered up the trap, and Milo promptly landed on him.

"Ow," the old man groaned, staggering to his feet.

"What the hell was that?" Cade demanded.

"Magical trap," Milo replied, brushing himself off briskly. "I think I handled it pretty well. Looks like it was made for taller people, since the brunt of the blast went right over my head. The chest should be open now, anyway. Somebody boost me up again."

Ana moved toward him, and Milo took a step away. "Not you," he muttered suspiciously.

Aust picked the halfling up from behind, and Milo squeaked nervously. Aust hurled him over his head, and the thief landed above them once again.

"It's open," Milo called. "Let's see, what's in here...gold, gold, gold gold, some gold encrusted rope, and more gold. And some jewels. Wait a sec...there's a trap door at the bottom of this chest. Lemme just pry it open..."

There was a loud grunt, and the sound of wood snapping. "It's open," Milo explained.

"Throw down the rope!" Ana called up. "And let's get out of here!"

"I'll check to see if the coast is clear," Hermit muttered, sliding down the trap door first. "If I say it's clear, the rest of you can come down."

"And if it's not?" Cade asked.

"Then I'll fight until it is," Hermit replied. He jumped down the hatch, and looked around. He was standing in the long narrow hall their cage was in. The difference was, he was on the other side of it.

"All clear!" he called, and everybody else jumped down.

"This is fun," Aust said cheerfully as he scrambled down. "Now let's give those scalawags the what-for!"

"Uh, aren't we forgetting something?" Cade pointed out. "We're four people on a very large ship in the middle of the ocean, surrounded by thousands of enemies, and with no idea where we're going. In other words, I think we're in trouble."

"Don't be so pessimistic," Aust replied cheerfully. "I'm sure the calvary is on its way as we speak!"

The calvary was, indeed, on its way.

"I see them!" Dave called. "What now?"

"Ram into the side of the ship!"

Dave shrugged. "You're the captain!" he replied.

With the first ram, the ship flipped over.

Lich was sitting in a small box in the captain's chambers, muttering restlessly. When the boat flipped over, the box slammed into the ceiling, and cracked a bit, rays of light streaming through. Focusing all of his mental energy, Lich exaggerated the crack...and it blew wide open.

The captain shrieked, and hobbled on his peg leg out the door. Lich followed him out of the chambers into a long hall, where the captain was pointing at a group of people dazedly rubbing their heads and staggering to their feet on the ceiling.

"You!" he shouted.

"Oh, shit," Ana replied.

Lich would have rolled his eyes if he had any. Sighing, he head-butted the captain, who collapsed to the ceiling. Then the group began to climb upward, toward the bottom of the boat.

Brottor roared, jumped off the boat, and began hacking at the underside of the pirate ship. Eventually, he managed to chip a fairly large hole into the wood. Much to his surprise, standing right underneath him was the rest of the party.

Milo tossed a rope up to Brottor.

"Tie that end to something," he ordered. "And get us out of here."

"Hey," Hermit muttered. "I thought he was afraid of water. What brought him up above?"

"A dwarf is afraid of nothing," Brottor replied as he searched for a place to tie the rope to.

"Well, we're here!" Aust called cheerfully, helping Dave dock the boat. "Yoo hoo! We're here! We've reached Risunbir!"

Blinking at the sunlight, the rest of the party came out. Brottor, mysteriously, had disappeared back into his quarters as soon as the pirates had been defeated, and remained there for the rest of the journey.

"We might actually have enough money to stay at a decent tavern too," Milo commented. "We did pull in a few valuable items from that treasure chest on the pirate ship."

"I'm just glad it's over," Brottor replied grumpily. "Now I know why most respectable dwarves stay underground."

"Why are we going to that castle up here again?" Hermit asked dazedly. "I forgot."

Everybody else just ignored him.

Aust and Hermit jumped off the boat, and began exploring the town, like small, inquisitive children.

Grumbling, Milo (with Lich in his re-sewn backpack) went off next in search of a pawn shop that would take gold encrusted rope. Brottor and Dave departed to argue with other boat owners for no real reason at all. Ana was just about to leave to see which tavern Milo had found, when she saw Cade still standing on the boat, gazing down. He was surprisingly, unafraid of the drop.

"Hey Cade!" she shouted. "C'mon, let's go! We need to find an inn to stay at for the night."

"As soon as I step off this boat," Cade replied quietly, "the journey will be over. We will have found our destination. And we both know what comes after that."

He looked up, and saw over the miles the village covered, a dark mountain rising, storm clouds clustered unnaturally around it. At the peak of the mountain was an enormous black castle.

"Cade." Ana tried to avoid being frustrated, and act as reasonably as possible. "Cade, we both knew this was coming. It's what we set out to do. You can't have gone this far to consider giving up. Go ahead, look behind you."

Cade turned, and looked at the vast sea stretching out behind him.

"You see?" Ana muttered. "There's just emptiness there. Turning back at this point is not an option."

"We've seen many different challenges," Cade replied. "Little 'bumps in the road,' for lack of a better phrase. But this..." He paused, and stared up at the castle. "None of us are prepared for what's ahead."

"Come in," Milo ordered, when he heard a knock at the door. Ana opened it, and jumped.

"Watch it!" she cried, seeing Milo standing on the bed, and pointing a crossbow at her. Apologetically, Milo lowered it.

"Sorry," he muttered, jumping off the bed. "I'm starting to get a little edgy around this town. Everybody acts completely emotionless here, and it's starting to freak me out."

"I see what you mean," Cade replied. "There was something strange about this place. The people here are all like zombies. Now that you mention it, it does seem strange that none of the children were playing."

"That doesn't mean anything," Ana replied. "It could be a very strict town to live in."

"A fishing village?" Cade shot back. "Doesn't seem likely. We need to find everybody else, see if they know what's going on."

"That could be problematic," Milo muttered. "We're looking for four people who could be scattered all over town."

"Where's Lich?" Cade asked.

"He's wandering around, doing this weird kind of thing with the shadows. Anyway, he's sneaking around, looking for information. It probably won't be of any use to us, but he enjoys gathering as much info as possible on anything."

"Strange hobby," Ana replied. "Well, we need to search for him. If there's anybody who knows what's going on, it's either him or Hermit."

"I'd be inclined to agree," Lich said thoughtfully, once

the entire group was assembled in Milo's room. "There's definitely something non-kosher going on here. Personally, I think everybody here has been brainwashed."

"That sounds right," Hermit replied. "But what do we do about it? We can't stay here long, but we have hardly any food at all for the trip tomorrow."

"We'll need to stay here at least one night," Cade said reluctantly. "But we should all be on our guard. I'd suggest you all lock your doors tonight."

Then he got up, and left the room.

Cade went downstairs, and knocked on the clerk's desk.

"One room, please," he said politely. The clerk shuffled around, and stared at him blankly. He was a pudgy, unshaved man with a wide, blank stare in his glossy eyes.

"Yes sir," he replied. "What kind of room would you like." There was no question in his words, the words evenly spaced.

"One bed," Cade replied. "An inexpensive one."

"Inex- inex—"

"Inexpensive. Cheap."

"Yes sir. Cheap room. Right this way sir."

Cade shivered, then followed the clerk. On his way down the hall, still following the clerk, he heard a scream from one of the rooms.

"What was that?" he exclaimed, jumping. The clerk stared at him blankly. Then, same blank expression on his face, he charged. Cade stepped out of the way, and punched the clerk in the back of the head. The clerk fell, and there was a sickening snapping sound as he broke his nose.

"Brainwashing doesn't make for great fighters," Cade muttered. "Even I could subdue this guy."

He turned, and then yelped when he felt a clammy hand on his shoulder. The clerk pulled himself to his feet as Cade turned around, and punched the wizard in the face, knocking him over. He felt a cold, comforting darkness cover him.

"Enough is enough," he growled. "I've had it with blacking out at the crucial moment." He kicked the clerk in the jaw, and the clerk staggered backward. Cade slowly got to his feet, and ducked another clumsy blow, planting both of his hands in the clerk's stomach, and focusing all his energy on creating one powerful electric blast. The clerk yelped, and flew across the hall, bouncing noisily down the stairs. One of the stairs broke as the clerk flopped limply onto the ground floor. A thin trail of blood ran from one of his nostrils, and Cade knew he was finished. The wizard turned, and cautiously opened the door the screaming had emitted from. Dave was standing before the door.

"Oh, thank the gods," Cade breathed. "I thought something serious was going on in here. What was all that screaming about?"

In response, Dave delivered a swift high kick aimed at Cade's throat. The wizard grabbed Dave's ankle with both hands, and frowned. Then he pulled upward, and Dave collapsed on the ground.

"You are extremely irritating," Cade muttered. "Now run."

Dave just lay there, staring up at the sky thoughtfully. Cade moved forward, thinking he was dead, and got that delayed blow in the throat. He fell back, slamming his head against the wall, and blacked out.

"Dave's gone," a voice in the darkness said, and Cade jumped, wide awake. Ana was standing over him.

Cade had a headache, and blinked dazedly at the light streaming through the solitary window in the hall. It was daytime already, and he was still lying in the hall.

"What happened?" he asked groggily.

Ana knelt beside him. "He knocked you out, then ran, apparently."

"What about the others?"

"You mean, are they drones too? No, not as far as I can tell. They seem pretty much normal. I guess after a little violence, even drones panic." Her expression quickly turned to concern. "Hey, are you okay? Looks like you took quite a beating."

"From the clerk and Dave," Cade groaned, staggering to his feet. "It hurt. A lot."

He grinned devilishly. "But I actually fought back! You should've seen me! Dave tried to kick me in the throat, and I grabbed his ankle, and—"

"Cade, could you tell me about it later? We have more pressing matters to attend to."

"Uh, guys?" Milo called. He was standing on an overturned wastebasket in his room, staring out the window. Cade and Ana ran in, soon joined by the rest of the group.

"We'd better leave," the thief muttered. "Soon."

"Why's that?" Ana asked skeptically.

Milo pointed toward the mob circling the inn. "The villagers seem pissed," he explained. "Really pissed."

There was a long, awkward silence. Finally, Aust called out, "Well, what are we waiting for? Let's get out of here!"

"And how do we intend to do that?" Cade replied skeptically. Aust grinned, and winked.

"Where there's a will, there's a way! Hermit, lead!"

"Wait!" Milo screamed desperately. "Those are still civilians down there, even if they are brainwashed! We don't wanna kill them!"

"Er, good point," Aust murmured after a while. He grabbed Hermit, who was jumping out the window, by the back of his shirt, and dragged him back in. As Hermit stumbled to the floor, an enormous crash sounded out from the very roots of the inn.

"Well, guess they're inside now," Milo muttered. "Nice knowing you all. I'm going to go back to my room and gather all the belongings I want to be buried with."

"Wait!" Cade cried. "That's it!" He grinned at the rest of the group.

"What?" Milo replied blankly. "What'd I say?"

"Actually, you didn't say anything," Cade replied. "Do you have a sturdy grappling rope on you?"

"I'm a thief, genius," Milo replied, removing one of the grappling rods from his utility belt. "'Course I have a grappling rope."

"Good. Go out the window, swing onto the roof, then send it back down to the next person."

"What?"

"They can't reach us on the roof—" Cade explained patiently.

"—and if they try, they'll bring the whole building down on themselves!" Hermit finished. "Wizard, you're a genius."

Milo shrugged. "Better plan than waiting to die," he said, and disappeared out the window. Lich followed him silently. The rest followed hastily one after the other, each time the rope came down. Hermit was last, and as he was about to climb up, the door slammed to the floor, its hinges flying right off.

"There they are," a villager called monotonously. "They're trying to get onto the roof." The rest of the villagers, pitchforks and torches in hand, slowly filed into the room. Hermit froze up for a second, then leapt at the rope and dragged himself to safety, just barely avoiding the uncomfortable end of a pitchfork.

The villagers patrolling outside began to throw rocks. Fortunately, they had horrible aim. Most of them, in fact, just crashed through the windows of the top floor, and injured other villagers.

"Well, that's that," Hermit said, brushing his hands off. "Now we just wait." He sat himself down on the straw roof (carefully to sit on a beam, for if he didn't he'd fall right into the lap of a murderous villager), and busily set about waiting.

The villagers inside the building began to file out, and circle the inn again.

"What they hell are they doing now?" Brottor grumbled.

Cade, fighting his ever-present fear of heights, leaned over the edge of the roof.

"They've got ropes," he muttered. "They're looping them into the crevices of the place... pulling...dear gods, they want to tear the walls down."

And the villagers tried. They pulled and pulled, never once showing any sign of exertion, and finally, the walls gave a little.

Aust phrased it best: "Oh, crap."

The roof fell inward as the walls collapsed outward. Villagers snapped out of whatever dark fog had compelled them to murder, and screamed as the walls collapsed on them.

The group of adventurers began to scream as well, as they fell through a sea of hay and wood splinters, crashing through the weak floorboards of the building, and slamming onto the first floor, shielding themselves from the falling wood chips.

When the last piece of straw had fluttered to the ground, it was Aust who spoke first.

"Ow," he stated. Milo concurred.

"Do you smell something burning?" he asked, struggling to his feet. He was standing on one of the tables in the inn dining area. He looked around, and shrieked. When he had fallen, his shirt sleeve had brushed against the candle on the table. He leapt off, ran across the room, beat his arm against a plaster wall now lying beside him, and sighed in relief.

"Uh..." Cade began. "Maybe we should get out of here."

Milo stared at him blankly, then looked at the floor. A burning piece of his shirt had hit the straw surrounding him, and it was slowly beginning to burn.

"Good idea," he said, and leapt over the straw as

it burst into a wall of fire. The rest of the group followed, Lich swooping in from above to take up the lead. Once they had gotten a few yards away from the fire, they watched as a large pillar of smoke surrounded by four fallen walls rose into the air.

Brottor heard a soft groaning by his feet, and glanced down. A villager was trapped under a fallen wall. Eyes narrowing, Brottor put his foot on the villager's throat.

"Talk," he growled. "Why were you attacking us?"

"W-we had no control over ourselves," the villager explained. "We were…compelled."

"By what?"

"What else?" Cade said hollowly. "Dark magic."

He knelt beside the dying villager, and his eyes quickly surveyed the man. Now the man's mouth was beginning to bleed as well. His eyes seemed to be sinking back into his skull.

"Rapid near-death deterioration," Cade said queasily. He looked away. "This is lich magic."

"I'm innocent!" Lich howled, as everybody turned to him.

"No, not that Lich," Cade explained. "A lich is a powerful wizard who uses dark magic to make himself immortal. Usually, he has his life essence, or his soul, contained in some kind of vessel, usually a crystal or a bottle. The trademark of a lich is rot. Their own bodies quickly began to rot after the first half century or so, until they are completely emaciated. But physical strength is not where their real power lies."

Cade glanced back at the villager, whose skin was now beginning to turn gray. He shuddered.

"If Kaos has a lich in his service," Cade whispered, "we sure have our work cut out for us."

"There is only one Lich I know of who is still living," Lich muttered. "An old enemy of my creator's. He was a coward. He was always a servant to evil, and he may still be one now."

Lich looked toward the castle in the distance. "His name was Yarthank."

"Please," the villager rasped weakly. "You have to believe me. It was the evil within that castle. None of us would ever kill. It was…" He trailed off, and began to cough up more blood.

"One of us, a knight, had a head start," Brottor snarled, leaning into close to the villager. "He probably got here first. What happened to him?"

"Sir…Bernard? He was led up to the castle. We that were taken are all linked. I saw through his eyes…he was talking to Kaos, but I can't remember what they were saying…then Kaos gave him a sword, and the link broke."

"So he's dead," Ana said.

"No…the sword was presented to him, still in its sheath, and he accepted it. Please, I never meant to…forgive me."

His flesh began to peel off, leaving a gleaming skull beneath, and he gave one final gasp. As he did, the rotting accelerated, until the adventurers ended up watching solemnly as the dust that was the villager slowly blew away.

"Well, that's that then," Aust said, after a long pause. "Time to begin the final hike."

With grim determination, the group approached the black mountain rising up before them, the smell of sulfur filling their nostrils. They looked up, and saw a clear sky from behind him slowly form into a cluster of dark storm clouds over the peak of the mountain.

"Luckily, this doesn't look too steep," Milo commented. "There are enough crevices and footholds to make this an easy hike. We should be halfway up by the end of the day."

"Hooray," Aust said hollowly. The mountain was affecting even his mood.

"Once we get up," Milo continued, "I want one thing understood. If we're going to live through this, we're going to have to do things my way."

"What do you mean?" Ana asked.

"Well, this whole time, we've been stomping down doors, running through places and randomly killing bad guys. We won't last two seconds if we try that up there. Let's sneak in, slide a knife into the base of Kaos's skull, then get the hell out of there. Agreed?"

"Certainly not," Brottor grumbled. "A dwarf never stabs anybody in the back, no matter how much they may deserve it. We are honorable creatures…I demand that we wage a fair fight against evil."

"Fair?" Milo screamed. "He's a freakin' god! You want a fair fight? Fine! Why don't you just amble into his throne room, glove slap him, and see how long you last!"

The rest of the trip up the mountain was a long, agonizing argument. Eventually, Milo declared himself winner. Even Brottor was too tired to object by then.

"We're not far from the castle now," Milo

announced. "Time to come up with a plan. Cade, lemme see your glasses."

"What?" the wizard said absently, and Milo snatched the glasses right off of his nose, placed them on his own, and them commenced struggling to operate them.

"Press the corners of the frame to zoom in and out," Cade explained. Milo nodded gratefully, and began observing the castle.

"Looks pretty heavily guarded," he decided. "If we could make a diversion on the western wall, then we could just grapple up the wall, creep inside, quietly deal with any other sentries, and make our way through. I don't know, this looks pretty tough. Usually, I need a good layout of the interior of a structure, and months of planning to pull something even half this big off."

"And we don't have either," Ana sighed. "Look, Milo, we'll do it your way, but if things go wrong, we're going to have to be prepared to try it Brottor's way. Agreed?"

"Agreed," Milo replied. "Hey, Lich, you wouldn't be able to set off a few diversionary fireworks, would you?"

"I could, if I tried," Lich said. "You want that to be the distraction?"

"Exactly. Judging from your size, you should be able to slip past the guards, and meet up with us inside the castle grounds again as well."

"Very well," Lich sighed.

"Now then," Milo muttered. "We wait until nightfall. Possibly around midnight. By then, most of the guards will probably be asleep anyway. So Lich, try to make those quiet fireworks. Quiet, but attention-grabbing for those with their eyes open."

"Can do," the skull replied.

"Okay, now everything's set," Milo decided. "Prepare yourselves, gentlemen. If we pull off tonight's break-in, it's going to be the greatest break-in ever performed."

EIGHTEEN
Endgame

Nightfall. Milo gave the signal to Lich, and the skull swooped around the castle of Kaos, to the western wall. There, it focused for a few moments, then released several enormous, yet oddly silent explosions. Milo watched through Cade's glasses as sentries clad in skeletal black armor fled to the western wall to watch as a dazzling sea of red and orange tore through the air, illuminating the night sky. Still, other guards just slept on.

"Gods," Milo muttered, watching as the guards stood there, staring off into space. A few slumped to the ground, but the others paid no attention. The lights were far more fascinating. "He's stunned them,"

Turning toward the rest of the group, he made one hand gesture, and began to creep toward the eastern wall.

"Showtime," he murmured. The endgame began.

Hermit scrambled over the wall, and glanced around,

the last to reach the top. Lich joined them shortly after.

"Well now," Hermit said cheerfully. "All those guards are already knocked out. Saves us a little work."

"Ssh!" Milo hissed, and affixing his grappling rod to the wall again, scaled down it, to the interior castle grounds. Everybody else followed.

Milo gestured for them all to halt not far from the entrance to the castle. Two guards were guarding a two-story wooden doorway. They were both armed with spears and swords. Neither of them had seen the fireworks.

"So how'd you get into this?" the one on the right asked.

"Well, you know, I majored in evil sidekicking in college..."

"Oh, really! That must have been interesting."

"Yes, well, there were no real positions available. You know, with today's job market and such. I applied for a few small time mad scientist sidekick positions, but they said I wasn't deformed enough."

"Ouch."

"Yes, well...I heard that this demon god or something was hiring sidekicks, so I signed up."

"But you didn't get the job."

"No, some joker named Yarthank got it..."

At the name "Yarthank,"
Lich's ruby eyes flashed with recognition. "Yarthank," he whispered, and cursed. "I knew he was involved in this somehow."

The guard in the process of explaining how he became a sentry cut himself off, and looked around.

"Did you hear something?" he muttered to the other guard.

"Why yes, as a matter of fact I did," the other guard said.

Slowly, they crept forward, until they saw Milo and Brottor standing before them.

"Intruders!" one of them gasped to the other. They both hefted their spears, and collapsed to the ground, unconscious. Ana and Hermit stood behind them, rubbing their fists.

"That was too close," Milo murmured. "Let's make an effort to avoid chatter from now on, shall we?"

Lich grumbled incoherently, then flashed Milo a telekinetic image of a hand with only its middle finger outstretched.

"Yarthank!" Kaos called. He was sitting at his throne, the tattered remains of his trainer lying before him.

"Yes?" the lich said timidly, creeping into the throne room.

"I want a status report," Kaos growled. "How far are my little puppets from the castle?"

"Well, er, actually, sir, according to my divinations…"

"Well, spit it out!"

"They're just about to enter the castle."

"Assuming they can scale the wall."

"Well, see, er, that's the thing." Lich rubbed the back of his neck nervously, being careful not to rub to hard, as his rotting neck was very fragile. "You see, they're already within the castle grounds. What I mean is, when you called me in, last I saw they were opening the doors to physically enter the castle."

Kaos considered this, then smiled under his spiked helmet. "Excellent," he purred. "Are all my plans in order?"

"Yes sir, everything is in place, as asked. Our best guards are waiting for them near—"

"Get rid of them."

"Sir?"

"Send the guards back to their quarters. I want to handle this personally. Tell me, where are they right now?"

Lich paused for a moment, drawing all his energy into a kind of telepathic lighthouse, sweeping the castle for adventurers.

"Eastern wing, main hall," he finally replied.

"Excellent. Teleport me. Something flashy. I want to make a dramatic entrance."

"As you wish, sir."

Obediently, the lich muttered a few incantations, and his master disappeared.

"Do you smell something?" Aust muttered. He turned to the rest of the group. They all shook their heads. The elf frowned. "It smells like…sulfur."

There was a fiery burst a few feet from where Aust was standing, and the elf was knocked to the floor. Dressed head-to-toe in full battle armor, and carrying an enormous sword, stood Kaos.

"I AM KAOS!" he boomed. The adventurers shrank back. Kaos grinned.

"Well, what are you people waiting for?" Brottor snapped. "He's there, he's outnumbered, and he's the reason we came here in the first place! Let's kill him!"

The group charged forward. Kaos waited until they were all within range, then with one swipe of the flat of his sword, knocked them all on their backs

"Fools," he muttered, and waited for some guards to carry them away.

When everybody awoke, they were within an enormous coliseum. Milo was inside the arena, sitting and blinking dazedly on the stone floor. Everybody else was chained to their seats in the spectator area.

"Front row," Hermit commented. "Classy."

Ana looked at him, and raised her eyebrows. "That's really not funny," she said.

Kaos appeared within the arena out of nowhere, arms folded, a burgundy cape flowing behind him.

"WELCOME TO MY ARENA!" he roared, throwing his hands into the air. Everybody cringed at the sound of his voice. Kaos turned to them, bright red eyes shining from beneath his helmet.

"I've selected two of you for a performance you'll never forget. I'll dispose of the rest of you after the show."

"Two of us?" Milo corrected. "Uh, Kasey, there's only one of us in the arena, namely, me."

Kaos kicked him the ribs, and Milo doubled over, gritting his teeth from the pain.

"Don't spoil the surprise," he purred. "And don't call me that," he added after, sharply.

"Yes sir," Milo muttered, willing himself out of the fetal position.

"Now then," Kaos continued, "I've prepared a special surprise for you. He's a lean, mean, justice machine! Give it up for...THE EXECUTIONER!"

One person clapped excitedly. Everybody stared at Aust.

"What?" he cried indignantly. "I like watching grown men beat the crap out of each other. So sue me."

The executioner arose from a tunnel off of the arena, an over-muscled and very hairy man wearing only a pair of ragged black pants, and a black mask. He was carrying a rather large axe.

"MILO PENNYWISE!" he boomed, stepping into the arena. "YOU HAVE BEEN ACCUSED OF ROBBERY, BREAKING AND ENTERING, AND DISTURBING THE PEACE! SENTENCE IS: DEATH BY EXECUTIONER!"

He roared, and swung the axe. Milo quickly sidestepped it.

"Is this the best a demigod can do?" he asked indignantly.

"No," Kaos replied. "It isn't."

Milo saw something out of the corner of his eye, and quickly did a backflip, landing a few feet away from an axe smashed into the ground where he was a second ago.

"I am no servant of Kaos!" he snarled. "I'm here for one reason: Milo Pennywise must pay for his sins!"

"Too bad I don't believe in sinning," Milo replied, and dodged another blow.

"No?" Executioner said shrewdly. "Then why do you steal?"

"Easy. To make a living."

"Then why do you continue to steal when you have no need to?"

"That's not true! I—"

"Oh no? Before you tried to steal the king's crown, and dumped all your money and resources into that, you were filthy rich. But you chanced it all just for the rush of robbing him of his crown."

"Alright, so it is true," Milo replied, leaping up and punching Executioner in the face. "I rob for the thrill of it. But he deserved it!"

"Who was going to get the money?"

"Well…me."

"Were you helping anybody?"

"No."

"Were you hurting anybody."

"Only that freak of a monarch!" Milo cried desperately, dodging another blow. "He got what he deserved!"

"Not all of your victims do, though. Do they?"

"Well actually, as a matter of fact, they do."

"The single mother?"

"Axe murderer."

"Oh. The countless politicians?"

"Every single one was corrupt."

"Hey! I voted for a few of those guys!"

Milo shrugged. "Sorry, but that's the truth," he said.

"But if you steal from them, that makes you no better than they are."

"Nuh-uh," Milo snapped back, kicking Executioner

in the face. This time, his nose gave. "There was a time when I would have fallen for that whole guilt trip thing, but there's one thing that separates me from them; I'm saving the world. So there!"

He leapt up onto Executioner's shoulder's from behind, grabbed his neck, and pulled upward. Then he reached into his boot, removing his hidden lock-pick set for emergencies. He removed a pick from it, and slammed it into Executioner's neck.

"Sorry, guy," he muttered. "You don't deserve to go like this, but I'm in a bit of a hurry."

Executioner collapsed. Kaos howled, and Milo bounded into the spectator's seats, picking the locks chaining everybody to their chairs.

"Er, the big guy's coming," Aust pointed out, rubbing his wrists.

"I'll free the rest!" Milo called to Aust, Brottor, Hermit, and Ana. "RUN!"

They ran. Milo turned back to Cade, and the small box holding Lich.

"Sorry, no time man," he said to Lich after quickly freeing Cade. He picked up the box holding Lich, and ran, Cade bringing up the rear. Behind them, Kaos charged.

"I wonder who the second challenger was," Lich said aloud. "Bet it was Dave."

Kaos stopped. "That gives me an idea," he said to himself, and turned to the arena. Then he ran to free his next challenger. This challenger was a fast one, and would be able to catch up with the intended victim in no time.

Outside of the arena, the group hit a long, and

fairly wide naturally formed bridge of what looked like asphalt over a lake of bubbling magma.

"We must be deep underground," Cade theorized, peering over the place where a balcony should be. The magma itself came up to ground level, and Cade could feel the suffocating heat on his face.

"CADE WELKLAND!" a familiar voice roared. Nobody in the group recognized the voice, except for Cade. It was much more feral and monstrous, which explained why the others didn't recognize it, but...Cade had heard this voice laugh many times, and he knew that this was just the inner beast which had been lying in wait within somebody he knew for so long. This was his challenger.

"Go," he whispered. Everybody else looked at him.

"GO!" he repeated loudly. Ana was the only one who didn't move, arms folded.

"Look, this is my challenge," he explained. "Ever since I was a child, I've waited for this moment. I need to face it alone."

"WELKLAND!" the voice repeated.

"It's Bernard, isn't it?" Ana said stiffly. Cade sighed.

"Yes, it is. Look, this is my fight now. You need to keep moving forward. If I'm still alive, I'll catch up with the rest of you later."

"Uh...heheh..." somebody chuckled nervously. The group ground to a halt at the end of the bridge. Hunched over nebbishly, Yarthank stared up at them, rotting face grinning broadly.

"None of you...heheh...are going anywhere..."

Bones began flying out of the lava, piling up around the group.

"YARTHANK!" Lich shouted. Yarthank, in between chants in a strange, ancient language, laughed.

The bones began to structure themselves purposefully into a kind of cage, with bars too narrow for Lich to fit through, and too strong for Brottor to knock over. Ana ran to the aid of her friends, when a skeletal hand shot out from the cage, bars briefly giving it a shape and a life. It grabbed Ana's shoulder, and sucked her in.

"Ana!" Cade staggered forward. From behind him, a maniacal laugh ran across the cavern. Cade turned, eyes narrowing angrily as he watched Bernard approach. His armor was still gleaming brilliantly, perhaps even more so then before.

"Hello, Bernard," Cade said tranquilly. Then he drew his sword.

"Cade, what the hell are you doing?" Ana shouted from within the cage. "Blast him!"

Cade shook his head, and beckoned for Bernard to come. The once great knight roared, and charged. Taking a tip he had picked up from watching Aust and Milo, Cade stepped to the side, and stuck his foot into Bernard's path. The knight slammed into the ground, and was up again in no time, wiping blood off his lip with a gauntlet.

"You'll...pay for that!" Bernard yelled. He charged again. Cade wasted no time, flipping up Bernard's visor as the knight got within range, and stepping aside again, poking him in the eyes. Bernard yelped, and kicked Cade in the shin. Cade fell over, and avoided a blow from Bernard's sword.

Now it was getting serious. Cade felt a gauntlet hit

him in the stomach, and was sent flying backward, eyes wide in shock. He was quickly on his feet again, however, and he struck forward blindly with his sword. Bernard let the sword bounce off his chest, and it clattered across the bridge. Cade dove for it, and Bernard laughed as he watched the wizard trip, then lunged toward it on his stomach. Cade found the sword just in time, and he leapt to his feet, whirling around and grinning triumphantly.

Bernard thrust his sword through Cade's abdomen, and forced it upward, until it pierced the wizard's heart.

Ana yelled Cade's name, and pounded against the bars. Lich lowered his head. Brottor roared, and started beating against the bars. Hermit, Aust, and Milo just stood there with stunned expressions on their faces, unable to even move.

Cade dangled there, lifted off the ground by Bernard's sword. Summoning all his strength, he spit into the knight's eye.

Bernard laughed, and removed his sword, wiping it on the bars of the cage holding the rest of the adventurers. Stunned, Ana brought her hand back covered with Cade's blood.

Cade staggered backward, removing a scroll from his belt. Slowly, he lifted it up, and began to read it, struggling to see the words from a foggy veil falling over his vision. The world seemed to grow cold, despite the lava, and he found himself not caring if he lived long enough to read the scroll. Still, he forced himself to continue. Bernard just stood there grinning triumphantly.

"...ich barlam na'a'say, setnaibus," Cade finished. His eyes rose to meet Bernard's, as he fought a losing war to keep them from clouding over. "And on a personal note," he added, "goddamn you."

Cade fell over, and died.

NINETEEN
Deus Ex Machina

Bernard waiting for a few seconds, expecting the scroll to take its toll. When nothing happened, he smiled confidently, and whirled around. Everybody in the cage was gaping at the corpse behind the gleaming knight. One small river of blood was running along the cavern floor.

"So what now?" Milo muttered.

"I think the world is doomed," Lich said. "I could transport us all to another dimension, but we wouldn't be able to go back."

"No," Ana said fiercely. "We stay. And we fight. For Cade's sake."

"Mm-hmm." Aust said absently. He was staring at the ground, beside Cade. Specifically, at the river of blood. It had stopped running, despite the fact that there was an ever so subtle downhill turn on the rock beneath it. What did that mean? Then, the blood did something even more unusual. It began to flow backward, every last drop lifting from the crevices it had sunken into. Cade's fingers twitched, and his eyes snapped open.

"Uh…guys?" Aust said, and pointed. Cade slowly got to his feet, leaving his glasses on the floor as he no longer had any use for them, blood floating off of the ground, and flying back into the wound, which was now beginning to close slowly, severed tendons reconnecting within the exposed muscle tissue. Blood began to leave the cage bars, flying across the room, droplet by droplet, and Bernard stopped smiling. Slowly, he followed the flying trail of blood to its destination, and screamed.

"I killed you!" he shrieked, tears running down his eyes. He began repeating that over and over again, and Cade smiled coldly, holding out his hand. In it, the scroll he had muttered before dying crumbled to dust.

"A scroll of resurrection," he explained, letting the dust fall through his fingers. "From GROMMP. Probably the only one ever seen by the outside world. Had I died a second sooner, I wouldn't be standing here now." Still smiling, he slowly lay his sword on the ground, and stood over it. "No self destructive wizard would ever survive without it.

"I have no use for this in combat anymore," he told Bernard, gesturing toward his sword. "The mind is mightier than any sword, and that is why I will ultimately defeat you. As clever as you may think you are, you are a stupid little child, trying to get whatever he wants. Not this time." Cade's eyes narrowed. "Not ever again." His eyes narrowed. They contained a hint of something incredibly frightening, something that made even the great knight Bernard shudder involuntarily. Perhaps it was because he had finally met somebody who he couldn't push around, somebody who he couldn't intimidate until he got what he wanted. And Bernard felt a completely alien feeling to him, one that chilled him to the bone: inferiority.

Cade held out his hand, and Bernard charged forward blindly, crying out with frustration. A blazing red bolt of fire hit him in the chest, and he was knocked back several feet. He looked down at his chest, and screamed. On his breast plate, the seal of King Devham had been melted off. Getting to his feet, he charged again.

"Don't make this any harder than it is," Cade demanded, and gestured at the ground. The floor beneath Bernard rippled, and the knight tripped.

"You're only tiring yourself out," the wizard said gently. "Give up."

Bernard's lips pulled into an enraged sneer, the facial expression Cade would always remember him for.

"Never," he snarled, and got to his feet, backing up a few steps from the wizard. Then, screaming, he charged. "I'll put you into a permanent grave now!" he shrieked. The wizard bowed his head, considered his only remaining option, and put his hands by his sides, slowly bringing them up into the air together, as if in prayer. When he did this, magma from either side of Bernard slowly rose into the air. The knight looked up, and howled. And for the first time in his life, during, ironically, the last minute of his life, he wet himself, as so many of his victims during grade school had. The magma closed in, and Bernard disappeared under it. When it slowly seeped away, all that remained was a polished white skeleton in syrupy melted armor.

"Never again," Cade repeated, dumbfounded at what he had just done. Slowly, he bent over and retrieved his sword and glasses, resheathing one, and putting the other back on his nose.

"Stand back," he advised. With one hand gesture, the entire bone cage shattered, as if from horrible tremors only it felt the effects of. Yarthank howled in fear, and prepared to make a break for it, when Lich lowered himself slowly in front of the lich's face, until their faces were almost touching.

"Hello sunshine!" he said cheerfully, and a wizard's duel began.

Yarthank backed away from Lich, and fired a green bolt in the skull's direction. It hit Lich in the face, and he went tumbling backward. He slowed to a stop not far from the naturally forming bridge, and sent out his own bolt of brilliant red energy. Yarthank waved his hand, and the bolt stopped mere inches away from the lich. Then Yarthank formulated his own counterattack, blasting Lich with another green bolt. This time Lich deflected as well, and countered with several small bolts of blue fire attacking the lich. They swarmed around him, dodging the shields and counters he set up, and burned him. Yarthank screamed, and collapsed.

"Well," Lich commented, "that was easy."

Yarthank leapt to his feet, and blasted Lich. Lich,

extremely startled, was sent flying backward. He hit the ground, and slowly rose up.

"I'm a real lich, remember?" Yarthank taunted. He held up the small bottle containing his life essence. "As long as this is around, I'm indestruc—"

"Yoinks!" Hermit cried as he swiped the bottle from Yarthank's hand. Yarthank turned around, planting one hand in Hermit's stomach, and blasted. Hermit's mouth dropped with shock. His stomach began to rot, until some of the brilliant light emanating from Yarthank's hand poked through the other side of him. Yarthank released his hand, and snatched the bottle of his life essence back. Lich howled, and charged at Yarthank.

As Lich charged, Hermit stared down at his chest, and took a few staggering steps backward. Finally, he fell.

"Goodnight, ladies and gentlemen," Hermit said, speaking his last words.

"I will blast you into oblivion," Yarthank snarled, whirling back on Lich. Lich continued to move forward, ignoring him. Yarthank was about to deliver the final blast when he felt an arm close around his neck, and pull. Yarthank staggered, and his blast hit the ceiling, letting little pieces of rubble rain down. He struggled to look up, and saw it was an elf.

"I'll take that," Aust said curtly, taking the bottle from Yarthank's open hand. Then he kneed the lich in the back. Pain bolted through Yarthank's spine, and he twisted around, attempting to blast the elf as well. But Aust was too fast, and the bolt hit only his shoulder. However, it was still powerful enough to send him flying, spinning through the air like a flying dreidle. He slammed into the ground near the edge of the magma.

"Aust!" Lich called, "drop it into the lava! Do it!"

Aust grinned, saluted, and did as he was told. Yarthank screamed, and Lich called for everybody to look away. Then he blasted Yarthank one last time.

A thin red line of light emerged from Lich's mouth. It hit Yarthank in the chest, and carried him backward, flying across the cavern. As he hurtled forward, his body seemed to almost glow, and shards of light poked through all his pores. He screamed, and in a flash of brilliant light, he exploded.

Lich watched Yarthank's smoldering corpse hit the ground, then rushed to the other corpse in the room.

"Hermit," he muttered.

"Hey, what's wrong with your eyes?" Cade asked Aust who was getting to his feet. His eyes were a milky white.

"Well, the blast of light and everything from Yarthank's death seems to have blinded me," Aust replied. "Elves having extra sensitive sense and everything. I can still 'see' fine, though. That's the benefit of having elven senses. One of them can always kick in to replace another."

"Are you gonna be okay?" Ana asked.

"Never felt better, actually. You know, in elven history, the greatest storytellers in Elven history were blind. Er, we should probably go now. Kill the dark god, and all."

"Stop!" somebody called from the cover of darkness. "Dave the destroyer will destroy you all!"

Ana fired her bow into the darkness, and killed Dave. "I wasn't in the mood for more evil sidekick battling," she explained. "Let's go."

The group ran through the cavern, slowly climbing upward.

"I think we're reaching the throne room," Aust said as they pressed forward.

"What makes you say that?" Ana replied.

"I can smell Kaos nearby. But it's an old smell, like this is where he spends most of his time."

"That sounds about right," Lich said. "Ruling from the throne. Typical evil mastermind."

Sure enough, the party soon reached a light at the end of the tunnel. It was a large iron door. After much heaving and pushing at the door, everybody turned expectantly to Cade.

"What?" he cried. "No, no, wait a sec, it probably won't even work again."

Everybody continued staring at him.

"I was on a magic high after being resurrected!"

The stares never faltered.

"It's not going to work," he muttered, no longer entirely convinced.

Kaos sat on his throne, sword clasped in both hands. He was waiting for Yarthank to come in and give a report, any report. Maybe even bring in a few corpses, or better yet, captives.

He heard something rattle, and glanced up. It was the heavy iron door leading to his throne room. He got to his feet, hefted his sword, and smiled. They would never break through. And if they tried, they'd have a nasty surprise waiting for them on the other side anyway.

The door gave, and his eyes widened in horror as the iron block flew at him across the room, standing proud as if it had fasted to two wheels and a pulley, then pushed by a very strong orc. Kaos realized soon that there was no time to get out of the way, and prepared for the coming blast, shielding his face with his arms.

The door slammed into him, and Kaos was lifted off his feet and hurled through three feet of solid stone, flailing wildly. Finally, he felt his back break through the surfaced, and his immortal stomach leapt into his throat as he felt himself fall twenty stories, into a pit of lava. There was a little sploosh, some bubbles, then nothing.

Cade was still standing in the doorway, hand outstretched. His jaw was dangling down to his collarbone.

"Wow," Milo said. There was a long, awed silence. Finally, Milo crept over to the hole where the throne should have been, and stared downward into the lava.

"Cade, don't let this get to your head, but you just killed a demigod with little or no effort on your side."

Cade turned pale. "Oh," he said, trying his hardest not to sound surprised. "That was easier than I thought."

"So...that's it?" Ana asked. "I though there would be more of a fight."

"There will be," Aust replied, sniffing the air. "He's not dead. I'd advise you all duck."

An inhuman roar began to grow from the far

reaches of the cavern. Everybody did as Aust advised, and Kaos swooped over them, snatching Ana off of the ground as he went.

"Ana!" Cade cried, flipping over onto his back and staring at the shape above him.

"Oh, shit," Milo growled. He aimed his crossbow.

Hovering above them was Kaos, holding Ana's wrist and dangling her five stories above the ground. His gauntlets had partially melted, revealing red reptilian hands with enormous claws and boils all over. The wings sprouting from his back were similar. His helmet had melted back around the mouth, into a shape that oddly resembled fangs. When he spoke, smoke arose from that hole.

"Put down your weapons!" he shouted to the adventurers, "or the girl drops to her death!"

Milo fired his crossbow, and Kaos responded by breathing a jet of flame at it. The bolt began to smolder, and disintegrated in midair.

Milo fired another one, and got the same result.

"Put that down!" Cade demanded, pushing the crossbow away. "You could hurt Ana!"

Milo shrugged. "It's no use anyway," he replied. "The only way to his vital organs is through that mouth, and he can easily turn any foreign object that tries to enter it to ash."

"Then what do we do?"

"You're the idea person, why ask me?"

Kaos was surprised to find that Ana was not struggling at all. He assumed that she must have fainted from the shock. Glancing down at her, he saw she was just dangling there calmly, not in the least bit frightened.

Ana looked up, and met his gaze.

"You stupid little chauvinistic bastard," she muttered. "I'm not your freakin' little damsel in distress."

With her free hand, she grabbed onto his wrist, lifted herself up, and kicked him in the chest. Kaos slammed against the wall, one of his wings snapping painfully under his own crushing weight. He roared, and tried to hit Ana with flame erupting from his mouth. When he opened his mouth, however, he found a strangely foreign object in it, with an odd, coppery taste. In fact, it tasted a little like gold.

Dropping Ana, he quickly spat the thing out. It was a golden skull, with winking rubies for eyes.

"You'll be glad to know that you don't have any cavities," the skull told him. "But, really, take some breath mints every once in a while! Well, cheerio!"

Then the skull dove after Ana.

"Grab on," Kaos could hear him yell, and when he looked down, he saw Ana slowly drift to the ground, clutching onto that odd little skull.

"He looks in bad shape," Aust commented, looking upward.

"Uh, you can't see him," Milo pointed out.

"No, but I can certainly feel his presence. His left wing is broken, and he's struggling to stay aloft. Looks like he's bracing at the wall now, trying slow down his fall. Not having much success by the looks of it."

Milo glanced upward, and indeed, Kaos was

struggling to push himself against the wall. Still, he continued to plummet.

"That's amazing," Brottor muttered.

Aust smiled. "I don't call myself 'Master Bard' for nothing," he said, and drew his sword. "Now, from what I know of yore, there's only one way really to get rid of this guy. First of all, as long as he's in his armor, there's no way we can really kill him. So, we're going to have to be able to hold him down, and unbuckle all the straps on his armor. Then, we need at least two wizards, very powerful ones, mind you, to put their might together, and severely weaken him, while we non-magical adventurers continue to beat on him. Once his magical protective field is disable by the wizards, Kaos needs to be decapitated. Okay?"

"Er...sounds relatively easy," Cade muttered. He was, of course, lying. "What a coincidence that we have two wizards here. That probably has something to do with Loki, again. Anyway, all we have to do is disrupt his protective field?"

"Not an easy task. Imagine killing a demigod."

"Okay..."

"Now imagine putting in that much effort just to disable his invincibility spell."

"Oh. Crap."

At that, Kaos finally hit the ground, and a tremor rippled beneath the feet of the adventurers.

"Ready?" Aust said.

"No, but what the hell," was Ana's reply. She raised her bow. "To the death!" Milo, Brottor, Ana, and Aust raised their weapons, and charged.

Lich and Cade glanced at each other.

"Right," Cade said nervously. "Right, then. So, we just hang back, and wait for them to remove his armor."

"I know that," Lich replied impatiently.

Milo leapt over Kaos, who tried to reach up and grab him on the trip over his head. He missed, and Milo landed on the other side, before leaping up onto the demigod's shoulders, and clawing at his helmet. It was, surprisingly, completely cool, even after its trip through the lava.

"Distract him!" he yelled at the rest of the group. Ana, Brottor, and Aust began throwing everything they had at Kaos. The demigod roared, and charged at them, as Milo unbuckled part of the helmet. He reached for the other buckle, and was hurled into the ground. Ana kicked Kaos in the stomach, and he fell over. Brottor smashed him in the stomach with an axe, which left a large dent. Aust was slashing excitedly back and forth with his rapier. Most of the jabs and slashes did not connect. In fact, almost none did.

"Well," Milo said to himself, lying on the other side of the room. "He is blind." He got to his feet, and ran over to Kaos, leaping onto his back again before the demigod got to his feet. He realized it was only a matter of seconds before he was thrown off again, and praying silently, he pulled on the second buckle. With one tug, the helmet came off, and Milo fell to the floor with it clutched against his chest.

Kaos looked around, and roared. Now his true face was revealed. Yellow eyes. Small horns growing from his face. Pointed ears. Red, tough skin with blisters and boils everywhere. In his mouth were rows and rows of filed, gleaming white fangs.

"Ugh," Aust said. "Judging from the gasps from everybody else in the room, I guess I should be glad I'm no longer burdened by sight."

Kaos roared, and charged at Aust, who stepped to the side. Kaos went tumbling right into Cade and Lich.

"This is for Hermit," Lich muttered, and the two wizards blasted Kaos with all their might. The two brilliant white beams emanating from Cade's hands merged with the brilliant white beams emanating from Lich's eyes. They melted together into one large ray of light, pointed at Kaos's head as the demigod hunched over, in a strangely feral position, roaring angrily.

The beam came in contact with some kind of shield, and tendrils of light played across an invisible dome protecting him.

"Push!" Cade shouted. Lich nodded, thinking he sounded like a midwife. The beam grew, and all kinds of colors became infused into it, dancing across the walls of the cave in all directions like a magical laser lights show. A few passed through the other adventurers harmlessly.

"Push!" Cade shouted again. A crack seemed to grow in the field, and one tiny ray of light cracked through and hit Kaos in the breastplate. He screamed as it cut through the armor, and smoke slowly wafted out. The crack widened, and finally, the field was destroyed. Lich stopped, and Cade collapsed, exhausted.

Kaos lunged, and leapt onto Brottor, snapping and biting at him like an animal.

"Help!" the dwarf howled, and Aust turned. He lifted his sword, and charged, not entirely sure if he was even running in the right direction.

"One shot at saving the world," he muttered as he grew closer to the screams. "Make it count."

He brought down the sword.

He heard Kaos scream, and the sound of chunks of stone ripping free of the ceiling. One crashed on the ground nearby, and a shard of debris smashed into the back of his head.

He felt no more.

Cade's eyes opened slowly, and he looked around. He was in complete and utter darkness. He held up his hand, and a single flame flickered into life from it. He got to his feet, looking around again.

"Hello!" a voice said. Cade screamed. Standing before him was a tall man with a goatee, and clever, reptilian eyes. He was dressed in long, flowing garments, and had a devilish smile.

"Who are you?" the wizard asked, and the where he was standing lit up. He was standing on a cloud, surrounded by hundreds of flickering stars in the night sky, which had spontaneously alighted on the command of this strange man.

"I'm Loki," the man replied. "Remember me? This is the form I tend to take in the immortal realms."

"Immortal—" Cade froze. "Am I dead?" he asked cautiously. Loki laughed.

"Nope!" he said cheerfully. "This is just an illusion. You're actually still in the Kaos's throne room."

"But...you said you couldn't reach us through there."

"I couldn't. Kaos's presence was too great. But now he's dead."

"We...actually did it?"

"Oh, yes. Fine job, if I do say so myself. Care to join the others now?"

"Are they all okay?"

"Well, you all have a few nasty scratches and bruises, and Aust appears to have gone blind since our last meeting, but besides that, yeah, pretty much."

"Then take me to them."

Cade's eyes snapped open again. He was lying in the throne room, now dimly lit by the rays of the sun glimmering from far above. He looked up, getting to his feet, and saw that an enormous chunk of the roof had been ripped apart, and was lying in a large crater in the center of the room.

"Cade," Ana said. Cade turned around. "Are you okay?"

Cade nodded dumbly. "You?"

"I'm fine. Kaos is dead."

"I know."

"And Loki is here."

"I figured."

Out of the crater emerged Loki and the others. Loki smiled charmingly. "Well, looks like you folks have all done a bang-up job," he said proudly, looking around. "I assume you all would like to be on your way back to Irrellia now."

"Oh, shit!" Milo screamed. Everybody looked at him. He ran a hand through his hair, and glanced around nervously. "I'm still wanted there, remember? Ohcrapcrapcrapcrapcrap! Why me, why me, why me."

"Calm down," Loki replied. "I wouldn't worry about that now. I've had the whole thing straightened out. By the time you get back, Irrellia will have gotten word of your brave accomplishments. Besides which, Devham isn't king anymore, nor is anybody else."

"What does that mean?" Milo demanded.

Loki grinned, and winked. "You'll see," he said. "This time 'round, I've been able to arrange for a faster mode of transportation as well, if Cade doesn't mind moving very high up at some very high speeds, that is."

"Oh, no," the wizard moaned. Loki grinned. A chariot swooped down from the hole in the ceiling, one of brilliant, gleaming gold, pulled by two white winged horses.

"Chariot of the sun god," Loki explained. "He wasn't willing to lend it to me the first time 'round, 'cause he though I was a moron for sending you guys to get the job done. So, I made a bet with him that you people would save the world. If I won, I got the chariot. If he won, I'd stop dating his sister. Well, hop in, and enjoy!"

"Wait a second," Milo demanded. "Why didn't you just use the chariot in the first place, borrow it, and deposit us right here? It would have saved us a lot of trouble!"

Loki sighed irritably. "Because, part of the bet was that you guys wouldn't even make it this far. Now, are you going to get into the chariot, or do you want to walk home?"

Everybody climbed in, Cade shivering noticeably. Lich was the only one who didn't budge.

"I'm not going," he said.

Everybody stared at him.

"Well, you can't stay here," Aust said.

"I don't intend to. It was nice tagging along on your adventure, and it made me realize I want to have a few of my own again. It's been a while, and I'm thinking of going on a trip to some other dimensions."

"Well, it's been nice knowing you," Ana said politely.

"Maybe we'll see you again sometime," Brottor said hopefully.

"Maybe in a few hundred years," Lich chuckled. He turned toward Loki.

"Loki," he said to the god.

"Lich," the god replied stiffly.

"You two know each other?" Milo muttered.

"We go back a long, long time, Lich and I," Loki replied. He turned back to the skull. "It's been good seeing you, old friend. Give my regards to the mischief gods of whatever worlds you visit."

"Will do," Lich replied. "Old friend."

With a burst of light, he disappeared.

EPILOGUE

The court of King Devham, with its air of complete decadence and overindulgence had been replaced, the throne trashed in favor of a long table with several politicians sitting at it, the paintings and banners thrown aside to provide an environment where the imposing symbolism of monarchy was nearly nonexistent. It was here that the heroes were welcomed home.

"We would much like to speak with the new king, if he is here," Cade said to the group of men sitting at the table. They looked around, and coughed uncomfortably. The man in the center spoke.

"There is no king," he explained. "The revolution was a bit more drastic than that. You see, it occurred to us that nobody really liked living under an absolute monarchy. So, we decided to try a new system. We're the charter group, with a new council being elected by the popular vote every other month or so. We make the decisions, but they have to be approved by, uh...I can see I'm kind of losing you right now, so I'll stop. By the way, where is Bernard? I assume he's not taking the news very well."

Cade shuddered. "He, uh...died."

The man nodded gravely. "I see," he muttered. He

began fiddling with a quill pen. "Well, you'll all receive great rewards for your good deeds, and I hope you'll stay in the employ of the new government of Irrellia. It's obvious you're very capable of what you do, and we could use your clear heads, your determination, and your strength. What do you say?"

Aust was the first. He shook his head. "First of all, in case you haven't noticed, I'm blind," he pointed out. The politician, who actually hadn't noticed, was obviously surprised. "Second of all," the elf continued, "saving the world once is enough for me. I have enough stories from this to keep tots entertained for the rest of my life. I'm returning to my old village, in the Eastern Woods. And any of my faithful sidekicks are welcome to join me anytime."

"'Faithful sidekicks?'" Cade muttered.

Aust shrugged. "Sorry, but we can't all be the main character."

Brottor refused as well. "I agree with elf boy on this one," he said. "I want to return to my own land, in the mountains, and retire there. Maybe tell a few stories, of course, making my part in the whole thing a little larger."

Milo grinned, as he approached the table. "I'll be happy to infiltrate a few places for you, but let's get one thing straight; I get to keep whatever I pocket once I break in. Understood?"

"I'm in, too," Ana added. "Not much of an equal opportunity job market out there, and this looks like it would pay pretty well. Besides, I'm starting to get addicted to the adrenaline of adventuring."

The politicians all turned toward Cade.

"Mr. Welkland?" one of them said. "Loki has told us your skills as a wizard are unmatched in this kingdom. It would be an honor to have you in service of our new order."

Cade looked around, and sighed. He thought for a long time, before giving his answer.

"I don't remember how else to live anymore," he finally said. The room responded with stifling silence. "Yes," Cade finally clarified.

The Fool's Tavern Group, as they had now begun to call themselves, met in the tavern in which all of them had changed the course of their lives forever. They toasted, and were bought numerous drinks by frequenters of the tavern, who insisted it was the least they could do. The group discussed their plans for the future, and their reflections on how the adventure changed them. Brottor pointed out he was now more willing to acknowledge the accomplishments of elves and women alike (though he still sometimes referred to them interchangeably, a practice both Ana and Aust found extremely annoying). Aust claimed he was now the "Master Bard" he had always just claimed to be before. Milo said that he had lost some of his kleptomania in favor of common sense and decency. Ana said she finally had figured out what she was going to do with her life. Cade was probably the one who had changed the most.

"I think I'm a little tougher now," he said. "A little more confrontational. And not so klutzy. Also, a little more optimistic about the world. I mean, think about it. If a bunch of schmucks like us can save the world from somebody who's practically a god, imagine what everybody else can do if they just work together, like we did?"

The group reflected on it for a little while.

"Well, I'm completely drunk," Aust announced. "And we all have a very large party we have to go to tomorrow. I'm off to my room in the inn. 'Night."

Everybody echoed "Goodnight," and watched him walk off, rarely bumping into anybody despite his blindness.

"I should get some sleep too," Brottor growled. "A good warrior always gets plenty of rest, so that he'll be ready for the perilous rigors of eating contests and such. Goodnight, fellow adventurers."

Milo was next. "I need sleep, and for once I'm not just using that as an excuse to sneak away and rob more people," he said matter-of-factly, then left as well. Finally, it was just Ana and Cade, sitting there and nursing their drinks.

"I should be going too," Ana said, and began to leave. Shivering noticeably, Cade spoke up.

"Wait," he said. Ana stopped. "Do you think," he began, then froze. He paused, trying to get his brain to work again, then started talking once again. "Do you think maybe you could stay a while? Maybe have another drink? Just…just the two of us?"

Ana smiled politely. "Sorry, but I really need to get some rest. You should, too."

"Oh." Cade was noticeably disappointed.

"But I'd be happy to take a rain check on that," Ana continued. "We have a lot to discuss. Remember, we may be working alongside of each other for the rest of our careers…"

"I'm looking forward to it."

Five years later…

Vampires are obnoxious little bloodsucking bastards.

One was hiding out in the castle, and of course, the Fool's Tavern team was called in on this one. The vampire operated in pitch black, so Aust was called back on as the scout for this search and destroy team, due to his gradually developed acute sense of blind sight.

"Over there," he muttered to the rest of the group, pointing down a long, spiral staircase. The rest of the group was composed of Cade Welkland and Ana Anastacion, as well as Milo, the thief, and Brottor Balderk, called in due to his expertise in weaponry. Behind them were a group of recruits specially trained by Ana, Cade, and Milo (called, ironically, "Irrellia's Fools," a name which the ministry had objected to, but on which they had finally relented, and compromised on calling it the IF).

The vampire hid in the shadows at the end of the staircase, in a large room. Devham's lost wine cellar. Aust could smell the vampire's scent of rot, almost completely covered by the smell of wine.

"Cade, give us a light source for the guys with working eyes to work with," Aust instructed. "He's down here."

Cade nodded, and flame began to alight across the entire, fireproof ceiling. Beneath the flames, the vampire roared.

"The IF!" it snarled. "I am nearly a god! You cannot destroy me and my minions!"

Out of the numerous barrels of wine burst hulking zombies, which shuffled toward the adventurers, mouths gaping, hands reaching out to attack.

"So that's what vampy was up to," Milo muttered. "An army of fermented zombies. Interesting."

Ana nodded at the rest of the group.

"I guess I should get at him from behind, as usual?" Milo asked.

"Sounds good," Cade muttered. "And get your thieves to arm their crossbows, and get ready to fire. We'll need some cover fire from them."

The zombies lunged forward. The IF raised their weapons.

"Just like good ol' times, huh?" Aust said.

Showtime.